because i remember you

a novel by
Trey Burwell

For my mom and all parents who love unconditionally,
My friends and all friends who offer support,
And most importantly,
My wonderful husband and all soulmates who have
been told they don't belong together.

Love the way you want.

CONTENTS

SUMMER

A life without love is like a year without summer.

–SWEDISH PROVERB.

CHAPTER 1: CATALYST

A violently rough vibration rippled across my cold pillow as a loud alarm sliced through the heavy silence around me. I cracked my crusty eyes open, and I found my bedroom untouched and devoid of life, as usual. It took only a few seconds for the aggravating beeping from deep beneath me to bring me back to life. The desire to find my phone and shut it up sent my hand digging under my pillow until I succeeded, and the air fell silent once again.

The sun peeked up over the mountain our house stood on, casting an eerie red glow over the world like I'd woken up in Hollywood's next big thriller, and the morning news grumbled softly behind my closed door, signifying somebody, probably Mama, had already gotten up.

I never wanted to leave my bed, where the warmth of the thick blankets shielded me from the fan's frigid gusts and my bedroom door kept me hidden from everyone on the other side of it, but I had an important day to get through. I brushed my fingers through my thick, oaky beard and shoved my glasses into place on my nose before unlocking my phone.

No notifications. As usual.

That's okay, I told myself, taking a deep breath. *I'm sure nobody gets notifications at 6:30.* I slithered out of bed and threw on some jeans and a T-shirt, but the look wasn't complete until I covered it up with my oversized senior hoodie. Time to face the world.

"Good mornin', Monte!" Mama exclaimed from across the island as I stepped onto the cool linoleum in the kitchen.

Adorned in one of her most beautiful sky-blue floral dresses, she stood over a sizzling griddle that filled the room with a melody of scents no expert candlemaker could've ever replicated: sweet cornbread muffins, smoky bacon, and the fluffiest scrambled eggs in Nicholas County, quite possibly even West Virginia.

From the television hanging on the wall in the living room, local news anchors warned viewers about some incoming storm and the nation's biggest threats, but Mama had no time to watch it herself. She'd probably turned it on so Dad could watch it when he got up.

"Mornin' Mama. That smells incredible."

"Thanks, sweetheart. Eat up. You've got a big day ahead of you." She put a plate made especially for me on the bar, which I quickly made my way to after pouring a glass of tart apple juice, and then she prepared three more plates before preparing one for herself—like every morning.

This morning, however, *was* different. It carried with it the heaviness of being the beginning of my final day of high school and the beginning of my last summer at home.

To have said I had butterflies in my stomach would've been a massive understatement; it was more like a load of gravel tumbling around in there. My life beyond graduation, or more accurately when I'd be moving out in August, seemed so uncertain. The only guarantees were my dorm room number and my class schedule. Everything else, from what I'd eat to where I'd shop to who I'd see every day would remain unknown.

Someone had always told me how to live, and though I found myself wondering why I always obeyed more frequently as I grew up, I had grown to sort of like the reliability of it. There was no uneasiness because the hard stuff—ya know, life's hardest decisions and Satan's biggest temptations and stuff like that—had already been taken care of for me.

But with adulthood on the horizon, I would certainly be given the power to alter the direction of my life and destination in the afterlife forever. The thought of giving in to anything made me sick in the stomach.

"You excited for your last day of high school?"

"Excited... nervous... sad... a lot of different feelings to be completely honest." I don't think I could've named the last time something genuinely excited me or if anything ever had, but unnecessarily worrying Mama seemed like a selfish thing to do.

Personal happiness wasn't of particular value to me, at least not as a top priority, and graduation provided me with the best excuse for wanting to be alone and do nothing. Pinning it all on senioritis saved me from a lot of awkward introspection and half-truth explanations and probably even therapy.

"Oh, that's okay, even perfectly normal. I know it feels like lots of things are ending, but it's only because God's got so much more in store for ya." She did her best to lift my spirits, as was normal for her since I was old enough to breathe, but I could tell by her red eyes and scratchy voice she'd been up all night.

Mama greeted Dad as he rounded the corner into the kitchen, reaching a plate and hot cup of coffee across the island to him with a ceremonial *Good Morning* kiss.

"Good mornin', Cath." Dad took his breakfast and kicked back in his recliner for what had been his morning ritual for as long as I could remember, probably since they got married in the early nineties. He worked long days as a logger and spent weekends preparing sermons for the Church, and he typically had little energy —or patience—for us in what little spare time he had between obligations. He'd come straight home from work to a hot plate of food, fall asleep in his recliner, wake up to study his Bible, and go to bed.

But he was a God-fearing man and kept us on the right path, so I bit my tongue and considered myself blessed to have a father who cared at all. "Spare the rod, spoil the child," he'd say. "Respect thy father and thy mother." Whatever.

Mama had equally warm offerings ready for both Juliet and Remington when they strode into the kitchen. Juliet, probably the smartest of the Lee children no matter how badly I hated to admit it, came out school-ready with plenty of time to spare. Remi, our youngest sibling and the one with the most heart, was homeschooled, so he simply rolled out of bed and came to breakfast in his pajamas whenever he felt like it. I always felt so jealous of him for that.

I picked up my phone once again and began my morning social-media catch-up, nibbling sparingly on my breakfast, giving attention to nothing around me but my screen. I enjoyed looking at things with the power to sort of force a smile or a chuckle out of me, like the r/ memes subreddit. I found over the years that the easiest way to ease my overworking mind was with a distraction or several, so I often sank into extended staring matches with my phone when I wound up on the meme boards.

"Get your shoes on, stupid. I will not be late again because of you." Juliet pulled me out of my trance some thirty minutes later, rushing me out the door and into the warm air, heavy with humidity.

We marched across the backyard, basically a hillside field surrounded by dense forest, to the expanse of gravel where I parked my dew-drenched car—a fifteen-year-old Chevrolet Impala. The dark blue paint had chipped away in places, revealing a layer of brown rust underneath, but I loved it like my own European sports car. My parents bought it for me to get to work after school and probably spent no more than a thousand dollars on it online, but none of that bothered me at all. I bopped around in my massive car with my chest puffed out and a smile on my face because it was my one *me* space.

The narrow mountain road down which we sped on our way to school twisted and waved with the undulating terrain of Appalachia, and the morning dew had risen to heavy fog on the mountaintops or thick clouds from the valleys.

Traffic crept down the street along the Cherry River behind log trucks until the sleepy lumber town of Richwood came into view. The town benefitted from having once been one of West Virginia's most productive small towns and sprawled along the river despite its current population of fifteen hundred, filling every inch of flat land in the valley for several miles. We had more sawmills in town than banks, and the one traffic light changed on a thirty-second timer.

My car rolled down the quiet streets of downtown Richwood, and I whipped into my parking space in the shadows of the giant tan brick building I'd come to every day for years. Every morning, the place either smelled like mildew or bleach. Nothing else.

My last morning was a bleach morning, probably since they were cleaning the school up for graduation.

Juliet and I made our squeaky trek down the freshly-waxed halls of the one-hundred-year-old school, my last one ever. Juliet continued into the cafeteria, but I split off toward the restroom and slipped my headphones into my ears, shuffling the Indie Pop playlist I saved on Apple Music. I stepped through the open door into the poorly lit boy's room and approached the slab of semi-reflective glass hanging above the sink, checking under the stall doors and around the corner at the urinals on my way to make sure I had the bathroom to myself.

Once certain of my solitude, I pulled my comb out of my backpack and leaned in toward the mirror so I could make some final touches to my beard and hair like I did most mornings. Just as I finished combing my hair and started on my beard, a sarcastic gasp from across the room sent my heart out of my chest and down the sink drain. I turned my head slowly to see who wanted to make sure I knew they were there.

There, in the doorway, stood Jonathan, the biggest bully in the Cherry River Valley. Easily two hundred and twenty pounds and standing six-foot-five, he was not a guy someone of my lanky stature wanted to trifle with. I'd seen him sink football players with one punch and knock any teacher who tried to stop him across the room without flinching, so I found it best to play it safe and take his abuse, especially now since I would soon never have to deal with him again and could watch him rot from afar.

"Oh my, fruitcake. Does preacher Daddy know you like to look good for all the boys?" He moseyed across the tile floor in my direction like some wild west sheriff, and my body temperature rose with each step until the blood pumping under my skin boiled violently. "Let me see that."

Jonathan yanked the comb out of my shaky hand and spat on it before brushing it through his greasy red hair and returning it to me, not that it was ever going to be of any use again.

"What do ya think, fairy? Would ya fuck me?"

I nearly vomited at the suggestion. I wanted to say everything but couldn't say anything, not if I wanted my face clear of a black eye or two in my graduation pictures. I bit my tongue and pitched my favorite comb in the trash can.

I came to the conclusion my odds were better with me out of this situation altogether, so I started in the direction of the door. With a painful firmness, Jonathan threw his hand on my shoulder and squeezed tightly, stopping me dead in my tracks. The sound of my gulp bounced off the walls at the end of the bathroom and echoed back into my ears. "I asked you a question, faggot. Now come on, it's our last day together. Don't make it mis'rable." He spun me around to face him. "Do I look fuckable to you?"

If I'd been carrying a can of mace, I'd have surely used it on him. Or even better—a cannon, but alas, all I had were my stupid words.

"I wouldn't know because I'm not gay, Jonathan." I winced, pulling my shoulder from his agonizing grip. "I'll pray for you."

I'll pray he goes straight to the fiery pits of hell.

He shoved me back into the wall as if he heard my hateful thought, but my bloated backpack catapulted me face-first to the ground. Thanks to cat-like reflexes from years of his crap, my arms shot upward, protecting my face from a head-on collision with the grimy floor. I rolled over on my back to make sure he wasn't on his way to kick me in the head.

He wasn't, thank God. He stood in the same place I'd just been, hands on his knees, breathless from laughter. My small moment of courage shattered around me, and I found myself fighting off tears, struggling to stand back up under the weight of the textbooks in my backpack.

I should've kept my mouth shut.

"You listen here, queer bait: I known Jesus since I's a youngin, and I don't need no homo prayers." He kicked me back down and gripped the jagged wooden cross hanging around his neck. "Not that my God hears what you're sending up, anyways. Have a good last day, fucker. You better hope we don't run into each other again." He walked out of the men's room.

I slipped out of the straps of my backpack and stood up once more, examining myself in the mirror over the sink. My hair was even more disheveled than it had been when I woke up, and now I had no comb to fix it with. Wet patches of what I hoped was only water from the bathroom floor seeped through to my skin like icy pins and needles. I brushed my fingers through my hair and tried to dry some of the wettest spots on my outfit up with paper towels, but most of my energy went to fighting back a flood of rageful tears. It wasn't uncommon for me to become the target of any bully I happened to cross paths with, but it rarely got physical like it had that day.

My stupid mouth.

I felt angry I said what I said; angry I hadn't said more; angry God allowed a jerk like him to live in the same world as me in the first place. The idiot got one thing right, though. I hoped with everything in me I would never see him again. I grabbed my backpack from the floor and headed back out into the hallway.

As I made the trek across the cafeteria to my friends' table, my mind rushed to the bullies, the ones like Jonathan, who sat scattered throughout the cafeteria watching me fumble across the giant room. Every last one of them, and even some people who weren't typical bullies, believed rumors they made up about me. My voice, my clothes, my music, my everything seemed to tell the world who I was before I had a chance to, and that person was someone I desperately didn't want to be.

The Bible laid out very explicitly who I was supposed to be, and so did my parents, and so did my peers. If I dared venture off course and indulge in any type of lustful or otherwise sinful temptation, God would've seen my every move, and I'd have been sure to pay a great price. I found it best to fight every urge not from the Bible and to pray long and hard over the gray areas—although Dad always told me there was never a gray area. "If it's not *Absolutely,* it's *Absolutely Not.*

"Good morning, Monte!" Meri yelled obnoxiously as I approached my friends' table in the corner of the cafeteria.

Meri, short for Merida, was my absolute best friend. I'd known her longer than I'd known any of my other friends, and I think I'd even known her longer than I'd had siblings. She reportedly spent hours every morning straightening her long brown hair and applying her makeup, and she liked, most of all, to wear yoga pants in public and to brag about her over-sexed relationship with Keith, this know-it-all from the next county over.

"Hey Meri," I said, wiggling into a spot on the bench.

"It's all drawing to a close!" She grabbed at her chest with one hand as if her heart would've fallen right out of her body if she didn't and wiped an imaginary tear from her eye.

"I know it. Last day of school. Last youth rally. Last summer vacation. I'm not ready." I tried my best to hide the damage from the morning's confrontation, and it wasn't hard since we were caught up in thinking about too many other things, things I needed to validate the brand I curated for the Church. I hoped for some re-assurance or something from Meri to let me know I wasn't alone in my pensiveness, but she left me drifting.

"Eh, I'm not letting it get me down. I'm ready to graduate and get ou—" Her phone lit up with a *Good morning* text from Keith. They met at the church they both went to, the same one that lent them sponsorship to lead the local churches' youth association with some other teens and me. My earliest memory of their relationship was fake-sleeping while they had sex in the back of the church bus. It wasn't pleasant—their relationship, I mean—but I couldn't have done anything about it.

At least they had a relationship. A relationship would have strengthened my claims to straightness the same way it did theirs.

"Ya know, when we get to college in the fall, maybe you'll find a babe you can chase God with," she said.

"I don't need anyone but me," I replied, hoping she didn't notice the way my voice faltered.

This was the part where most church-goers gave me some stock response. "God has created someone for all of us. You'll find her." Meri was a church-goer, so she fell in line.

Before I could cringe at her cliché but well-intentioned sentiment, the bell went off, and the student shuffle in the direction of first period began.

Our school was rather small even for West Virginia, maybe four hundred students total, and my senior class made up a large one hundred and ten of those. Any new student was almost immediately recognized and labeled so the appropriate clique may absorb them. Everyone who's ever been to or even seen a movie about an American high school would've known how this process worked.

I usually didn't pay too much attention to new students since my friend group sat somewhere between the cool kids and skanks on the desirability meter, and that was fine with me. Taking on new kids was a gamble, especially for someone who feared rejection the way I did.

Meri and I made our way down the main hallway to our lockers like we did every morning when someone coming out of the main office caught my attention.

"...and that should just about cover all you need to know for your first and last day at Richwood High

School. If you have any questions, you know where my office is." Ms. McMullens, our school counselor, spouted off annoyingly joyfully as she handed an orange binder full of informational pamphlets to a new senior. "And sorry, again, for making you come out for one day, but if I understand correctly, you want to participate in graduation, and it's something the principal thought would help us justify allowing it since you didn't actually earn any credits here."

I paused for only a brief moment and watched from across the hall, but it felt like much more than a moment—sort of like a slow-motion scene from a movie. Any stress about the morning's negativity or the uncertainty of the future vanished, replaced by intrigue and a strange, new feeling deep in my chest and stomach, kind of like if something inside me caught on fire.

The new guy held his head high and possessed a firm, decisive glare as he scanned the halls behind Ms. McMullens. Light brown curls billowed out on the top of his head, adding an inch or so to his height, and faded down into a handsome, closely-shaven caramel-colored beard. Even his eyebrows seemed to have been given special attention in his grooming routine with the way they arched sharply over his brown eyes.

His demeanor and put-togetherness filled me with awe, but I also felt a hint of something else, some other sensation I couldn't quite understand, a sensation I had never experienced before. There was a heat and a feeling like I stood in the face of something powerful that overworked my heart and sent chills down my arms.

As I recollected myself and resumed marching down the hallway next to Meri, I got close enough to the new kid to smell his name-brand cologne. His skin-tight blue jeans were set against a flowy, blue chambray button-down loosely tucked in and only halfway buttoned, revealing a clean white V-neck underneath. He appeared ready to take the pontoon out on Summersville Lake or whatever snobby stuff rich folks did.

Oh crap.

He turned his head and looked at me. I tried to look as if I'd been admiring the senior art projects hanging on the walls down the hall, but my initial hesitation had to have given me away. I'm almost positive he saw me staring at him. I only hoped it didn't give him the wrong idea or promote his excessive cologne usage.

I visited my locker for the first time that morning, and the new guy, luckily—or maybe unluckily—had been given a locker for the day just a few down from mine, even closer than Meri's. I couldn't quite put my finger on what about him intrigued me so much, but I couldn't keep myself from looking at him one more time before class.

He looked back. And then the tardy bell rang, sending me on a mad dash to first period.

CHAPTER 2:
ROSE PETALS

I never visited my locker as much as I did the last day of school, but every time I did, he stood at his with that nice little grin curling up charmingly under his nose—so close I could smell his cologne. I didn't have anything to do at my locker other than stand there, lost in the mysterious aura around the new guy. I didn't let it bother me too much, though, because he didn't seem to be doing anything, either. He'd just stand there and maybe shuffle through his empty locker, but he smiled every time he noticed me looking at him. I eventually learned his name from some kids talking in homeroom: Amias Parker. I loved his name, his unique name.

Amias Parker.

Amias. Parker.

Amias.

Parker.

His name somehow tasted sweet on my tongue when I whispered it into my locker, and my body felt like I imagined it might've felt on drugs if ever I found myself on them. Each time we passed, I couldn't stop looking at him, studying him, and getting caught nearly every time, but the more it happened, the more it felt like a game between us—Who Could Catch Who Staring the Most? It became my new favorite game.

The bell to dismiss us from fourth period rang, and the dingy halls filled wall to wall with bodies and overstuffed backpacks as nearly all four hundred students eagerly marched toward the cafeteria for lunch or to advisors for study hall. I made a beeline for my locker, hoping to catch Amias one last time before noon and perhaps—or hopefully—to learn we shared a lunch period.

I stood at my locker for a couple minutes before concluding Amias either skipped for the hour, like a lot of seniors did the last week of school, or he went straight to study hall. The smile I hadn't noticed I put on faded away, and the day suddenly reverted to feeling like any other day I'd ever lived.

I'd heard at the Church numerous times of people crossing paths and having obsessive thoughts about them because God needed them to do something together. It sounded so divine—to have been hand-selected by God to do something miraculous for someone who possessed so much intrigue and charm.

I stopped by the bathroom for a quick prayer on my way to the cafeteria. Prayer brought me some sort of comfort in unsteady times, making me feel as if I could still call some of the shots. And even when life didn't feel out of control, reaching out to God throughout the day made me feel wiser and more prepared, even if I didn't get much of anything out of it. Self-validation.

I walked into the foul-smelling bathroom, sat on the

cleanest available toilet, and bowed my head for silent prayer.

Dear God, I come to You humbly, asking You to please reveal if You have sent Amias into my life for a reason. I know You can and do work in mysterious ways, and Dad tells me all the time about how You send people to trigger events in our lives to effect change.

When I met Amias today, I felt something. I can't quite explain the feelings I'm having or if I should use them to befriend him or get him to the Church, but these are some of the most positive feelings I've felt for a person in a while, or maybe ever. Please, if You're listening to me despite my shortcomings, hear my question and show me a sign.

Is Amias Parker in my life for a purpose?

Then, I whispered a quick *Amen* and sat for a while to see if any new epiphanies or revelations had come exploding from the palpitating depths of my heart or if a pattern in the crusty yellow grime on the floor would prove to me once and for all that God was out there somewhere, hearing and reacting to me.

Nothing, as usual.

I came to find over my eighteen years God rarely answered prayers in a noticeable way, and He never spoke directly to me like He had people in the Bible through visions or burning bushes. Every plea and request I made seemed to go no higher than the ceiling, making it hard for me not to believe the things Jonathan said. Maybe God couldn't hear me because He knew me more than I did, and He knew better than to believe the lies I told myself.

I settled to stop wallowing and expecting so much of God since He wasn't meant to be my on-call life coach anyway and stepped out of the stall. I washed my hands in the airy stream of warm water bubbling out of the faucet and was rubbing a thin paper towel around my hands to sop up the water when a voice from the entrance to the bathroom sent a hot chill down my spine.

"Hey there."

I turned to face him, but I already knew who it was. Jonathan, again, meandered across the bathroom with a creepy smile under his patchy red mustache.

He kicked the door stopper out of the way on the bathroom door and let it fall shut. "Remember what I told you earlier, fairy?"

I did, and my number one wish had been to not run into him again, but my wishes didn't seem to mean anything anymore. He kept up his slow march until he backed me into a corner. My eyelids became as heavy as anvils as my body instinctively tensed up, readying itself to face the consequences of being in the wrong place at the wrong time two times in the same day.

"Hey, it ain't gonna be that bad," he said, shrugging his shoulders and chuckling. "Today's the last day after all, and this'll probably be our last time *hanging out*. I'm kinda glad you hit me up again. I ain't ever hit somebody who has a crush on me before."

"I just want to go to lunch... Please, Jonathan."

The sound of my begging sparked a sickeningly merciless glimmer in his eye and a wicked smile, and I knew I'd just bought a one-way ticket to the hospital. I'd cemented myself in Amias's memory as the kid who got pummeled on the last day ever of high school, ruining whatever plans God may have originally had for the two of us. My heart thudded faster and louder than it had since the last time I saw Amias at his locker, and my tongue burned with stomach acid. I threw up my arms and tried to push past him to get to the door.

"I don't think so homo." Jonathan grabbed my shoulder and shoved me into the wall. "I'm not done wi—"

Just then, a flying fist from nowhere flashed into view behind Jonathan's fat head, plowing forcefully into the back of his thick, freckled cheek.

I stood in disbelief as his gargantuan body fell to the ground, his head slamming off the cruddy tile, knocked out cold. I turned my attention to the person whose fist saved me and found Amias Parker—*the* Amias Parker—in a fighting stance with his fists up in case Jonathan tried to wake back up.

"Grab your backpack," Amias said sternly but with a tremble in his voice. The cloud of scent from his cologne got to my nose when he reached his arm out for me. "Let's get out of here before he wakes up."

I turned to grab my backpack off the floor and noticed a reddish-purplish welt forming on the back of Jonathan's cheek where Amias's fist slammed into it, and a sweetness suddenly spread across my tongue like the sugary coating of a warm glazed doughnut.

He *had* been seeing me all day.

We quickly got out into the hallway and started downstairs toward the cafeteria.

"Thanks. I've never... well, I've never really stood up to anyone like that."

He squinted at his reddened knuckles as we disappeared into the crowded main hallway. "Don't mention it. People like him don't deserve the chance to defend themselves." He looked back up and shook it all off as if stepping out of a trance. "Forget that asshole. What's your name?"

A faint smile crept onto my face, replacing the grimace that persisted well after we were out of sight of the bathroom.

"I'm Monte. That's short for Montgomery." I choked on my saliva. *Jesus. Did I just introduce myself by explaining my name?*

He let out a cute laugh, the real kind that causes your cheeks to crinkle and your eyes to sort of close, and flashed me another half-grin, his perfect teeth shining bright white. "I'm Amias. That's short for Amias. Nice to meet you."

I struggled to put any other words together in his presence as my entire vocabulary was reduced to a mess of garbled sounds and gibberish. It seemed I'd lost control of myself, but I didn't exactly hate the way it felt. "Nice to meet you, too."

"I gotta stop at the office and talk with Ms. McMullens before lunch. I'll catch you later, Monte!"

My name sounded so wonderful rolling off his tongue, even if it came at the end of a sentence that made me feel a little insecure because it put me in the face of the confusing feelings he pulled from the deepest parts of me. It felt good for a moment, like something I needed but never knew about or my first-ever massage.

But that pesky self-doubt. It always came back like a twisted boomerang, and Dad always told me it served a purpose. "Humility and obedience contribute to a closer walk with God."

"I think we should be friends with the new guy," I suggested to Meri when we met up in our usual spot outside the cafeteria doors. "Or at least invite him to the rally with us on Sunday."

"But why? I heard he doesn't go to church, and you won't believe what else I heard about him."

"What now, Meri?" I struggled not to let it show how much I judged her for saying things like that because, quite frankly, I didn't care what she heard about him. He had already shown me enough of who he was to earn my respect. "You know you can't believe everything people say."

"Well apparently…" She glanced over her shoulders. "… he used to go to Keith's school, so I fact-checked with him, and he says it's all true. Amias—that's his name— is gay." That tidbit of information slithered out of her mouth with the special tone most Christians liked to use when talking about *worldly* people. And I'll admit, the information shocked me a tiny bit at first, but it did make sense the more I thought about the way he targeted Jonathan. He could've said something to trigger Amias, and Amias walked in on the perfect opportunity to exact his revenge. Or it could've been something else, something more uncomfortable. It occurred to me he might've stood up for me because of a crush and that I might've given him the wrong idea with my ambiguous staring and smiles all morning.

"Keith told me he transferred from East because someone saw him at the movies with another guy and followed them to Applebee's, where he beat the shit out of them."

"Oh my gosh. Are you sure?" The story she told me sounded too extreme to be true.

"Yeah, the guy followed them to Applebee's after the movie because he suspected they might be 'gaying.' He saw them outside definitely 'gaying' and beat the shit out of them."

"Jesus H. Christ. That's terrible."

"Yeah. I mean, I know what they were doing is sinful and not something to mess around with, but that reaction seems a little harsh to me, too."

"A little harsh? It's completely ridiculous is what it is. He followed them? And then attacked them? Because he thought they might be gay?" I couldn't understand why she would think Amias and his date were to blame for that for even one second, but I was also reminded why I never asked for her help when I became the target of a bully. She wouldn't have done anything.

Another reminder of how very alone I was—they seemed to come so frequently anymore.

"I know, I know. It's just, ya know…" Meri tensed up, mirroring me. "You know how I feel about these types of things. Why the hell would someone choose to be something like that around here? It's like asking the bullies to target you."

I wished a response like hers would've baffled me, but it didn't. It sounded perfectly normal and perhaps even a little compassionate compared to the way other people in my life had referred to gay people.

"Whatever, Meri. It shouldn't have happened, period, and I'm gonna ask him to sit with us at lunch and maybe invite him to the rally this weekend." She looked uneasy at my suggestion, but I was determined to do it anyway. I think she knew that.

We pushed through the double doors and into the now fajita-scented cafeteria where we jumped in the back of the growing line. I used this time by the wall to nonchalantly scan the cafeteria for Amias. It took a little longer than I had hoped it would because Meri noticed just as I found him sitting at a table on the far edge of the room.

"Who're you looking for?"

"I'm just looking." I hoped she would give it no extra thought.

"You're so weird Monte," she said with a giggle. She, quite reliably actually, gave it very little thought.

After we got our trays, I sat down at our table in a way that guaranteed I could see Amias. I told myself if we made eye contact for any amount of time, I would consider it a sign and approach him. If he avoided me, I'd know he was going out of his way to do it and forget about him. All I had to do was halfway engage in conversation with Meri so I could keep my objective to myself.

"I think this Sunday, I'll talk about relationships, but the underlying message is going to be about finding love," Meri said, explaining the topic of her upcoming devotional at our last-ever youth rally.

Meri, vice president of our youth association, did a devotional every month in front of our churches' youth rallies. This one carried the extra weight of being the final one, the one everyone would remember her by, which explained why she couldn't shut up about it.

Ah. He finally looked at me, and he didn't look away. Our gazes locked in on one another like heat-seeking missiles.

"Hey Meri, sorry to cut you off," I said half-heartedly. "I'm gonna go talk to Amias and see if he wants to come to the rally with me."

We kept our eyes on one another, and the densely filled room faded to fuzzy blackness. Breathing became laborious as I raised my leg over the bench across from his, and the smell of his otherworldly cologne silenced the voice in the back of my head telling me to turn and run.

"Hi again." I extended my hand for a handshake, unwittingly revealing my trembling muscles.

"Hey again." Amias grabbed my hand and shook it firmly.

"I wanted to thank you again for doing what you did for me. In the bathroom, I mean. It meant a lot that you'd do something like that for someone you've never met." I felt his strong legs press against mine beneath the table. "I was just sitting over there with my friend Meri and thought I'd come see how your first day's going. Or your last day? Whichever."

"It's going okay, I guess. This school has a lot fewer students than East does."

"Yeah. A smaller school comes with a unique set of pros and cons. Just be glad you don't have to be here for more than one day. Anyway, I also wanted to see if you had any plans for Sunday night. Meri and I have this youth rally we're going to, and I wanted—I mean *we* wanted to see if you maybe wanted to join me—uh, *us*."

"A 'youth rally'? Care to explain it to me?"

"It's one night every month where all the youth groups from the churches in our association get together and do a service for teenagers. We rotate churches every month, and the host church usually puts on a small skit and gives out food. It's a lot of fun."

"And you go every month?"

"Yeah. I'm the president, so I start and end it all and do a little speaking when they need someone to stall." I laughed anxiously, trying desperately to keep it from seeming like I was fishing to impress him or coercing him into meeting Jesus because I detected any interest he initially had evaporating. "It's our last one since we're graduating, but I still thought I'd see if you wanted to join since you're new. It'd be a great way to introduce yourself to the community before walking across the stage."

"Hmm." He looked up with an indiscernible expression, sending my stomach to the floor. I braced for rejection. "Sure, I'd love to go with you."

"Really? That's awesome!" I immediately got self-conscious and dialed it back. "I think you'll have a lot of fun."

"I'm sure we'll have a blast. So how do I go about getting there? Can I meet you at your place and ride with you?"

"That sounds perfect. I have to be there around fifteen till seven so how about you meet at my place at fifteen till six on Sunday?"

"I like it. I'll be there."

My muscles relaxed for a moment before firming up again. A meet-up meant we'd need to exchange numbers, and asking for his number meant another chance at rejection.

"So, can I get your number?" he asked.

I took a deep breath. "Absolutely." I spouted off my phone number and had him call me so I could send him my address. I almost didn't do it, but I followed up with an invitation to come with me to my friends' table. He bagged up his lunch and came along.

When we got back to the table, I introduced Meri and Amias to each other and explained that Amias would ride to the rally with me. I couldn't tell you what happened for the rest of lunch because Amias put me under some sort of spell.

He pulled out a deep red, shiny apple and wrapped his

lips, pink like dewy rose petals, around the side of it, biting firmly, sucking the tart apple juices into his mouth and off of his lips. My eyes couldn't have been forced in any other direction. They were stuck. He took his time, chewing deliberately and with so much force the muscles in his cheeks stiffened furiously with each upward motion of his jaw. The drool created by the sweet sourness of the apple and the juice dripping between his teeth had his lips shimmering in the fluorescent lights like an expensive lip gloss until they were so saturated he had to lick them to keep the sugary wetness from running down his fuzzy chin. He'd take his tongue and lick his lips in a slow, circular motion between bites, starting and ending in the same corner each time. Every once in a while, I swear he noticed me concentrating on his apple-munching and playfully bit his upper lip or used his tongue to slowly lick up the trail of juices dripping down his forearm, though he never broke eye contact with Meri as she rambled on about her devotional. She couldn't control herself. But that was okay because I couldn't stop watching Amias.

The bell rang and knocked me out of my reverie, and I fell back to the real world where I had a horrifying new problem to deal with: a throbbing erection. Aside from being worried that standing up would reveal my raging hard-on to my classmates, I also began worrying about what set this one off. I didn't want to, but I knew exactly who the culprit was.

My insides twisted as a thought came to the forefront of my mind that I regularly dealt with but buried every time.

Yeah, I didn't want to go there.

I quickly adjusted myself, tucking the nuisance down

beside my leg, and got off to class behind everyone else. The day progressed and I had my regular encounters with Amias at our lockers. The sickening thought that he could somehow read my mind and knew what I'd been thinking in the cafeteria made me second-guess my decision to keep returning to my locker, but he didn't seem to know anything. Or maybe he did and didn't care. Either way, our grins and hopeful stares at one another evolved into something I liked even more.

"Hey bro, your shirt is unbuttoned," I said sarcastically in a brief moment of courage when we passed between fifth and sixth periods. I would've cringed, but I received the open-mouth smile I hoped for.

We were gathering our things from our lockers to head home after sixth period when I saw him again.

"It's still okay if I tag along with you to your rally on Sunday, right Monte?" He spoke so confidently while rummaging through his locker as if he knew I'd been paying a great deal of attention to him.

"Of course it is. Just remember to be at my house by 5:45 so we can make it to the Church on time. And you got my text?"

"Sure did, I'll be there."

"Can't wait."

"Me neither."

I walked down the hall toward the student parking lot, filled with back-and-forth thoughts and a weird okay-ness with myself.

CHAPTER 3: CURIOSITY

The first weekend of my last summer at home dragged by in periods of nothingness punctuated by daydreams of Amias. I didn't understand this new interest I'd taken in him, but I felt as though I walked the line between interested and obsessed.

There was something about him I couldn't quite put my finger on. There were obvious things like the fact he chose to save me from one of the most aggressive bullies in Richwood at great risk to himself, and not just because of the punch. Jonathan had a special hatred for anyone who wasn't a straight, white Christian, the kind that made me wonder what in the world could've happened to make him feel that way, and if he found out a gay guy knocked him out, he would've unleashed every bit of homophobic rage that'd been building behind his fists since before he met me.

The words Jonathan dropped in every other sentence pierced through my flesh and bones like sharp arrows, so to Amias, I imagined they had to have a much more personal impact, one he couldn't resist firing back against. I wished I'd had the courage to do what he did years ago, but I didn't have the courage to do or change much of anything. Something happened to me when I met Amias, though.

Something big.

Something different.

Something I didn't want to ignore but needed to.

One of my biggest *Absolutely nots* was homosexuality according to the Church and Dad, not that there was much of a difference. Allowing something so blatantly sinful to dominate my life and soil my ability to spread God's love spelled certain doom in both this life and the next, but I couldn't just let his baggage erase the good he'd already done. It seemed even more sinful to let it go because of a label he'd been assigned by the stupid world. He risked so much to defend me, and the least I could do was risk a little for him.

Sunday morning started the way Sunday mornings always had with Dad bursting through my door around 8:30 singing a hymn—a different one every week. On that particular Sunday, he chose I'll Fly Away, bellowing loudly with his baritone voice and off-beat melody, making me wish I had a lock on my door and a two-mile hallway between it and the rest of the house.

My eyes adjusted sleepily to the blinding light flooding my room from the overhead light and now-open drapes as I sat up in bed, sleepy and aggravated.

"Time to get ready for church, son!" he yelled on his way out of my bedroom, slapping the top of the door-frame as he exited.

Sunday mornings were Dad's mornings. He handled the wakeup routines, which were much more abrupt than Mama's had ever been, and cooked breakfast, almost always cheesy scrambled eggs and buttered toast, and Mama told me the reason he had so much energy on Sunday mornings was he saved it up by being lazy every other morning. I figured it was really because he was about to do what he loved the most: lead a large group of people. He put so much time into preparing sermons and so much effort into his appearance every Sunday morning that it left room for very little doubt about how highly he felt about his job as Shepherd of the flock, Father of the House, Pastor.

By the time I finished getting ready, most of the morning had passed. The only breakfast left was cold oily eggs and soggy toast sitting uncovered in the kitchen, which had to be eaten with nausea-inducing speed since Dad insisted on being about thirty minutes early for every service to greet everyone on their way in.

I guess I understood why a pastor would need to be early for every service, but I loathed that my dad just had to be a pastor. It felt unfair for his decision to lead a life dictated by the whim of the Church to affect my whole family in nearly every way, but nobody ever said anything.

It didn't only bring additional and often unwanted responsibilities, though; no, it also meant we lived under a sort of "microscope" as Dad liked to put it—a microscope under which the World and the Church liked to examine us intently to ensure maximum adherence to Christ-like principles. If we dared stray from the commands of the Written Word and backslide into a sinful lifestyle, it reflected poorly on Dad's spirituality and could've cost him his pastorship, which would've resulted in punitive action from both God and Dad, and I couldn't ever decide which one I feared the most.

If I spent too much time thinking about it, the constant pressure made me question things I had no business questioning. So, I never spent too much time thinking about it. There was nothing I could've done to change the way things were because things were the way things had always been. Nobody else had ever changed them, and I didn't feel like being the first one to ask questions.

I put a plastic smile on my face every Sunday, walked into the sanctuary, and played the part of *The Pastor's Kid*, equal parts unrelenting obedience and painful predictability.

We cruised up the hill toward the Church, and at first, I could only see the clean white siding reflecting the sun's bright rays through the woods. Then, the bell tower rose above the trees, and the sea of cracked pavement spilled out before us, littered with groups of fellowshipping churchgoers who liked to see who could get there first. Dad steered the car into his assigned parking spot and led us inside.

First came Sunday School, with its corny but important lessons about how a life devoted to God would, or at least should, bring us peace. I'd always done everything I'd been told, though, and the peace everyone talked about still seemed to evade me. I followed every rule, suppressed every temptation, and showed up every time the Church doors were open, but still, I found myself adrift in a tempestuous sea of conflicting thoughts and mismatched identities. The only certain thing was there were rules, and the rules had to be followed.

Following dismissal from Sunday School came the most excruciatingly boring part of every Sunday morning service: the Worship Hour, though it did help a tiny bit that I'd been granted a sliver of freedom in being allowed to abandon my family on the front pew to sit with my peers in the back. From there, safe from the glare of the elders of the Church and Dad's direct eye-line, I could comfortably zone out or catch a few glances at my phone to help pass the time. It wasn't much of an escape, but I'd have done anything if it meant forgetting about where I was even if only for a few seconds at a time.

The hour started with a few folks sharing testimonies about something, anything really, relating to their walk with God while the rest of us sat back and listened quietly from the cushioned pews.

Mrs. Sorek, the longest-standing Sunday School teacher at Old Prospects Baptist, led the congregation in the moaning of a few hymns, meaningless from over-use, to fill the lulls between testimonies. We supposedly sang to God or the people around us, but gazes remained locked dourly into crispy, yellowed hymnals through every song. Smiles could've been counted on one hand as we sang of joy and dancing and excitement in a room with a heavier atmosphere than most funeral homes.

It rarely felt like the place to focus on my one-on-one relationship with the Creator like everyone said it was supposed to be. It felt more like a club to earn the approval of people.

But I couldn't go there. I often found myself riding wild trains of thought I felt it best to jump off of as quickly as possible, trains of thought that only led to a life of worldly pleasure and spiritual destruction. I regained control of my thoughts to find Dad spouting off his God-given message for the week. He spoke loudly, wandering around the front of the sanctuary, delivering a message related to Jeremiah 29:11.

"And God wants everyone in the Church to remember He has your future under control, and everything that's happening is happening for a reason. There's no need to fear *anything* because He's allowing it. God is always with you."

He bowed his head to lead the closing prayer, but I rattled away on another train of thought. That last part, the part about God always being with me, never seemed to have the effect Dad intended. It always felt more menacing or threatening than anything else, like driving in front of a cop. If God was truly always with me, then I could plan on having a hard time answering questions at the pearly gates of Heaven. Thank God Dad's prayer ended, and the room filled with the noise of laughter and conversation. We could finally go home.

When I got back to my room, I realized I didn't have to do much primping since I could just stay in my church clothes. I plopped down on my bed, ready to spend the afternoon thinking about what I'd do when Amias arrived. First impressions had given me a nice look at who he was on the surface, but I wanted to know more.

I pulled out my phone and opened Facebook. Finding his profile took almost no time at all as if somehow he wanted me to find it, and it revealed what I suspected about him from the get-go. He never looked bad. That boy always had clean haircuts and trendy clothes, though he often posted pictures of himself shirtless, and that didn't look bad either.

There were pictures with other boys sprinkled all over, but his featured photos were of him and his girl friends hiking around places like Long Point or Beauty Mountain. Lyrics to Fleetwood Mac songs had been written beneath nearly every photo, but the only concert I could find photos of were taken at a LANY concert. He posted very few pictures with his family, who I could only tell were his family because of the last name "Parker," but it didn't surprise me much—I got the sense his lifestyle called for a lot of independence. Everywhere I looked, it seemed he indulged in showing the world who he wanted to be. And to my bewilderment, he looked happy to live that way.

I decided it was time to stop stalking him and, after going back and forth with myself over it, add him as a friend when a notification popped up at the top of my screen.

Amias Parker added you as a friend.

I immediately clicked the notification and tapped the "Accept" button, a decision that ended up inspiring a bout of anxious self-doubt. I accepted the request almost as quickly as I could read it. Would he suspect me of sitting by my phone, pathetic and lifeless? Or worse— would he figure out I had been perusing his profile? Had I accidentally tapped the like button on one of his old pictures?

A text from Amias disrupted my normal pattern of overthinking.

"Hey."

"Hey," I wrote back after a cautious amount of time. It was our first time texting since I had given him my number, so naturally, I feared coming off as a lame piece of garbage.

"You think I could come over a little early and get to know the guy driving me to a church I've never been to?"

"Sure," I responded. "Well actually, let me ask my mom

first," I added, suddenly remembering I didn't live alone. I made my way to the kitchen where I found Mama about to put a couple homemade pizzas in the oven, filling the room with the mouth-watering aroma of spicy pepperoni and savory garlic.

"Uh, hey Mom."

"Yes, hon?" She slid a raw pizza onto the oven rack.

"You remember that new guy I told you about, Amias, who I invited to the rally tonight?" She nodded. "I was wondering if he could come over a little early to hang out."

"Sure, just make sure he's okay with scratch-made pizza for dinner!"

"Sure thing, Mama. You're the best."

I shot Amias one more text to let him know he was good to come over whenever on the way back to my room, actually feeling excited about something for once, and of course, the universe knew it. Each second seemed to pass more slowly than the previous one, and nothing I could do helped.

As naturally as if it had been a lifelong habit of mine, I was back scrolling through his Facebook again when I came across an album named "Senior Year Beach Trip" and figured I'd examine if a trip to a hot, sandy beach might have exacerbated his fascinating habit of going topless. I was not surprised to see his toned torso completely uncovered in nearly every photo.

Amias had the smallest amount of body hair, enough to darken his chest to a golden color, and a denser, brown trail led down the center of his stomach, disappearing under whatever piece of fabric covered his hips. The summer sun danced through his fluffy hair and traipsed warmly down his body, illuminating every muscle, vein, and bulge. The details of his physique curved into and out of the beachy sunlight, revealing the sculpture of a body like the ones depicted in ancient works of art—solid yet untrained, unattainably attainable.

All of a sudden, a familiar yet unwelcome friend interrupted my scrolling: my erect penis. I rolled over to grab the lotion off my nightstand, lubed up my right hand, and began stroking my cock, and with my dry hand, I looked up whatever straight porn I could find.

As usual, I found myself disenchanted with everything I clicked on. They all had the same things going on—a beautiful woman and a man with an iron body, some overdone "plot," and a weird power differential that always creeped me out more than it turned me on. With each effeminate moan and masculine demand, my dick went limper in my hand despite the most intense of strokes.

In a moment of animalistic desire, blinded by fiery lust, I switched back to Amias's beach pictures, and instantly, the blood pumped back into my cock, every heartbeat expanding it a little more in my hand.

I frantically scrolled through picture after picture, trying to find the one with the most power, when I came across one that wiped my mind clear and made me want nothing but him. His half-grin, his faint abs, and his happy trail guided my imagination to design what forbidden treasure laid hidden beneath his towel.

My skin started to tingle.

My toes curled, and my legs stretched.

My lungs pumped powerfully and sporadically.

My mind started, without effort, fantasizing about how I would feel if he were watching from the foot of the bed or perhaps stroking my dick from his spot next to me.

His spot.

Maybe he was stroking his dick to my pictures, too.

That final swell crashed over me, my eyes rolled back in my head, and I let out a victorious groan signaling I finished. Hot goop exploded from my dick, splashing onto my stomach and thighs. Simultaneously, my vision flashed out, and I could feel my back arching so severely I'm surprised I didn't break it.

My vision returned.

The pleasure existed for a moment, but in a flash, it was gone, and I was worse off for ever having felt it.

Standard sequence.

I felt ugly, disgusting even, as I instantly thought about God standing next to the bed. He certainly knew what I'd been doing, and it was horribly, blatantly sinful—a slap right in His face and a lashing on Jesus's back.

I closed the app, grabbed a few tissues to wipe up the sticky aftermath, and went to the bathroom to wash everything down the drain where it belonged. It was easier when I didn't let myself lie there and think about anything.

There was another text from Amias on my phone when I checked the time, one I'd been excitedly awaiting but suddenly felt underprepared for. He had arrived.

Oh crap, I thought, pulling my pants up quickly and drying my hands roughly.

I walked slowly to let him in, brushing my hair with my fingers, flattening my beard, and forgetting completely what my face looked like when I'd seen it in the mirror a few seconds earlier. Was there any evidence left of what I had just done on my face? Dirty white stains on my clothes? Knots in my hair? Guilt in my eyes? In my voice?

I could only hope I had cleaned it all up as I dragged myself across the laundry room to the back door, where his knocking came from. I pulled back the curtain covering the window on the back door and standing there in broad daylight was the boy who saved me on Friday, the boy with whom I had been so excited to spend time again, the boy whose pictures I had just used for... for something vile. I wanted to go back thirty minutes and *not* do that. It felt gross, but I now had a much clearer picture of what my interest in him was all about.

Not good. Or it felt good, but it wasn't supposed to.

"Hey, Monte." He greeted me with that half-grin I caught myself looking forward to.

Oh God, he knows. The redness across my face had to have revealed my dirty little secret.

"Hey, Amias." I motioned for him to step inside. "Take your shoes off by the door if you don't mind. Family rule. Mama prefers to keep the floors clean, and Dad likes it best when she's happy."

Words seemed to flow out of my mouth before they had the time to run through my brain, but he smiled again, stopping me in my tracks, and kicked his yellow sneakers off. This time he wore a fully-buttoned blue-and-white flannel doused in the same striking amount of cologne he'd sprayed on before school Friday. His snug chinos hugged him a little more loosely than the jeans he had on the first time I saw him, but his athletic legs still consumed my attention from the other side of the folds and stitches in the tan fabric. That was the *best* Sunday best I'd ever seen.

"You guys live in the middle of nowhere, huh?" He looked out the window at our giant backyard.

I turned to look out the window, too, embarrassed because I hadn't thought to be embarrassed about the isolation. "Sure do. No visible neighbors, either. It's liberating some days and downright horrifying others."

"I'd kill for this amount of space. Plus, I see so much forest to explore in your backyard." He spoke so genuinely I almost felt like I could stop doubting myself around him.

I smiled back. "Yeah, we love it. There are trails everywhere, and there's a beautiful little creek up on the hill, and Dad even built us a treehouse up there years ago."

"A treehouse?" Amias looked at me with wide eyes. The treehouse was one of the first things I wanted to share with him because it never ceased to be a valuable conversation starter. My castle in the sky, as I liked to call it, was a place I usually spent time alone, reading a book or napping, thinking about or doing whatever I wanted, but I liked taking friends up with me on the rare occasion one wanted to make the hike.

"Yeah, it's honestly just a small platform in a tree, but we loved that thing growing up. I still go up there on occasion for some alone time."

"I have to see it," he demanded as we came through the doorway into the kitchen.

"You must be Amias." Mama welcomed him with her usual warm expression, sliding two slices of pizza wrapped in a paper towel and a plastic cup filled to the brim with ice-cold lemonade across the counter to him.

"That's me. Nice to meet you, Mrs. Lee." He extended his arm for a handshake, something Mama wasn't particularly used to from my other friends who often came

in and made themselves at home without so much as a
Hey.

"Oh honey, call me Cathy." She spoke to Amias with a
soft friendliness as if they were old friends, flicking her
done-up eyelashes and returning his handshake.

"Hey Mom, I think we'll take our pizza to-go. Amias
wants to see the treehouse." She nodded before turning
to make herself a plate.

Amias and I looked at one another.

"Follow me," I said.

CHAPTER 4: PERSPECTIVE

From the moment we stepped outside, Amias couldn't seem to take his eyes off the trees surrounding the yard like an army of giant green trolls, and his enthrallment sent my eyes zooming around as if it were my first time there again. The thick, sun-bathed grass fanned out beneath my feet, growing patchier until giving way to shaded dirt and dead leaves. A squirrel leaping between treetops and a creek bubbling down the mountain in the distance created the kind of sounds most people had to buy noise machines to hear.

And the glory didn't stop there. I told him to follow me, but he wound up in front of me at a distance so tempting I couldn't keep my eyes from drifting. The way his shirt sat on top of his round butt, bouncy but not jiggly, called my eyes lower than they should've been. *The motion.* Forward then backward, up and down, again and again.

I couldn't *not* look. Real-life was so much better than pictures online, and with his cologne washing over me in the breeze with ribbons of rhododendron, I thought for a second I may have actually died and gone to heaven before I had the chance to do anything sinful.

As we trudged along the worn-in trail through scattered thickets and over the occasional fallen tree, I thought of all the places I loved going to be by myself: the hillside where I could watch the sun dip below the mountains across the valley, the loft in the abandoned barn on the edge of our property where I could sneak away to read, or the moss-covered stone in the middle of the creek where I could dip my toes in the crystal clear water flowing from the mountainside.

But something felt off now—now, I wanted to take Amias. I wanted him to see what I saw, to go where I went, and to sit where I sat. I wanted to see the places he ran to when he needed to be alone. I wanted our alone to be together and our together to be alone.

I wanted him, but that was all it could ever be—a burning, itching, distracting want.

He turned back and flashed me another half-grin, and I thought maybe he'd heard my thoughts. "I never want to leave this place."

He never wants to leave this place.

Oh, he happened to say the exact thing I wanted to hear and the last thing I needed to. I never wanted him to leave this place, either, but at the same time, I wanted us to run away from it, to find somewhere we could be free and open and normal. I couldn't find the right words to say, so I smiled back and kept going.

The treehouse came into view at first in slices peeping between brown and gray tree trunks. The crooked boards nailed between three trees and flapping blue tarps came together humbly if not messily, but we still

BECAUSE I REMEMBER YOU

had a room fifteen feet off the ground, which automatically made it cool.

"We made it," he said with a single fist pump. "Can we go up in it?"

I froze. I wanted it, but I wasn't ready to be that close to him, not after the sins I committed with his pictures, not with the possibility of my secret feelings about him becoming completely visible under the zipper on my pants.

God, why does this have to be so complicated? I looked to the sky through the green leaves.

Silence.

One of the worst things I could've done was knowingly and willingly engage in something so sinful, no matter how good it felt. But it didn't only feel good; it felt natural. It felt like the thing I should've done and the person I should've been, or maybe the person I would've been had I been raised to dig out my own way in this life.

But I can't because I wasn't.

"We can definitely go up in it," I responded, gesturing for him to climb the ladder. The urge to watch him climb became too irresistible for even my strongest of fights. I looked, and it was worth every drop of self-hatred. With each rung, the khaki fabric flexed around his butt cheeks and thighs, and one lucky seam stretched between them, struggling to hold the two sides together around his voluptuous butt.

Oh, Christ. He looked down at me between his legs on the ladder. My cheeks grew hot, and I nearly broke my neck looking away as quickly as humanly possible. He didn't say anything, though. He let me suffer silently.

When I got to the top, he stood at the rail made of flimsy boards staring out through the shady, expansive

43

forest. "So this is the place Montgomery Lee goes to hide?"

I smiled helplessly at the sound of my full name rolling tastily off his tongue. "Sure is. Or one of the places anyway."

"It's amazing out here." He turned away from the rail to face me. "I'm so jealous of all this. It's nature as far as you can see."

"It's great up here, for sure, but you shouldn't be jealous of me." I thought about how I felt jealous of him. He could live how he wanted and love who he wanted in a life he seemingly controlled by himself. I at once craved a life like his and feared I might backslide if given it. I feared an eternity of suffering in the life after this one, but the fantasy playing out in the back of my head with him and me and some good music made me feel... unusual.

Amias joined me on the floor and scooted across the plywood, coming so close the only thing separating his flesh from mine was the thin fabric of our pants. I redirected my gaze forward to keep the closeness from getting awkward as my heart did a dizzying dance, but awkward didn't seem to be a concept with much influence over Amias.

"It's so private out here. My backyard is basically a grass closet. I have no privacy whatsoever." He let out a sigh, the first one I'd heard from him.

"I don't know. I think I'd love to live in town. It'd be nice to live closer to people my age," I said, gulping so loudly it hurt my throat.

Amias reached his hand over and rested it on my leg, and it felt sickeningly good. Nobody had ever touched me that way.

"So, who is Monte? Tell me more about who you are when nobody else is around." He turned to face me, sliding his legs over mine, and with his chin propped up on his fist, he shifted so that his face was inches from mine. I didn't know whether to wig out and move or be still and act normal, so I went with the latter.

"Well, what do you wanna know? I'm pretty much an open book, some say to a fault."

"Ya know, I want to understand you better. You intrigue me."

My eyes shot wide open, and I shook my head ever so slightly in disbelief. *I intrigue him?* Did he find me an odd person? Had I been too mysterious or too heavy on the smiling? Did he know too much? Did he *like* like me?

"You seem like a cool guy. I just wanna know what's fueling your fire. What is it that makes you happy?" he asked.

Nothing anymore, I wanted to blurt out with the deafening volume of the crow screaming above us. But I didn't.

"Well, Dad preaches at Old Prospects Baptist down the street, and the Church is pretty much the center of our lives anymore. I think I told you Friday I'm the president of our youth group association, so that comes with some responsibilities..." I looked back at him with squinted eyes.

"Well... okay, but what about you without all of that?"

I realized at that moment I had absolutely no idea who to tell him I was without "all of that." I stared at the tarp waving about in the slight summer breeze across the treehouse, unable to think of anything to say, and thank God I didn't have to. The alarm I set on my phone began blaring from my pocket, prompting me to hastily climb out of the treehouse. "Time to head to the rally. Bet I can beat you to the car!"

No sooner than I could start running did Amias leap out of the treehouse and roll across the fern bed a few feet from the ladder. I let out a gasp I didn't expect but sped to a sprint when he jumped up and dashed toward me. As he passed at full speed, I got a whiff of that cologne he must've bathed in, which at this point had become my favorite scent in the world.

When I got to my car, Amias had already been there for a few seconds and leaned against the driver's door, patting some invisible wristwatch.

"I thought you said you could beat me," he said, grinning ear to ear. I wouldn't dare stroke his ego, so I ignored him, pulled the car door open a few inches behind him, and slid inside.

"Beatcha." I mouthed out the window at him. He ran to the passenger side, but I locked the doors and cracked the window. "You're gonna have to dance."

"Play some Britney."

Perplexed, I did as he said, opting for a classic with a good beat: Oops!... I Did It Again at full volume. And sure enough, he bopped next to the car like we'd been friends forever. He didn't resist, he didn't beg or plea, and he didn't care.

Amias seemed to have two rules in this life: have fun no matter the place and live as authentically as possible. I had seen people like that in movies and read about them in books, but I had never met anybody like that in the real world. I assumed they were entirely fictional like fairy godmothers or superheroes. The people in my life always followed the same rules I did, living their lives in a way that others and God wanted them to.

"Dedicating this life to Him is a small price to pay for an eternity in heaven!" was what they'd always say.

But what good is this life if we're miserable?

I could never have asked it, but I thought it every time. Amias would've asked it, though. I could tell.

I turned the music down and let him in a minute or so into the song because my alarm really had gone off before, meaning we really did need to get to the rally. On the drive, I worried about how Amias would like the version of me I had to be around my church friends or if they would like him.

I always thought the Church was supposed to be an open place where anybody could go, but it suddenly felt incredibly exclusive.

* * *

For a fella allegedly not raised in the Church, Amias sure seemed to know exactly who to pay respect to. He broke beyond his reputation and seemed to put my friends at ease, specifically Meri. He listened as she rambled about things that were entirely too personal and that he probably had no interest in, and he spoke with respect for the Church and our beliefs without soiling his own authenticity.

When asked about why he transferred to Richwood High on the last day by Keith—who definitely already knew—he spoke candidly about the evening he ran into his bully, saying he and his date for the night had been followed by him and attacked at Applebee's. He didn't regret pushing the drunk boy who'd been harassing him all night over a wheel stop, breaking his left arm. He didn't regret that doing so forced him to transfer schools at the end of his senior year if he wanted any part of a normal graduation ceremony. He didn't regret doing what it took to stand up for himself or others. He didn't have a single regret.

For a long time, we hung out in the shadow of the brick church tower in the boggy evening air, and I got to watch Amias and the way he interacted with other people. He smiled at most of them, but the smile he showed them looked different from the one he showed me. When he smiled at others, his mouth moved in a consistent, blueprinted way that seemed to say, "This smile is for you and everyone else, like a Hallmark Christmas card." It meant something nice, but so did the one he sent everybody else. It was the way I smiled at people my whole life.

But when Amias smiled at me, it was unique and rarely ever a perfect smile. He'd raise his lip on one side just slightly, cracking his mouth enough for a teasing glimpse at his beautiful teeth, wrinkling his forehead and the outer corners of his eyes as if to say, "This smile is for you and only you because you make me happier, and it's yours as much as yours is mine."

But why me? And why him? I looked around the groups of kids in the front yard for a new face, one hopefully belonging to a girl my age. I found one. *Why not her, God? Why does it feel like him?*

The bell chimed from the tower, ushering everyone inside, and a group of young boys, probably in middle school, stampeded past us like a herd of bison. One kid from the middle of the pre-pubescent group of greasy-haired, squeaky-voice idiots, covering his identity with a red hat and the rest of his rambunctious gang, shouted "FAGGOT!" and cowardly dashed through the pine doors of the Church.

Although a name hadn't accompanied the slur, we all knew exactly who the target had been, and we turned robotically to face him.

"That's just awesome," Amias said, tucking his hands into his pockets.

Meri ran to him and hugged him. "Oh my gosh. I'm so sorry you had to hear that. Keith, go get somebody!"

"It sucks, but we can't do anything," Keith said curtly. "We don't even really know who said it. Just let it go."

While everyone else busied themselves giving their renditions of what happened and debating over what, if anything, could be done to bring justice, I kept my focus on him. His smile, every version of it, had vanished, and his eyebrows sagged in the middle like a flimsy curtain rod. I didn't like seeing him that way. I wanted to grab him and hug him or take him aside and let him tell me what happened in his perspective, but I couldn't risk it, not with the rumors already floating around about my sexuality.

When we got inside, I sat in my usual spot in the front row near the center aisle, and Meri normally sat next to me so she could lead her devotional after I finished with my opening. There was no requirement for it or any-thing—it was just the way things had always been done.

On this night, however, Amias sat next to me, bliss-fully unaware he was throwing off a years-old tradition. Meri was my best friend, and I loved her dearly, but she had been known, on occasion, to go ballistic on in-nocent folks who accidentally did harmless things like taking her seat, her parking space, or anything else she felt belonged to her. But it didn't happen that way with Amias. She came in quietly, smiled, and took a seat next to him.

"I am very glad you came," she said, patting Amias on the back.

It baffled me, but I didn't spend much time thinking about it. Instead, I scanned the sanctuary for a little boy with a red hat, hoping he forgot to take it off before coming inside. He didn't forget, or he didn't come in. Either way, his identity would go unknown, which left me with a sour feeling in the pit of my stomach. I loathed being associated with people like him and that the boy was probably a regular churchgoer, regular enough to be at extra services like rallies. He obviously never listened to anything, though, which wasn't all that uncommon. Some people only attended because they had to—not to get anything out of it or to learn or to develop a relationship with God. They saw the rules as suggestions for themselves and as laws for other people.

When the people in the sanctuary quieted down, I played my usual part: opening with a prayer, leading some corny ice breaker, reading from the Bible—that night I read 1 Peter 4:8—and introducing the host church. Everything seemed to be back on track.

Or so I thought.

Merida took her position behind the podium directly after me and started a loud prayer.

"Dear Lord, I come to You today, thanking You for Your Grace and Mercy. I'm filled with joy over the fact that we can lay our sins at the foot of the cross You suffered on for us. I know there are people here who don't normally attend who need to confess their shortcomings and conform to Your Will, people who need to know what real love looks like and where it comes from—"

My eyes shot open, and Merida's voice muted behind my thoughts. It was suddenly clear to me why she was *very glad* he came—for the same reason a snake would've been *very glad* for a mouse to come along.

"Amen," the Church proclaimed in a disorganized roar at the end of her prayer, though I silently raised my head to find Amias staring at the red carpet.

It didn't stop with the prayer, though. Throughout her devotional, Merida rattled on about how the meaning behind marriage was equal parts Christ-like love and God's gift of reproduction and about how marriage was something God created for the "real love" felt by a man and a woman designed to be together. She even resorted to illustrating loosely-constructed parallels between the modern LGBTQ+ community and the mob of horny men who wanted to break down Lot's front door for sex with the angels inside.

As she went on, my usual tactic of reassigning the sins I heard about to people outside of the Church lost its effect. I began drawing lines between what she said, what the people in the Church agreed with, and my own behavior. She explained every unrepented sin added a lash on Jesus's back the day He faced a bloody death on the cross, and the guilt began eating me alive, right there on the pew.

If they had only known what things brought me joy just a few hours earlier or the feelings I had for the boy whose thighs touched mine, whose thighs were still touching mine, they would not have had me as their president.

I needed to escape.

I discretely turned my attention to Amias, who had slumped so low he couldn't see Merida over the podium.

I couldn't find relief in him anymore. It hurt me to think I brought the person who saved me from my bully to a place filled with his bullies.

He'll never want to see me again, I thought.

Merida's devotional finally ended, and she returned to her seat next to Amias, giving him a pathetically phony grin. He kept looking down. I'm not sure if he paid any attention for the rest of the service aside from the few times Merida threw her arm around his neck, presumably because she thought something someone said applied directly to him. She seemed incapable of showing him anything but this petty type of brotherly love, the only kind many Christians knew how to show in my experience. That kind of love fully depended on a person's willingness to conform to the Church's idea of who they needed to be.

I felt ashamed for ever having looked at his pictures online, for bringing him with me, or for ever thinking to approach him in the first place. Every decision I made was exactly the wrong one, as usual.

The hosting church's pastor went forward to extend the Invitation—a period at the end of a service where those with imperfections were implored to take them to the altar. The Invitation typically elicited an emotional response from everyone because the person giving it reminded us we may die on the way home and that if we hadn't covered our sins in Jesus's blood, we'd be doomed to an eternity in Hell.

Nobody could hide from the earnest pleas of the Church elders to fall to their knees at the altar. If it hit you, it hit you.

And by God, it hit me.

I couldn't outrun the consequences of what I had done

earlier; the consequences of the thoughts and feelings I had for Amias; the consequences of being an unfiltered version of myself. If Jesus was with me, He knew I was a member of the viciously horny mob outside of Lot's door. He knew I had been adding lashes to His back. He knew I didn't deserve passage into Heaven.

Keith's acoustic version of Amazing Grace grew louder, and a surge of feverish chills pushed down my back like lightning from the Great Above. I reached around Amias and grabbed Merida by the forearm, pulling her with me to the altar. I don't remember what all I said to God that night through my weeping, but I prayed for freedom.

Meri looked over at me with joyous tears when I whispered *Amen* and said to me, "You can leave whatever it is with God tonight!"

And just like that, I was cured, free at last—as long as I didn't give in to those temptations anymore.

After I regained control of my emotions and gave a brief closing statement, I once again found myself looking for Amias in a crowded room. I scanned endlessly over people's shoulders and around their heads until I spotted him squeezing through the mob in the direction of the sanctuary doors. Worried about how the messages of the night may have affected him, I brushed off my responsibility to speak with everyone else and ran after him.

"Hey, wait!" I ran up to him on the sidewalk. The sun was long gone now, chased away by the moon, stars, and fireflies, and the crickets competed with the bullfrogs for the Loudest Creature of the Year Award. "Is everything okay?"

"Not really, Monte." He spun around to face me under the flickering parking lot light. "I'd like to go if that's okay."

"Yeah, uh, I mean..." I couldn't understand the tears trailing down his cheeks or his lack of remorse. I looked up at the stars, at God, for guidance. Nothing. "I don't mind heading out early with you, but don't you wanna stay for the food or to talk?"

"I'm good," he whispered. "It was a mistake for me to come here. It was a mistake for me to think my history wouldn't follow me to church or that these people could tolerate me... I'm not a project for everyone to work on."

He didn't see it as harsh love. He saw hate. He didn't see it as an act of consideration from those who didn't want him to die and go to Hell. He saw judgment.

Perhaps he saw it correctly, but I couldn't let myself think on that for too long.

It became clear to me our paths were too different. He was concerned only with how he could be happy right now, and I didn't have room for clouds like that impeding on my relationship with God or my reputation.

So, I took him home.

CHAPTER 5: CHERRY

I figured it'd be best for my relationship with God to cut off whatever caused it harm, *pluck out thy right eye and all*, but it wasn't like I had much of a choice by the time the night was over. Amias probably wrote me off as some brainwashed basket case from the boonies who wasn't worth his time, and I felt certain we'd never speak again. The last thing I remembered about him that night was how he got in his car and left without saying goodbye, leaving me in the dark to think about what never could have been a thing anyway.

His body and all of its lines and bulges; his raspy yet high-pitched voice; his pink lips and fuzzy chin—I couldn't get him out of my head. He ate at my brain for days like a really bad car accident, replaying over and over again no matter how badly I wanted to forget.

I didn't *really* want to forget, though. I'd stretch out in bed, having completed my nightly Bible reading, and would pull out my phone to obsessively scroll around on social media until the stinging of my tired eyes forced them shut.

I hoped to see something like a status update, a shared post, a photo, anything as long as long as it came from Amias, and sure enough, I almost always did. Helpless, I'd tap on his name, and his profile would come up, and I'd get giddy like a kid in a candy store, forgetting for a moment God was watching my every move. A tap at the photos section would show me just what I wanted to see, but it was also the place I felt things I knew I shouldn't feel. I preferred to scroll around his timeline to see his statuses, and if the occasional photo popped up, it wasn't my fault.

In some weird way, it felt like we were having conversations that helped me get to know him. He only ever shared music from three sources: Fleetwood Mac, LANY, and Troye Sivan. There were more memes and hilarious GIFs than anything, which didn't surprise me given his charming sense of humor, but I could tell from the scattered photos he'd been hard at work to establish his aesthetic—Polaroids, records, whitewashed jeans, gloriously floppy hair, the whole nine yards. It would have looked like corny hipster garbage from anyone else, but it didn't look like that on him. It looked like the best thing in the world.

I told myself nightly I was innocently checking to see how summer had been treating him, but it became increasingly difficult to believe my own lies. I knew my motives were sinful. I checked his profile because it was the only way I could get lost in his captivating eyes and his enchanting smile, imagine the smell of his wavy hair by the sea, and feel the forbidden but consuming closeness to him I craved.

I had to stop, and I did a good job avoiding him until graduation day. Everyone was scrambling to get into position before the ceremony when I ran smack into somebody else in a graduation cap and gown. *Amias.* He'd been looking down at something on his phone when he looked up at me, his wide eyes brown like a sandy beach after a rain shower, and I couldn't do anything but stare into them. I couldn't smile. I couldn't look away. I couldn't apologize. I couldn't breathe. I stood there.

"Oh gosh, I'm sorry Monte," he said, halfway smiling, erasing everything negative for a few blissful seconds in the magical way only he could. It didn't last long, though. Ms. McMullens screeched it was the last time she'd tell us to get into position, and we ducked away from each other, hurrying to our assigned places in line.

That was the last time I saw him. He collected his diploma and went on with his life, and I did the same, though going on with my life didn't feel so liberating at first. In the first few weeks of summer, I kept to myself like I always had. Merida and Keith filled their time with couples' crap I had no interest in joining them for, so I was left in front of my computer or staring at my phone, thinking about things I couldn't be thinking about. I ended up volunteering to lead young adult Bible study every other Tuesday evening in hopes of strengthening my standing with the Church and God. It wasn't a huge step, but every step was a step further away from the darkness.

Being at the Church more frequently gave me, in addition to favor with the elders, more exposure to the lower-level leaders I often admired from afar. One particularly powerful person, Delilah Sorek, took me under her wing as a sort of apprentice for the summer and even invited me to help her teach youth group classes.

She was only a few years older than me, but her parents had been involved in leadership at Old Prospects longer than anyone else and had accumulated a certain amount of prestige—and oddly enough, wealth, too—giving them power over most of the congregation, including Dad. I wouldn't have dreamed of wasting the chance to work with Delilah.

Dad pulled Delilah and me out of class as the sun beat through the dusty room where we met for Sunday school one scorching morning in June. He asked us to start planning a curriculum for Vacation Bible School—a week of popular nightly services the Church hosted every July including activities and food for the community. The event drew in churchgoers and non-churchgoers alike every night, which made ministering to the nightly crowds much more impactful than regular services, but it also made it an incredibly daunting responsibility.

I accepted the opportunity to teach on such a prestigious level alongside Delilah with my chest puffed out, feeling like I meant something to somebody in the Church for once.

We planned meetings in the weeks following so we could get prepared, and during one of them, we decided to divulge struggles from our pasts to one another in a candid, judgment-free way to aid in designing a more relatable lesson plan. Delilah shared with me a story about when she first graduated and embarked on a weeklong booze-fueled mess of a vacation with some friends at the beach. She spoke freely about having sex that week with men from all over, sending herself on track for a pregnancy scare after she got home. She, "thankfully," as she put it, wasn't pregnant, but it scared her nonetheless.

It was wild to me hearing all this from Delilah, a person I'd long regarded as angelic and Biblically heroic, but it made me feel less terrible about myself and the things I failed at as if maybe my demons hadn't been so evil after all.

"I guess I've never really partied or anything like that, but I recently had to deal with some, uh, *unnatural* thoughts." My cheeks went a hot shade of red as those words tumbled off my tongue and into existence. It meant they were real, and it meant I believed in them.

"Unnatural thoughts?" Delilah asked, forking her skinny fingers through her silky blonde hair. "Be more specific."

I hated myself for starting, but I couldn't stop now. "Well, last month, Satan tempted me with this new kid at school, a boy."

"Monte! What? Are you..." She glanced around the empty sanctuary to make sure we were alone, giving my heart enough time to do a few somersaults. "...still a virgin?"

"Of course I am!"

"Well then, explain. You can say anything here."

I turned my attention to the floor to hide the tears gathering in the corners of my eyes. "I... uh, well... I found his pictures online, and—and something came over me. I was weak, and I sinned, but it was a one-time thing."

For a long second, the air fell so silent I swear I heard the ants marching along the edge of the windowsill on the other side of the room. I knew she wouldn't believe I hadn't done anything more serious, and even if she did, she'd know the labels everyone had always put on me were accurate.

"Well…" Delilah dropped her hands from her mouth, revealing a slight grin. "I guess we all have our battles. What's important is that you're here now, and you're learning to do better."

The heaviness triggered by Delilah's initial reluctance to speak lifted, leaving me comforted in the idea that I hadn't committed an unforgivable sin and could still be a good Christian. She slipped into the world as much as I had, or more to be honest, and came right back. All I had to do was focus on the Church like she did, and I could get away from that darkness.

The next Sunday, I watched as the ceiling fans spun in wobbly circles, trying desperately to stay glued to my seat like everyone else, but it seemed God wouldn't let go of my transgressions the way Delilah and I had.

My palms heated up.

A weight dropped down my throat,

And my body began shuddering uncontrollably.

The back of my tongue burned as I found myself struggling to swallow,

And my mind failed to conjure up a distraction.

I had to stand and confess my sins.

I had to do better.

With my fists clasped to the bench in front of me, I pulled myself to my feet and broke the punishing silence in the sanctuary.

"Church," I rattled, choking over a river of tears. "I betrayed Jesus, myself, and everyone here who depends on me to walk the straight and narrow. I have faltered and need forgiveness." Nobody reacted to my heartfelt confession, and some even yawned. I focused on the cross hanging at the front of the room and swallowed what must've been a gallon of saliva. I didn't want to come off as dramatic or unstable, so my next reaction was humor. "Unlike you old farts, I haven't quite learned how to be happy here. Please pray for me." I fell back into the pew, feeling like a two-ton weight had been lifted off of my shoulders.

Clear skies ahead, I thought.

The following Tuesday evening, when I was on my way to lead the young adult Bible study class, Deacon Sorek, Delilah's father, pulled me into a dingy storage room to "have a word." I assumed he was about to ask me to do even more to support the Church, that the Church respected the boldness I'd exhibited on Sunday, that I'd remain a crucial part of the Church community. I was so prepared to say Yes to any responsibility he might've asked me to handle.

"Yeah, um... Monte," Deacon Sorek spoke, turning to shut the door with a shaky hand.

"Yeah?" I asked, but I didn't particularly wanna hear—or quite frankly live through—his response.

"There've been a few complaints about what you said the other day." He seemingly developed an inability to look me in the eye.

I choked on nothing. I wanted to ask, *Is everyone disgusted with me?* but my vocal cords wouldn't turn on.

He pulled away from the wobbly table he'd been leaning on to face me directly, slapping the dust off his hands. "Now don't take this personally Monte, but on Sunday, you stood up and gave a testimony in which you inadvertently spoke with disrespect. I believe you called some members of the Church 'old farts,' which ticked some people off. You know you can't speak so casually in the Lord's House."

I jerked my head back in shock and crossed my arms, but he babbled on, watering down the details of who said what to the point of near-incoherency. Confusion transformed to grief as I considered what members of the Church I offended so severely they complained to Deacon Sorek. The room got quiet again and blurrier behind the lakes filling my eyes.

"I am so sorry Tim. I promise I will not slip up again." I just wanted to get to the class I was supposed to be teaching and forget about all this, relieved it wasn't about what I feared it was going to be about.

"Well, there is one more thing." He pulled out his handkerchief and dabbed the beads of sweat off his balding head. "Delilah requested a special meeting with the elders of the Church before the bells rang tonight, and what she informed us of was rather... concerning."

Fuck. Brace for impact.

"She approached us—me, the other deacons, and, uh, your father..." He looked away again as if I had some plague he could've caught by making eye contact with me. "And she told us what you've been doing and looking at on your phone. Would you like to take this time to explain, or may I continue?"

I could only shake my head, or vibrate it really.

"Well, leadership talked it over, and—now keep in mind Monte none of this has been easy—we think it would be best if you stepped down from your positions of leadership in the Church. It's not wise to have someone who's still learning teaching people, especially at Vacation Bible School. Plus, we really can't have someone with your particular demons working around developing minds. Think of the young boys."

What? Am I a monster now? Am I diseased? Do you realize

what you sound like? But my mouth remained closed.

"You don't have to tell anybody why, Lord knows we won't, but this is non-negotiable. All of your responsibilities will be transferred to Delilah, but you're welcome and expected to remain an active member of general congregation." He sped through his final scripted remarks and made his way back to normal.

I, on the other hand, was incapable of walking away from this. Like lenses on a kaleidoscope, a mosaic of emotions took turns affecting my perception. It baffled me how the Church forgot about all of my efforts because of one shortfall and a poorly timed crack at humor. Rage bubbled within me like a molten core when I thought about how Delilah had deliberately betrayed me, probably intending to keep the power to herself. "You can say anything here," she'd said.

Filthy viper. I thought about running straight to Deacon Sorek in the hallway and sharing Delilah's pregnancy scare with him, but it wouldn't have done any good. The Church would've swept that one under the rug since she struggled in a way they could relate to.

Mercy? Nope. Grace? Not for me.

I had been stabbed in the back. With a bloody crucifix.

But I swiftly remembered I had something much worse to freak out about.

Dad knew.

Aware I'd have to sit through a lesson prepared by Delilah if I stayed, I skipped out early. I didn't know exactly what my plan was, but I knew I had to get out of the Church. I high-tailed it out into the damp heat to my car and took a road trip to anywhere else.

I rolled all the windows down, and the crushing wind roared through them, prompting me to indignantly roar back through heavy sobs. Head aching, eyes squinted, and heart racing, I found a wide spot by the road to pull over.

My life is effectively over, I thought, slamming my hands on the steering wheel.

A sharp pain shot up my arms.

I couldn't go home.

I couldn't go to the Church.

So, I tried Grandma's.

Grandma, my dad's mom, taught me my whole life about the importance of an open heart, and she viewed her relationship with God as something to be kept private. Grandma's discernment of the rules of religion felt much more individualistic in approach than the punitive dogma of the Church, which had an image to maintain, as she put it. They had to remain vigilant, defending their righteousness against slander and darkness. Otherwise, the world would have had no shortage of ammo to use against them.

Grandma didn't care about any of that. She cared about love.

When I came around the curve and within sight of her homestead, I peered through the green branches of the weeping willow standing between her house and the driveway. There wasn't a light on in the whole place, but the brilliant evening sun lit the meadow up with its deep orange rays. I continued across the crackling gravel, along the ditch echoing with the chirping of crickets, hoping I might find her around a bonfire in the backyard or picking apples from the trees up on the hill. She was nowhere to be found.

I was completely alone. I couldn't call Merida because I wasn't so sure she would make me feel any better. I couldn't go to Mama because then Dad would know my location. So, I pulled out my phone and texted the only person I could think of who would understand the hell I was going through.

"Hey, are you free?" was the text I sent to Amias, my first text to him since the day of the rally. I didn't know what to do—I just needed another human being.

"Hi," he sent back within a few minutes. "I am. Is everything okay?"

"Not really. Can we see each other right now?"

"Sure. My parents are home, though, so let's meet at City Park."

Desperate for a connection and absent of a clear mind, I made the trip to Richwood. There was a moment when I pulled into the parking lot and saw Amias swaying back and forth on the swings when I considered turning around, but I needed a rock then more than I ever had before. And there he was.

"Hey!" he shouted at me, standing up from the swing, glowing in one of the final rays of sunlight. "Everything alright?"

I didn't say a word until I could smell him. I felt better with him, but that made me feel worse. "Nope."

"What happened? You can tell me, but you don't have to." That sentiment sounded familiar, but I felt like I could trust it from him for some reason. He seemed so much more human than anyone at the Church.

I broke down and fell to my knees. There I was, all but banned from the Church over masturbating to pictures of a boy with the boy himself.

"Hey, hey, Monte you're going to be okay. You're strong enough, but I'm right here for you when you're ready to talk." He hunched over me and wiped the tears from my face, embracing me in the tightest hug ever.

I had to keep it as vague as possible. "I've had some, um, unnatural thoughts ab—"

"Say no more Monte. Come here." He cut me off and fell back, pulling me onto him.

For what I swore was an eternity in heaven, we laid in the mulch holding each other, my head pressed against his chest so closely I could feel every beat of his heart. My sobbing intensified at first when he squeezed me, but it gradually dulled out as the darkness and coldness fled his light and warmth.

I pulled back and looked at him, and he looked at me in a way nobody ever had. The blue-purple glow of twilight danced across his face from west to east, only illuminating half of it, but he had more unintentional beauty in the twilit slivers of his face alone than most people had in their entire bodies. He grabbed his ear and tenderly tugged downward, leading my eyes along his chiseled jawline through his thick, light brown beard to his lips—his tight, supple lips. I closed my eyes and leaned in.

Something warm. Something soft. Something wet.
Something meant to be.

I forgot everything. Delicate taps progressed to rough, sensual lip-sucking as his hands slid from the back of my neck to the top of my head. His fingers scratched my scalp, flicking their way through my feathery brown hair, and his gravity pulled me closer and closer until he grabbed my bottom lip with his teeth.

I rolled onto the playground mulch, and he crawled over me with the grace and power of a mountain lion, never once breaking eye contact and only once pulling his lips away from my body to readjust.

His rock-hard dick shoved against my waist, pressing upward through his silky black shorts, and mine grew hard in return, drawing Amias's attention away from my face. He pulled up my shirt, and his long, turbulent smooches reverted to wispy pecks as he began a journey down my neck and along my fuzzy happy trail. While working his way down my torso, he began to unbuckle my belt.

I jolted back to life and jumped up from our mulchy bed when the noise in my mind could no longer be ignored.

Fuck remembering.

God, how I wanted to forget so I could feel something, anything, with Amias. I wanted to be with him, to feel him, to love him, even to have my heart broken by him. Anything with him would've been better than nothing by myself. I hurriedly wiped the saliva from my face and recomposed my hair, flicking flakes of mulch everywhere.

"I can't do this Amias." My bloodshot, dry eyes fought to stay open in the cool breeze.

"I know you can't Monte. I'm so sorry, I just... I thought this was—"

"I know. Trust me—I know. But it's not. And it can never be. I'm sorry I asked you to meet me out here. This was my mistake." It didn't feel like one, though.

"Can we at least talk Monte? I want to make sure you're okay."

Silent as a ghost, I turned and ran back to my car with tears once again streaming down my face and neck, soaking the collar of my shirt. I couldn't bear the thought of turning around and seeing him alone on the ground or, even worse, walking toward me with tears in his eyes. I had to keep running.

I had never smoked a cigarette in my life, but I'd sur-passed the realm of just wanting an escape. I needed one. I didn't even know why. I just knew I couldn't go on feeling the way I was without a filter. I would not make it. So, I stopped and bought a lighter and a pack of menthols.

I found myself parked in a wide spot by the road and wriggled out into the cool night air, facing the un-knowns of the dark forest on the steep slope dropping sharply on the other side of the guard rail. The moon-less night offered little light, but I didn't feel scared. A serial killer or sci-fi monster coming out of the woods and taking me away didn't sound that bad. I grabbed the pack of cigs, smacked it against my thigh because I'd seen people do that, and took out a fresh cigarette.

The smell surprised me. A hint of something leafy, like a tea, with some sort of freshness about it?

How terrible could it be?

I raised the cigarette to my lips, lit the tip, and inhaled.

Fuck.

I coughed and coughed so much my lungs nearly flopped out of my chest and into the sea of gravel and bits of litter around me. The dewy air tried to soothe my burning lungs but not before wheezing could de-prive my body of oxygen. The light from my headlights faded in and out with each failed gasp, and I leaned over, hands on my knees, hoping I'd recover before I passed out.

As I regained control of my panting, my vision re-turned and so did the ability to stand. I found the light-headedness unnerving, but it was some sort of escape from reality. So, I kept puffing that stupid beautiful cigarette.

The cherry entranced me, the way it argued with everything threatening to put it out. Against the mightiest of summer night gusts and my strongest puffs, the glowing tip of the cigarette fought back harder, blazing more brightly than it did during the calm. It should've stopped burning and gone dark. That would've made more sense, but it never did. It kept going.

I was only able to smoke about three-quarters of it before the light-headed sensation mutated into a deep-throated nausea. I dropped the remainder into the cold gravel near the guardrail. It was time to go home.

The cigarette dulled my senses, but it did next to nothing to calm my mind. No matter which direction I tried to come at it from, there was no fathoming the way my leaked secrets would affect my entire life. I wondered how much discretion Dad and the deacons might use or if Mama, Juliet, or Remi would ever look at me the same. I panicked about the likelihood I'd lose my best friend if she ever found out. Would I ever be allowed to hold a position of leadership again? Could I regain the trust of my community? Only time would tell, but I didn't want to know. I felt like I already did.

I remember passing under a traffic light, giving attention to whether or not it was even green only after I saw it in the rearview mirror. The clunk of the tires rolling over the metal lip of a bridge sent my imagination to work showing me how it might've felt to veer over the edge and into the deep river valley below, but I fought against every dark thought, struggling to keep my car centered between the yellow and white lines.

I temporarily pacified my mind with fantasies about

Dad receiving me with an open mind. Fantasies where nobody but Dad and the elders knew. Fantasies where I never revealed my secrets to begin with. Fantasies where I didn't have thoughts like that. Fantasies where I was never born. Pipe dreams.

The bright red reflectors at the end of the driveway came into view. As the car decelerated, my heart did the opposite. I gripped the steering wheel with my sticky palms and turned into our driveway, which suddenly felt like *their* driveway. It was long, but I wished it had been longer. By thousands of miles.

The parking area was so full I had to park in the front yard.

What the actual fuck?

CHAPTER 6: MEMORIES

My legs trembled like a high rise in an earthquake when they hit the ground next to my car. Cars I recognized from the Church and family reunions were crammed into the driveway by the house where I normally parked, so I left my car in the front yard. I dreamt of jumping behind the steering wheel and high-tailing it back to City Park to be with Amias but doing so would've only prolonged the inevitable. I had to face everybody at some point.

I pulled the creaky back door open and stepped inside. While quietly pulling my shoes off, I bumped into the metal dryer, muting the energetic conversations that had been taking place around the corner. After the reverb stopped, I walked at a snail's pace from the laundry room to the kitchen where I could finally see everyone. Dad had gathered some of our most puritanical family members and friends from the Church in a circle around the middle of the living room, including Delilah and her parents.

I stood motionless, staring from the kitchen.

Dad stepped forward from his spot in the circle.

My heart stopped.

"I'm sure you know why we're here," he said.

I nodded.

"Well, is what you shared with Delilah all there is, or is there anything else you'd like to share?" My head shot up and my eyes caught him staring through me like I'd have expected a detective to stare through a suspected murderer. Nothing about me seemed safe anymore: my life online, my history, my thoughts, anything I could think of that he might know about. I only wanted to say whatever would make everything end, but I couldn't for the life of me figure out what he wanted to hear.

Incensed by my silence, he grabbed my laptop off the bar, placed it on the kitchen island where everyone could see it, and slowly raised the screen. Every tap on the keyboard sent me further into my personal hell, one where Dad knew all of my passwords and could see my entire web history.

"What is this?" He wagged his finger at my computer, and my eyes zoomed along the imaginary line from the tip of his index finger to the bright screen. The most over-bearing parts of his brain had apparently been stirred to action by the discoveries of the evening because there, on my laptop, was a list of everything I'd been searching for on the internet—and not just Facebook pictures. Dad, and everyone else in the living room, saw things I wouldn't have dared share with another breathing person. Things I was only curious about. Things I thought I could leave in the past.

I couldn't breathe. I couldn't see. I couldn't exist. But I had to.

"We want to help you, Montgomery."

I still couldn't figure out why my father invited his prayer meeting friends, people he only reached out to in the worst of circumstances, to stand in a circle in the middle of our living room.

"Is all this because of that queer boy you had over last month? Is that why he's in your computer so much? Demons spread, son, and that's why we have to watch who we associate with. But Jesus'll rid you of this one."

This was terminology he liked to use when praying for substance users or domestic abusers, people he prayed for so he could feel nice about looking down on them, not for family or friends. Now suddenly everyone looked at me like Satan pulled my strings.

Are they right? They've never been wrong.

Sweat began to bleed through my shirt, creating large patches of wet, sticky fabric, and a bitter film coated my tongue as I peeled it away from the roof of my mouth.

"Monte, this ho-mo-sexual demon latched onto you wants to ruin us, to ruin everything I've worked hard to build for us." He didn't sound right to me anymore. He sounded like the nutjobs in cult documentaries. "There is a cure. All you have to do is want it."

All I had to do was want it? Fuck man, all I'd ever wanted was to rid myself of those thoughts; to make my parents proud; to have an unimpeded relationship with God; to look, sound, and be normal in the eyes of everyone else. I spent years trying to force myself into the happy life everyone else lived. I tried everything to forget about the way some boys made me feel and no girl ever had, and I wanted to have never met that *queer boy* who made me feel better despite making everything worse. If I wouldn't have met him, it wouldn't have been possible for me to miss him as much as I did. I'd have kept going on blindly.

I'd turned away every ounce of happiness I knew I could find outside the Church doors to live like Christ, and not one soul wanted to see that.

I looked into the living room, scanning familiar faces for even the slightest hint of an open mind. Mama stood quietly in the corner with her Bible firmly in her hand. She stared at the floor, perhaps to say a prayer, but she was definitely crying, clearing the evidence as quickly as she could with the mascara-stained tissue wrapped around her fingers. The deacons, Delilah, Mrs. Sorek, and my maternal grandmother stood in a small circle with their Bibles held firmly at their stomachs or chests to shield them from the spiritual pollutants radiating from within me. The contemporary gospel music dancing softly through the air tried desperately to cleanse the house of negativity, but its efforts were useless. I could only find the tiniest sliver of comfort in the fact that Dad excluded Juliet and Remi from this process.

"At your age, you can't possibly know what you want, and same goes for what you need. Let us show you," said Deacon Sorek, urging me out of silence. He struck a chord with the others, who verbalized their support in a mess of "Amens" and "Mhms".

My face caught on fire and went blood red. Red with shame. Red with misery. Red with rage. Red with frustration. Blood. Red.

"Well, Monte?" Dad asked, maybe to make sure I was still alive.

My eyes ran out of tears. My breathing grew similar to the sporadic backfiring of an old car exhaust, and every muscle in my body ached from relentlessly cycling between tense and tenser. People surrounded me, but I'd never felt lonelier.

"Come over here, son. We want to pray over you."

I dragged one foot in front of the other, making my way across the kitchen with the steadiness of a toddler, and crossed the border between the kitchen linoleum and the living room carpeting, and Dad spoke once again, charging me with sins grave enough to warrant spiritual intervention from his prayer circle.

"Dad..." I stopped, aware any pleas to him would fall on deaf ears, and turned my attention to the one person who hadn't looked at me with the lifeless eyes of a robot. "But Mama, I *am* committed to my work at the Church. I didn't ask to be this way. I never wanted any of this. I promise I'll do—" Dad cut my begging short and stepped between Mama and me. All she could do was sob silently. All I could do was obey.

"Son, I can't have this demon in my house, around the kids at the Church, or wreaking havoc on the work we do for the Lord."

It became clear Dad would've chosen to lose me over losing a fraction of the empire he'd built for himself. But it didn't matter. He may have been able to afford to lose me, but I could not afford to lose him and everything else I'd ever known.

I broke through the circle and made my way to the center, and the bright, sweltering ceiling light roasted me like the summer sun. Everyone stepped closer to me —everyone but Mama—and extended their arms, placing their hands on some part of my body, pressing my clothes against my steamy skin. Some rested their palms on my shoulders and back, some on my head, and some scattered across my arms and legs. Mama prayed with her arms raised in my direction.

Simultaneously, everyone began praying aloud, so loudly I couldn't tune them out.

"...free Monte from this demon..."

"...make Monte as miserable as he needs to be..."

"...please Lord, rid Monte of this disgustingly evil spirit..."

Each phrase cut through me like a dull sword. What once existed only as a private struggle now stood over me like an almighty demon with the power to destroy my family, the Church, and my life as I knew it. I hated myself with every fiber of my being. I wanted to stop existing, but I didn't want to give them the victory. So, I thought about how what I really wanted to do was run away to a world where I called my own shots, and I wanted to take Amias with me.

No matter how hard I tried to prevent it, prayers got to me. Some became so enveloped they smacked my back or pushed on my shoulders, demanding the demon leave me alone. I stood there, motionless, as my eyes tapped into reserves and tears I didn't know I had returned to my face. Slow trickles turned to violent bawling. I needed nothing more than a simple hug, a warm embrace. And all I got was a never-ending prayer for suffering.

When the mobbish shouting diminished to a dull rumble of hushed voices, Dad disappeared behind me. I thought he may come back with a belt or a switch or a lockbox for me to put my phone in, but he returned moments later with a small glass bottle. The circle grew to reabsorb him, careful not to break the line between God, them, and my body, but this time Dad stepped into the middle with me. He looked at me, then at the ceiling light, then back at me.

After whispering some unintelligible prayer, he removed the cork from the bottle and dabbed some of its contents onto his fingers, adequately moistening his own and passing the bottle around for everyone else to do the same.

The hushed praying ceased, and I stood alone in the center again. Everyone turned their attention to Dad, who began the final stages of the prayer by rubbing his thumb across his oily fingers in slow, rhythmic circles. He placed his hands on my head and began wiping the oil across my forehead. "With this anointing oil and in Jesus's name, I hereby command you to be gone, to return to hell!"

His thundering voice set off a chain reaction, and in sloppy unison, everyone softly smacked the anointing oil all over my head and body, screaming commands at the demon who allegedly controlled me. It sounded more like everyone begging me to send a part of myself to hell. And to hell I went, drowning in a cacophony of prayers.

"...nobody here can love you..."

"...go back to hell where you belong..."

"...there's no place for a thing like you in heaven..."

Fuck me. I began to hurt in a way I didn't understand.

I wanted everything to stop.

And then—quiet.

One by one, they pulled their hands away from my body, leaving my clothes clinging hotly to my skin. They gave me a few empty pats on the back and disingenuous offerings of *Thoughts and prayers* before migrating to the kitchen with Dad to celebrate the success of their spiritual warfare over a hot pot of late-night coffee. Mama wrapped me in a brief but tearfully warm embrace and disappeared into her bedroom for the night. As quickly as it had begun, the prayer was over.

Drenched in a foul mixture of holy oils and bodily fluids, I crept into the bathroom and looked in the mirror to assess the damage. Their incessant rubbing on my head disheveled my oaky brown hair, and the oil left dark blotches all over my clothes. Dark red stripes of raw skin ran down my cheeks and disappeared behind my scraggly beard, which dripped with tears, sweat, and snot. I stared into myself with cold scrutiny, peering through my dry, red eyes, beyond my pupils, and into my core.

Everything I saw was ugly, but only because those people told me it was. I'd never feel the same around them again, and I didn't have it in me to pray to the god who allowed—or maybe encouraged—them to treat me the way they just had.

I was still alone, but for the first time, I preferred it that way.

Desperate to wash the greasy concoction off my skin, I turned on the hot water and stared as it rushed down the shower drain, thinking about how nice it would've been to be a drop of water, one in a gazillion, always on the move and constantly changing forms, able to disappear within the crowd. Nobody could tell me where not to go or who not to be. Nobody could tell me they cared about me one minute only to stab me in the back the next or pray at me like I couldn't hear them. Nobody.

I thought about how I'd have felt at that exact moment if I'd have stayed with Amias in City Park or taken him on a cross-country trip to get away from the hate. I thought about looking over from the driver's seat to catch him looking at me, eyes sparkling in the passing headlights above a subtle smile as we passed a sign reading "Welcome to Any Other State." I thought about his cologne, his jaw, and his hair. I thought about hearing him laugh, touching his hand, and tasting his tongue under a cotton candy sunrise in a place we could call ours. I needed to feel that happiness, no matter the cost.

My glasses were coated in a thick, gray layer of steam when I reentered my body. I dragged myself out of a slump and pulled back the shower curtain, stepping into the boiling deluge. I stood there for a lifetime or two letting the water bounce off the oils and roll down my body, but my loofa was like a magic sponge when I wanted to rid myself of all physical evidence. Once it oozed and dripped its soapy froth, the oils stood no chance. I scrubbed and scrubbed and scrubbed them away.

* * *

Over the next several weeks, I struggled to keep my eyes closed long enough to sleep. I would lie awake, eyes burning and mind weary, sometimes thinking about everything and sometimes thinking about nothing. I'd ponder what could've been with Amias and check his profile to find some small escape from the bedroom where I now felt imprisoned. Fear of securing my spot in hell quickly followed fantasies about biting his shimmery lips or putting my hands down his tight pants, but the memory of that traumatic night in June would come to mind and wipe every last bit of fear away. The memory of guilt lingered, but I no longer believed in those who told me I needed to feel guilty. I actually felt good about that.

I spent most of my days dragging along, mind dysfunctional and muscles achy, finding comfort in the knowledge that college was just over the horizon. When I wasn't at church, I locked myself away in my room because I wasn't allowed to do much else. Interactions with anyone else, even my family, became short and pointless, and I stopped putting in any effort at church. I stopped reading my Bible. I stopped looking down for prayers. I stopped looking up for sermons. I no longer identified as a churchgoer, and I didn't want to—never, ever again. I never wanted to be associated with the types of people I'd learned liked to hang out there.

Questions with the power to kill my faith had always lurked in the back of my mind, but experiencing firsthand the venomous strike of the vipers I once called friends obliterated my will to keep them there. Nothing about what anybody at church ever told me made any sense. There was no love or mercy. I had not been shown grace and kindness. Jesus's blood hadn't been shed for me.

It became clear I'd been following the most hateful bunch of pricks in the world straight to an afterlife they couldn't even confirm the existence of. Pathetic.

I went to church. I came home. That was it. I was happy to have an excuse to disengage. My parents seemed generally okay with it so long as I attended church when they did. They also demanded nightly digital checks during which any device I could access the internet with was taken and searched thoroughly. They read through my texts, my web history, my profiles, and flipped through any new pictures. They even went as far as searching my gaming consoles to make sure my demon had been prayed away in every form.

It was what it was. I couldn't have done a thing to stop them.

Minutes felt like days and days like months. My favorite way to pass time became our family day trips to the larger centers of West Virginia, where bigger and more diverse crowds than we had back in Richwood afforded me tasty samplings of the freedom I craved. Being surrounded by people with colorful hair or fifty piercings made me feel like less of an outsider, and that was a feeling I'd always longed for.

The Town Center Mall in Charleston was a family favorite because the mall gave us each the ability to seek out whatever interested us. Mama and Juliet usually fell prey to the bright, colorful displays and enticing sales of shoe stores and boutiques while Dad and Remi meandered through the more outdoor-oriented parts of the mall, sometimes even wandering outside to admire the glass-clad high rises surrounding the plaza or noisy construction equipment across the street. This left me by myself, which I didn't mind.

On our last trip to the Town Center Mall that summer, I was bopping along the crowded concourse, eager to blow my movie theater paycheck on clothes I didn't need at the most expensive stores in the mall, when a familiar scent stopped me in my tracks. I took another big whiff; it was that cologne, the cologne I yearned for every day, the cologne Amias had worn every time I saw him—a prominent scent in a sea of them.

I looked around frantically, hoping with everything in me I might spot him walking around or browsing the racks in a nearby store. It took me only a few moments to pinpoint the store from which his heavenly aroma emanated, and I hurried inside and glanced over every shelf and rack, nonchalantly scanning each dimly lit aisle for the boy who changed everything. I realized when I got to the back of the store the smell wasn't coming from Amias. It was coming from a shelf of men's fragrances.

I grabbed a few test strips and began a desperate search for the right one. The last bottle I picked up felt odd —a black glass bottle wrapped in brown, tan, and blue plaid flannel. There was no brand name and no scent information, just a fancy bottle and a magnificent scent. With an itchy nose and watery eyes, I picked it up, pumped a spritz onto the paper strip, and took a whiff.

It immediately transported me back to the last time I experienced something good. I felt his beard scratching against my cheeks, his lips between mine, his fingertips twirling up the back of my neck. I felt happy for having met him and regret for having let him go. I didn't mind feeling happy-sad because I felt alive again.

Checking the price didn't even occur to me; I went straight to the checkout counter and purchased it, spending nearly my entire paycheck on one bottle of cologne. The fragrance of my dreams would now sit on my bedside table where I could always see and smell it, and its significance would remain my dirty little secret. To the world, I'd be wearing a nice cologne from an expensive store, but to me, I'd be wearing *him,* warm like an embrace and tingly like a first kiss. I covered my chest in a few spritzes of his cologne and pumped an extra spray onto the back of my wrist before heading back out into the mall.

Bank account practically empty and heart skipping beats, I meandered down the bright, massive corridor, excited by the bottle hidden at the bottom of my paper bag. I dawdled aimlessly past all the shops I normally loved, giving my wrist a sniff every few seconds.

Then, the spray-painted entrance of a young adult store I often ignored caught my attention. From edible miniatures to a variety of pop-culture-inspired merch, that store contained wall-to-wall shelves loaded with some of the best, most colorful dopamine activators in the world. In the rear, however, was a section my parents always told me was strictly off-limits. Hidden behind the cash registers existed a section stocked with sex toys, lubricants, gummy genitalia, and even edible underwear. I never really had the desire to venture back that far, but I took a whiff of his cologne on my wrist and wanted to do something new.

I scanned the hooks on the giant wall of sex toys, studying the difference between each product. The vagina must've been a crowd-pleaser judging by the more than two dozen rubber vaginas in every color of the rainbow. Then, the seemingly never-ending hooks of equally colorful vibrators and dildos grabbed my attention. I pulled a giant blue dildo off the top rack.

Jesus Christ. Its smooth, sparsely veined shaft rounded off on one end with a mushroom-shaped cap I presumed to be the head and on the other end with what appeared to be a suction cup. The way it looked and the way I imagined it might feel inside me made me hot and sweaty, and I shifted uncomfortably in my clothes.

There's no way I could take something like this home, I thought. But I took another whiff of my wrist, slipped the package under my arm, and headed to the register to spend my last few dollars. I dropped both of my new purchases into one bag and folded the top closed, guarding it with my life. The cologne wouldn't have been a big deal had my family discovered it, but if they knew what else I'd stuffed into the bottom of my bag, my life would've ended on the spot.

When we got home, I told everyone I wanted to try on some of my new clothes and disappeared into the bathroom. Mama asked what clothes since she hadn't seen me buy any, and for a moment, I thought she smelled my sin, but I got away without revealing what goodies hid inside my bag.

I locked the door, sat the bag on the floor, and dug the vibrant box out. It took me several minutes of contemplation and one more whiff of my wrist to finally undress and break the rubber dick out of its plastic jail.

For a moment, I rolled it around in my hands, caressing each soft curve and rivet, sniffing its squishy sides. I didn't want any surprises since I already felt a sickness in my stomach as I worried innately about what God and Dad and Mama would've thought about this ugly beautiful new toy of mine. It didn't matter anymore, but I had a hard time remembering that. I dropped my head to the floor and closed my eyes, trying to ignore the tears forming under my eyelids, but when I opened them, I saw *his* bottle shimmering faintly in the harsh bathroom lights at the bottom of my paper bag. I picked it up and sprayed it on my bare chest, rubbing it into my hair and down to my belly button.

I raised my hand to my nose for a long, desperate inhale. He filled my lungs and leaked into my veins before taking over my heart and mind. I felt him with me, his warm, steamy breath on my neck and his soft skin on mine.

A chill swept up my back, and I hurried into the shower. I took the suction cup end and slapped it onto the wall of the shower an inch or so lower than my dick, at the perfect height to get it in by myself. My untested aim had me probing myself most uncomfortably until the head of the dildo finally got caught in my asshole.

The cold-hot rawness of the rubber felt violating at first. As it slid inside, I let out a silent moan and reached for the shower wall in front of me, and a wave of Amias's fragrance wafted across my face. I imagined him behind me, inching his dick into my ass ever so delicately. With every centimeter, my dick grew larger until I could go no further. I thrust forward and backward, forward and backward, moving with more speed each time.

My hand slipped loosely over my nose, and I closed my eyes. He stood behind me, holding my waist, pulling me back onto him. His dick penetrated me long and hard as I imagined him with a breathless, open-mouth smile and a painfully, pleasantly large cock. I spat into my hand and started aggressively stroking my dick. Every muscle in my body simultaneously flexed and relaxed, and each breath grew deeper until the walls echoed with my breathy moans. My toes rolled up under my feet, my back arched, and my vision faded from purple to blue to black. A sharp, intense muscle spasm exploded in my groin, and out came a flood of sticky, white goop. Euphoria.

As per usual, my mind instantly went to the pits. I thought about how guilty I was and how disgusted everyone would've been with me if they knew I'd been doing *it* and worse again. At one point, I even looked on the other side of the shower curtain to see if I could spot a demon or perhaps Jesus there to scold me.

Nothing.

I abruptly remembered that terrible night in late June and felt relieved to be able to let go of the rules; I just wished I could let go of the trauma. I wanted to forget the internalized rules and stress I associated with living freely. I wanted to have more room for thinking about *him.*

What's the opposite of kryptonite? Because that's what he was for me.

FALL

The first breath of autumn was in the air, a prodigal feeling, a feeling of wanting, taking, and keeping before it is too late.

–J.L. CARR.

CHAPTER 7: FREE

S leep never returned to me—not at appropriate times, anyway—even when the cool autumn breezes came to blow the blistering summer humidity away. Memories of family board game nights in the den or of our day-long kayaking trips down the Greenbrier River kept me awake when longing for Amias's touch didn't, which was rarely.

During those brief moments of emptiness, I occasionally remembered weeklong campouts in the living room after storms knocked our power out and family hikes up the street to see the fall foliage from the mountaintop, and my eagerness to leave for college would dim slightly. But those windows of nostalgia never lasted longer than fifteen minutes or so as I inevitably wound up imagining a place where I could create a life worth living. There was too much in the future for me to spend all my time looking back.

My desire to be elsewhere became so intense that playing with my new rubber toy became a real challenge. I tried, but getting a handle on my focus for more than a few seconds at a time seemed impossible. My mind ran uncontrollably to whatever happened to pass through it, and that's why I wore his cologne every day—to feel his warmth and taste his musk, and to catch a glimpse at what heaven felt like when my mind wanted to obsess over other things. All it took was a whiff to transport me back to the best worst night of my life.

On my last night at home, I took a sleeping pill to guarantee some rest, but I woke up an hour or so after I dozed off drenched in sweat and nauseous as could be. I'd only ever known one school with a couple hundred kids in a town where everybody knew everybody, but Morgantown, the place I'd soon call home, had a population of over thirty thousand and an additional student population of about twenty-five thousand. My classes would be in buildings across two campuses in different neighborhoods, and the commute would require either a ride on the bus or the railway system on campus, which blogs and message boards assured me consistently ran late or broke down. I couldn't begin to imagine what my life would look like in just a few hours, but my mind certainly got to work drawing up some worst-case scenarios.

Wednesday night gave way to Thursday morning as the sun gradually came alive over the mountain. I sat on the edge of my bed for the last time and rubbed my dry hands over my face and back through my messy hair, thinking about how I'd suffered through my last night in my bed and would now suffer through my last morning at home.

So many lasts.

I limped into the kitchen where Mama frantically stirred a pot of bubbling, peppery country gravy and pried apart fluffy, buttery biscuits knowing she probably wouldn't have the stomach to eat any herself. She greeted me with a difficult smile—one she forced into existence beneath her red eyes and puffy cheeks. She donned one of her most prized black dresses and a beautiful blue butterfly broach she only ever broke out for major events, and her hair curled up and flowed out the way it did in her high school pageant-winning photos. I knew I'd miss waking up to her comforting breakfasts every morning.

Mama and I had always had a special relationship, one where she was a little more human than anybody else cared to be. When Dad grounded me from my electronics for a month or so at a time, she gave me time with them while he was away under the agreement that if he caught me, she had no idea. Her go-to words of encouragement if we faced a tough test at school were always, "Don't worry too much. They can't eat you."

She was great like that, and it didn't stop there. Once when leadership at church raised Cain over me dyeing my hair blonde and using a "girly" phone case in middle school, she told them where to stick their unwanted opinions, and then she'd look at me and say, "Don't forget what it's like to be a kid, okay?" There'd been times I felt she could've done or said more than she did, but I respected her for standing up at all. Nobody else ever did.

After everyone else woke up and devoured breakfast, Dad and Remi grabbed the last of my bags and hustled out the door behind Juliet, and Mama and I swung by my bedroom to do one last check for any important belongings. We scanned the closet, under the bed, and in all the drawers for anything I may have forgotten, trying to get the most out of our final moments in my room together.

"Well," Mama said, voice quivering. "Your room... It's

never been so empty."

"I know, but it's not really. There are a lot of memories here." I glanced around. "I'm gonna miss this room."

She looked at me with tears streaming down her face, and my eyes started watering. "I'm gonna miss you, Monte. You have no idea." She paused, and the pressure in my chest grew immensely. "Parents are not perfect people, and sometimes we do horrible things we'll have to carry with us for the rest of our lives... I just wanted to tell you— how—" She stopped, her voice too broken to continue.

"I will always love you, Mama."

She wrapped her arms around me and held onto me tightly, and my mind cleared as her warmth replaced the coldness I'd come to accept as normal. "Psalms 139:13 to 16—When you read it, think of me, and think of you. If you remember one thing I've ever told you, please let it be this: I love you the way you are—*exactly* the way you were born."

Mama knew me, perhaps better than I did, but she too lived in a place where her opinion had to stay suppressed beneath the church and Dad since he'd been given Head of Household status by Everyone's Favorite Book. That's not to say she didn't act with strength and courage when she needed to, though; no, it was quite the opposite. To speak out for what one believes in when not born into a role of God-given power is one of the strongest things any person can do, and that's exactly who she was—one of the strongest people.

I don't know where she got it, but Mama handed me a canvas with thick layers of colorful paint on it. I held it tightly and examined the image brushed onto it.

Standing on a stony, caramel-colored shore at the edge

of a stormy blue sea was a man wearing a colorful sweater. A dark, violent storm raged around him, whipping up whitecaps and puffy, black clouds, and centered in the distance, a tornado of explosive rainbow colors whirled around. But the man didn't seem fearful. He faced it head-on, awaiting its arrival from his sturdy perch atop the high rock. On the back, Mama had written "Psalm 139:13-16. I Love You The Way You Are, My Sweet Montgomery."

I held it closely and thought about what Mama must've been thinking about when she got it. She picked it out specifically for me. She picked the Bible verse out with my circumstances in mind. I looked up at her and felt like she might have the ability to see the future based on the glint of hope in her eyes. I hoped she could see a future where I brought someone familiar home with me.

"Time to go!" Dad yelled from the door. We wiped away our tears, and I left our home out the holler behind for a new life.

* * *

"Bye, love ya."

"Bye. Love ya."

"Bye... Love ya."

A broken record.

That was what we sounded like before my family left me to adjust to life in busy Morgantown by myself. I'd chosen one of the few co-ed dorms on the downtown campus with air conditioning—Honors Hall, thanks to my high school G.P.A.—so I didn't mind hanging out there while I waited on somebody I knew to arrive. Honors students got a few extra benefits to sweeten the deal, and one of them was the ability to move in a day ahead of everyone else, which seemed pointless to me, but I did it anyway.

I didn't mind my room, either. It stretched twenty feet or so from the door and couldn't have been more than ten feet wide, and my roommate's closet protruding into the middle of the room served as a partition to separate our living spaces. He'd settled in with the bed by the window, leaving me with the bed by the door. About halfway down the wall opposite his closet was a door to a small hallway leading to three doors: one with a toilet, one with a shower, and one locked, which I presumed to be my suitemates' room. I retreated into my room and locked the door to the bathroom hallway.

The yellow walls and wooden-looking linoleum did little to make the place feel homey, and my roommate's posters of half-naked women drinking beer on random beaches annoyed me more than they comforted me.

I added a few small decorations, which helped a little: a succulent on my bedside table, a picture of the ocean I took on a trip to Florida beside my closet door, and of course, my new painting from Mama directly above my bed where everyone who came in would be sure to see it. I placed my Bible in my bottom desk drawer and my laptop on top, and Amias's cologne went in the drawer on my bedside table with my dildo.

I suppose the time was barely after 5 p.m. when I got the last of my things unpacked. I wandered over to our fifth-story window, daunted by the layers upon layers of concrete and brick before me and the narrow, bustling alleyways and streets crisscrossing them. The nearest patch of wilderness was several miles upriver, and my car was parked in my space up the hill in a university lot

—a whole bus ride away. No kitchen. No private bathroom. No living room or porch.

Everything changed, but I mostly liked it.

To soothe the pang of homesickness festering in the pits of my stomach, I stripped down to my underwear and slid under my new comforter and into my chilly, crisp sheets for some much-needed rest. My eyes had been closed for about five minutes when the least charming individual in Morgantown exploded through the door, blaring some Hozier song from the Bluetooth speaker clipped to his belt loop. He walked in without a care and flipped on the lights on my side of the room.

"Oh, hey bro." He turned and flashed me a dopey smile. "Are you asleep?"

"I was," I whispered, thinking about how stupid of a question that was to ask a person. "You must be Samuel."

"That's Sam, man. Montgomery, right? Nice to meetcha." When he leaned in for a handshake, I noticed four purple hickeys circling his neck like a scarf, one visible from every angle. My only exposure to beer, or alcohol at all, up to that point had been when Dad had a drinking problem in my earliest years, but his beer-scented body odor told me that was changing effective immediately.

Sam fumbled to our shared mini-fridge-microwave hybrid and pulled out a six-pack of some generic beer. "Wanna brewski, broski?"

"Uh, no thanks. I'm good, *broski*. Maybe later."

He let out a chuckle that ended in a burp and let me know his plan for paying me back his half of our only appliance involved access to "bottomless brewskis," doughnuts, and ramen, and a guaranteed "chill ass time." Aiming to be "one hundred percent real as fuck," he also let me know he planned on having lots of "female traffic" in and out, but he made up for that by telling me I could come in as long as I knew they wouldn't be stopping.

Sam chugged his second beer and shot out the door with a thunderous belch, slapping the top of the doorframe on his way. I needed a minute to process everything that just happened, but I took relief in knowing Sam probably wouldn't be back for a while and flipped the lights back off, naively hoping I might be able to get back to sleep.

I spent all summer wishing I could escape my family, but now I missed them more than I thought possible. I couldn't stop thinking about Mama getting home and seeing my empty bedroom. It couldn't have been easy for her to support me the way she did, and I knew it wouldn't be easy for me to adjust to life without her, either. If Sam had been any kind of indication of the people I now lived with, I was doomed to never like anybody. Crass, rude, and inconsiderate didn't sound like ideal qualities to me. At least people at church had manners.

I struggled to comprehend the amount of control I now had to grapple with, too. There I was at the biggest school in West Virginia, a short walk or ride to anything I could ever want with more money than ever and nobody to tell me where to spend it. It scared me more than it empowered me, though—the thought I could do anything I wanted.

My eyelids flopped open. Suddenly, I remembered Sam's offer and that people on T.V. often drank alcohol to fall asleep.

I'm not getting drunk; I just need sleep. This is what people do.

I pulled the fridge open and an ice-cold can of beer practically fell into my hand.

It sat on my nightstand where I could watch it for a long while. I finally decided the can itself posed no risk to my health and picked it up to get a better look. It felt abnormally cold, colder than soda usually felt. I took my index finger and pried it under the stiff tab on the top, cracking it open, sending droplets of beer all over my hand.

I took a sniff from the small black hole. Chemically or maybe wheaty? It smelled unlike anything I'd ever sniffed before—a little fresher than the nasty odor riding along on heavy drinkers like Sam but still not pleasant. I pulled the can to my lips, raised it to the sky, and took a big gulp.

Fuh-uh-uck.

Sam's beer tasted nasty even ice-cold. Think cat piss mixed with watered-down Sprite blended with stale bread and you'll understand what his cheap beer tasted like. I took another giant swig and was surprised it didn't taste any better the second time. I wanted nothing more than to fall asleep, so I decided to chug the whole can, belching as horrifically as Sam had on his way out. A few minutes went by, and still, I felt nothing but nauseous and a little bloated. I wondered if a person could be immune to the effects of alcohol but suddenly remembered the massive lunch buffet we hit on our way into town.

I just need one more.

By the time the last drink of the second one fizzled down my throat, the effects of the first one had begun working through my veins. I felt it first in the back of my neck like a massage, and then my body heated up from head to toe. The symptoms I felt intrigued me, so I turned on Over the Garden Wall and sat back to enjoy the journey.

I woke up the next morning around noon with blurry memories and dozens of missed phone calls and texts from Merida. I didn't have the energy to sit and read through them all, but a quick skim of the thread revealed she and Keith moved in early and wanted to get lunch. My head throbbed and my mouth felt dry, so I grabbed a Tylenol and a sip of apple juice before responding to her messages. I looked into the mirror, worried she might notice I'd been drinking, but ultimately decided I didn't care if she knew and walked out without much preparation.

I regretted not getting up in time to go somewhere for a bottle of Gatorade when the heat dried out my tongue. The sun never seemed brighter, and I realized how loud cars were walking down the sidewalk inches from nonstop traffic.

On my first ride on the university's railway system, I saw more cars and city buses than I'd ever seen in my life. The small rail car meandered across town on the winding tracks, packed tightly with students new and old, and we passed over road after road of bumper-to-bumper traffic and overfilled parking lots. Every street was backed up with cars, moving vans, and droves of students partying wildly between them. Bedsheets spray-painted with phrases so explicit you'd never want to read them with your parents hung proudly from the windows in every other house, and I suddenly understood why the university considered early move-in a bonus for Honors students.

I finally arrived at the suburban campus and found Merida and Keith waiting in their car outside of their dorm after a muggy slog across two courtyards.

"Thanks for coming to get me guys," I said sarcastically, sliding into the backseat and snapping my seatbelt into place.

"I wasn't messing with traffic downtown or I would've come to get you," said Keith. "Let's just go get lunch."

A quick sniff of my fist reminded me why I had been so excited to get to Morgantown in the first place, and the last place I wanted to be was hanging out with people I knew wanted me to stay the same. I wanted new friends in my new town for my new life.

Soon enough, I thought.

"So Monte, we found the perfect church for Sunday," Merida said as soon as the server left us at our booth in the corner of the adobe-style dining room. The words "Los Amigos" glowed bright red above her. "It's right downtown, probably a fifteen-minute walk from Honors, and Keith's parents went there when they lived in Morgantown."

"Yeah, it's an awesome church. Bigger than what we're used to," Keith added.

"And listen to this Monte. They have a dating program designed to help single people meet other single people in churches across Morgantown. You'll love it."

"Sure, that sounds great," I said half-assedly, but she didn't notice. I just wanted to get through lunch, and thankfully, I eventually did. I managed to butter Keith up enough he offered to drive me back downtown. The ride to Honors passed quietly and quickly, but the silence felt more awkward than it did peaceful.

I reached for the front door of Honors, thinking about how lucky I'd been to make it all day without a formal invitation to church when Keith rolled down his window and hollered my name.

"We'll be here at 9:30 Sunday morning to pick you up!"

I paused briefly, but I didn't say anything and continued inside to the elevator, thinking maybe I could act like I didn't hear his announcement to get out of going.

"Hey, hey man!" someone shouted from the student lounge as I stepped off the elevator on the fifth floor. I turned to see what was going on, and a girl burst through the archway to the lounge, waving her hands like a runway worker at the airport. Her long, thick, curly brown hair blew behind her as she dashed down the hall to me. "Any chance you've got an HDMI cable? You can watch penile enlargement videos on the lounge T.V. with us if you do."

It took a second or two of nervous laughter for me to realize she wasn't joking. "Sure, let me go grab it." She showed her gratitude with a couple swear words and a high-five and told me her name was Imani before running back to her friends.

I ran by my room for my HDMI cord and jogged back to the lounge where Imani stood over a laptop with real penile enlargement videos, and her friends sat on blankets on the floor.

"Hey guy, I'm Ryder. This is Avery, and you've already met Imani." The tallest guy I'd ever met introduced everyone to me before offering me a hit of his banana nut bread flavored vape, which I nearly choked to death on.

Once Imani's laptop played over the T.V., she ran to join us on the floor. The group seemingly had no qualms about the real-life gore in the videos we spent several hours watching. They laughed at points. I, on the other hand, found it hard to stomach most of it so I preferred the ads or short conversations we'd engage in. The subject made me feel oddly comfortable, though. I knew I was in the presence of people who really wouldn't judge me for seeking out whatever happiness I wanted.

As the night progressed, I learned that Imani and Avery grew up together in the southern West Virginia town of Chapmanville, but Ryder, who they met the night before, was from a small town in Connecticut.

We'd only been watching videos for an hour when Avery disappeared into the elevator.

"So, what's his deal?" I asked. "Seems pretty quiet."

Imani looked up at me with a smile that read something like *You Dumb Fucking Idiot.* "Um... Avery is non-binary and prefers the pronouns 'they' and 'them.'"

I had heard the term non-binary before, but I never really understood what it meant. Most of the people at my church either laughed at folks with different backgrounds or, as Amias had cleverly put it, treated them like special projects. I'd always been taught to show them love—if you could call it that—from a safe distance, where the demons and spirits wreaking havoc in their lives could never touch me.

I didn't give it any more thought. They were happy, and I didn't see why everyone shouldn't be happy.

By 3 a.m., we turned off the penile enlargement videos, and Imani turned on live streams of something she called "vaporwave," a new kind of music I came to enjoy over the course of the night. We laid there until Avery finally returned—proudly carrying a giant box of freshly baked cookies.

Imani threw her arms into the air and jumped up. "That's where you fucking went, you goddamned angel! These are gonna be delicious."

She sounded vulgar, but she spoke the truth. Every cookie melted in my mouth, and chocolate chips erupted like molten craters throughout them. We ate the whole box with the help of the half-gallon of milk my parents left for me and laid back to listen to more music. Life felt genuinely good for once.

The sun shining softly through the windows of the lounge woke us up early the next morning. I couldn't believe I fell asleep with so many people, something my parents never would've been okay with.

Another chain is broken, I thought.

Imani shared her plans for the day before heading back to her room. She'd heard about an all-day party in the afternoon, so we swapped phone numbers to link back up later in the day. I went back to my room, too, excited to have found new friends so quickly.

After waking up from my nap, I saw a group chat on my phone Imani named "Blunt Bros." She added everyone to it, and they were already at the dining hall across the street grabbing lunch when I woke up. I hurriedly freshened up, threw on another outfit, spritzed on some of *his* cologne, and ran to join them.

I arrived as everyone scraped the last of their scraps into the garbage cans and left their dishes in the kitchen window, but they stayed to hang out while I ate. I'd never had friends prioritize me like that. It made me smile. It made me feel like maybe I did belong somewhere after all.

Imani told me to expect another fun night, a much wilder night than the one I'd just woken up from, if I was up for it.

"It's Morgantown's first weekend back from the dead of summer. All the parties and clubs are gonna be insane," said Avery.

"It's your choice," said Ryder.

But what if Dad finds out? I wondered. *And I'm supposed to go to church with Merida and Keith in the morning.*

I sniffed his cologne on my wrist.

"I can't wait."

CHAPTER 8:
JUST A TASTE

I had no experience at house parties, much less frat parties, so my mind raced as I hobbled across town in the blistering midday heat with a stomach so full of greasy dining hall food I thought it might explode. The bass from the frat houses pounded across town like a never-ending earthquake, vibrating my chest more intensely with each step we took toward the address on Imani's phone.

By the time we turned the corner onto the steep brick street aptly dubbed "Frat Row," the music threatened to burst my eardrums. My shirt clung to my sticky, damp skin as Imani led us up my new least favorite hill to the frat house—a giant brick building resembling a wealthy church from back home.

Imani strolled past the shirtless muscular dudes on the shaded porch who drunkenly shouted, "Chicks drink free!" before handing her a red plastic cup, but they demanded five dollars apiece from the rest of us. Our fivers earned us each one single cup, and plastic cups acted as two things: our ticket inside and our ticket to the heavily guarded kegs in the basement.

I hoped the inside would provide some relief from the heat lingering in Morgantown, but I was sorely disappointed. The hosting fraternity had some industrial fans going full force, but thanks to Morgantown's rainforest-like climate, they only blew more smelly, humid air around. The smell was pretty nauseating on a sober and full stomach—cheap incense overpowered by a mixture of body odor, body spray, and beer.

Ah, beer. Everywhere I looked, the piss-colored beverage filled red plastic cups to the brim.

Imani directed us through a red door in the back of a massive, stainless-steel kitchen, and we shuffled down the squeaky wooden stairs to the nastiest basement I'd ever seen. The blinding sunbeams and scalding heat failed to penetrate that far into the home, saving me from having to see how dirty it was, but they obviously had a mildew problem because I could smell it over everything else.

A long, dimly lit hallway stretched out at the bottom of the stairs, eerily silent and devoid of life. I followed my new friends closely past several closed doors, and a chill crept up my arms as I imagined what horror stories they could've told if doors could talk. I thought it best not to linger in that corner of my mind for too long.

We finally made it to the end of the hallway, which opened up to a large room with equally poor lighting. Scattered throughout the room were four kiddie pools containing a tapped keg and loads of ice, each closely guarded by a different frat member filling red cups as quickly as people could hand them over.

"Are y'all sure about this?" I asked.

"I mean, I'm gonna drink, but you guys don't have to."

Imani went straight for the kiddie pool in the far corner. "Just remember we're only here to get drunk. We'll hit the clubs after," Avery reminded me. "Beer'll probably smooth the edges on this place a little if you know what I mean."

The short line went quickly, which was nice because it gave me less time to think about running back to Nicholas County and confessing my sins to people who didn't deserve my time. The guy at the keg yanked the cup from my clammy palm without even looking at me and filled it to the top, and I followed Avery, Ryder, and Imani to the hallway. I watched as they chugged every last drop.

Seems safe enough. They weren't foaming at the mouth. They didn't pass out or start puking. They laughed and had a good ass time. I closed my eyes, plugged my nose, and quickly downed mine, too.

We fetched a few more refills, and the place felt less skeevy with each one, just like Avery said it would. The muscles in my back relaxed the way only beer could make them, only this time, it didn't stop there. I began to notice after the third refill I had a hard time standing still, and walking grew more challenging every minute.

Fourth, fifth, sixth—it got hard to keep track. The vibe of the main room shifted considerably when we stumbled back up with our umpteenth refill. I had scarcely enough time to notice if there was even a smell anymore before the beat began moving through me rather than booming around me. Hips everywhere gyrated in sync with mine and countless arms reached to the sky as I melted into the crowd, and I forgot I didn't know the people around me.

I ran out of beer but only for a minute or two. Someone

knocked my empty cup out of my hand and replaced it with a half-full one, and I chugged it, too. I forgot how to worry, how to cry, how to hide. I forgot about filters and inhibitions. I forgot about god.

I forgot about anything that didn't make me happy.

Ryder rounded us up and told us to meet him outside, so we rushed out into the heavy air and huddled on the sidewalk. The sun had set some time ago and given way to a starless Morgantown night. Ryder fumbled to the middle of our group screaming, "Club Time, bitches!" and the name of a nightclub he heard about down High Street.

High Street led a sort of double life. In the daytime, committed students, hardworking townies, and a wide array of visitors explored the quaint boutiques, exotic restaurants, and casual sports bars, but things worked very differently on weekend nights.

On Frat Row, which was actually North High Street, people seeking a cheap drink in the form of a frat party keg or an impromptu block party loaded the street from one sidewalk to the other, and south of Willey Street— where North High ended—High Street's sidewalks were lined with people waiting to get into hazy nightclubs, crowded bars, and restaurants open specifically to serve Morgantown's drunk college students. From pole-dancing scenes and gay bars to mellow tobacco clubs and drunk arcades, High Street had a little bit of everything according to Ryder, Imani, and Avery.

Our first and only club stop that night was one of the ones more popular with the underaged crowd because, according to Ryder's friend from Connecticut, anybody could drink. We waited in line under the bright neon lights so long I thought my knees might give out on me, and I wanted to do anything else with my alcohol-inspired energy.

The mouthwatering aroma from the carnival food stand across the street made my stomach gurgle as loudly as the cars whooshing past on their way down High Street. The vintage video game store down the alley we waited in line next to begged me to spend my student loan money there, but I had to wait in a stupid line.

We eventually made it to the front, and once again, Imani walked in and downstairs free of charge and without any harassment. The rest of us, however, coughed up ten dollars and consented to a pat-down before being rewarded with an ugly green stamp on the back of our hands and being shoved downstairs.

Avery and I followed Ryder across two overcrowded dancefloors and found Imani smooth-talking one of her hometown friends out of the glowing band around his arm—the only way to get service at the bar. It took some seriously stupid flattery and a crisp ten-dollar bill, but he finally handed over his wristband. She carefully slipped it on and disappeared in the direction of the nearest bar.

I looked around the dark room, which felt more like a basement with pretty lights and loud music than it did a nightclub, and considered telling my new friends I needed to go because of something imaginary, but I stayed. The guilt from back home plaguing the back of my mind couldn't last forever. I just needed to keep adding distance—distance and alcohol.

Imani returned moments later and slammed a pitcher full of some icy blue beverage on the table in front of us. "Drink up, shitheads!"

"What is that?" I became soberingly paranoid as Mama's dramatic true-crime specials often featured victims who accepted unknown drinks in seedy locales.

"It's a trashcan, Monte!" Imani bent over and started slurping from a straw. That name didn't answer my question, but her eagerness to drink it did. Avery leaned in for a straw, too.

"It tastes like juice but fucks you up. Best club drink by a mile, my dude," Ryder said, tonguing a straw into his mouth.

I grabbed one of the remaining straws and leaned in to drink before everyone else finished it without me. Ryder was right—the refreshing blue drink tasted like fruit punch, a pleasant change from the watery beer I'd been drinking.

We emptied the pitcher in a matter of minutes, and the club morphed into a dreamy light show like the scenes in Imani's vaporwave videos. I stumbled onto the dancefloor and danced more energetically than I ever had to songs I'd never heard before. Faces blended sloppily, and I could no longer tell my friends from the crowd. My arms and legs turned to raw dough and flowed loosely, reacting to the movement of my torso and the pulse of the music with the same rhythm as the guy next to me and the girl next to him and the person behind her. I danced with everybody, but really, I danced with Nobody.

Nobody to judge me.

Nobody to stop me.

Nobody to fear.

Nobody.

A group of Nobodies near the fan I'd taken shelter under absorbed me with the offer of a straw in their pitcher, and I sucked down alcohol until their pitcher bubbled emptily at the bottom of my straw. I looked up and, at that exact moment, caught a boy at the end of a straw on the other side grinning at me.

His dark brown hair was long on the top, swooping back in that glorious 1980s fashion I loved, and it flopped about on his head like wet pasta as he shook himself carelessly in my direction. The slim white tee shirt he wore tucked loosely into a pair of skinny jeans drew my attention to his small beer belly, but he carried it with more confidence and charisma than I'd been targeted by in a while. The way he thrust and jived and smiled at me as if he'd known me for lifetimes captivated my attention, charming me in a way only one person ever had.

Just a taste, I thought.

From behind, he began pumping his waist in sync with mine, pulling me back onto his hips before running his hands up my body and through my hair. With his stomach pressed into the small of my back and the music thumping louder and louder, our thrusting intensified, and I felt something new growing in his pants and then something new growing in mine.

I turned my head to look when he grabbed the back of my head and pressed my lips to his. Wet with sweat and drunk as could be, we danced on each other and kissed a thousand kisses. I felt alive again. Mr. Nobody wasn't the Somebody I missed, but his taste gave me hope.

Around midnight, the lights swooped into the most hectic rainbow explosion possible, and kaleidoscopic patterns of color flashed over me as bartenders hit us with streams of brightly colored water from their water squirters. The D.J., hidden safely behind a plexiglass shield, made demands the crowd obeyed in return for a heavier beat. I imagined Amias dancing around me and rubbing against me, that it was him who I'd just had my lips pressed against. I wanted nothing more than to suck his face off.

Imani, Ryder, and Avery pulled me out of the club before I could sober up enough to ask for Mr. Nobody's number, and I was too far gone to resist. I'm not sure why, but I expected some sort of shaming or disgust from them.

That wasn't them, though.

"Fuck man, you were getting it!" Imani swung around a tree growing through a square patch of soil in the sidewalk outside the club entrance.

Ryder bent over to dry heave and looked up at me briefly. "Beginner's luck."

"Call it what you want, I'm—" I hit the alley next to him and puked my brains out.

I woke up the following morning with a busting headache to my room spinning around me. The white morning sun peeked through the closed blinds across the room, piercing into the darkest corners of my skull. I couldn't remember a thing.

I spotted a glass of water someone apparently poured for me and decided to take a drink, or a hundred, but before I could get it to my mouth, a flailing muscle began to wriggle up from my stomach to the back of my throat. I jumped out of bed hastily and nearly landed on Imani's head. She and Avery slept soundly on the floor, using one of Sam's tapestries as a blanket, and Ryder slept pressed against the wall behind me in the bed. My admiration was brief as my stomach gurgled to remind me why I leapt out of bed in the first place.

I checked my phone when I returned to my bed, making sure not to wake everyone else up, and found over two dozen texts and missed calls from Merida and Keith. I couldn't help but roll my eyes. They were on their way and planned to be at Honors around 9:30 to pick me up for church.

I checked the top of my screen.

9:16. Damn it.

I came up with a fib for Merida about being sick to get out of it and turned off my phone, rolling back over to go to sleep.

Within fifteen minutes, all four of us were shaken awake by knocking at the door and yelling from the other side. I instantly knew who it was: Merida and Keith, ignoring my messages the way I ignored theirs.

I fought back against their coercion and guilt-tripping with every weapon in my arsenal, but it wasn't good enough.

"You have to come with us, Montgomery. It's the first Sunday morning of the semester, and this is when they're gonna be taking on the most new people," Keith said as I stood in my underwear in the doorway.

Merida stepped in front of Keith. "Keith's parents told us it's crucial to be there the first Sunday because if you start a week late, you'll be behind everyone else. Plus, it's harder to fall away if you don't give yourself the chance."

I would've done anything to get them to shut up, so I caved.

Imani, Ryder, and Avery were sitting on the bed talking when I went back in to get dressed. They didn't seem frustrated, offended, or judgmental like I expected them to be, like my friends in the past had always been.

They told me to have a good morning; all they asked for was a text in the group chat when I got back on campus. I began to understand there were people out there who wouldn't want to fix me, and I might've already found them. I liked knowing I had open-minded people in my life.

I noticed a heaviness in the air when I sat back in Keith's car like someone had gotten divorced or died or something. I didn't know why, and I didn't care to figure it out.

"Umm... Monte, I need to ask you a question," Merida said, breaking the silence once we were out of sight of Honors.

"Okay?" I couldn't help but roll my eyes, knowing I was about to learn why the car felt the way it did.

She turned off the radio. "Who were those people in your bed?"

"Just some new friends I made in Honors."

Merida stiffened up.

"Why'd they stay with you if you're sick?" Keith asked from the driver's seat.

"Oh, uh." I hadn't even considered that connection. "They're sick, too." I knew that smelled like bullshit as it slipped through my lips.

"They're sick, too? Really, Monte? You expect us to believe that?" Merida smelled it, too.

After a small window of quiet, Keith took a deep breath. "Ya know, Monte, we decided to walk down High Street last night to see what kind of people hang out around there after dark, and you won't believe who we saw waiting in line at some club."

They looked at each other and smiled connivingly like cops who'd caught an elusive criminal red-handed.

BECAUSE I REMEMBER YOU

Then, he raised his eyes in the rearview mirror to make eye contact with me. "Have anything you want us to pray for at church today, Monte?"

My heart stopped. I could feel an energy welling up inside me, but I couldn't tell if it was going to lead me to scream or to cry or to commit a murder. My body temperature rose sharply, and my skin went from dry to dripping in seconds. I never once thought I'd have to worry about Merida and Keith seeing me on High Street on a Saturday night.

"Were you guys spying on me?"

Merida turned around with a straight face. "Not exactly, but you should know we have been asked to keep an eye on you."

"You've been what?"

She turned back around to face the windshield, leaving me without any answer for the rest of the car ride. I didn't care to ask again. I didn't care to speak to them again. My heart turned to stone and weighed a million pounds in my chest. I couldn't decide what felt worse: that someone asked them to "keep an eye" on me or that they were actually doing it.

Screw this, and screw y'all, I wanted to say but didn't.

We got there in time for Sunday school in a dark auditorium off of a massive sanctuary, but no matter how hard I tried, I couldn't bring myself to focus on anything. I read over the material they handed me a dozen times and still couldn't remember what it said. Feelings of betrayal and infuriation, and not to mention a hangover, clouded my mind into oblivion.

Time crept by like it hadn't since the last time I sat in a church, and it didn't get any better when the preacher started hooting about desires of the flesh, condemning things like drunkenness, lust, and, of course, homo-sexuality. The more he spouted, the more I considered how little harm those things had done to me.

Being raised in the church had done much more harm than any of those things, but nobody ever wanted to talk about that. Leaving and never coming back sounded like the best idea in the world.

When the last "Amen" was uttered, I essentially sprinted back to the car, but Merida and Keith stopped at the exit to talk to some overly enthusiastic young people. They signed us up for a luncheon at someone's apartment immediately after the service, and once again, I found myself wrapped up in a life someone else was planning for me.

The luncheon part of the meeting only lasted about thirty minutes, but the remainder of the meeting ran on for hours. It ended up being some sort of orientation to the young adult group for new members who wanted to eventually take on a leading role. Eager to regain the au-thority they lost when we graduated from high school and our churches' leadership cabinet, Keith and Merida signed up for every opportunity to help, but I used more caution when writing my name down, so much caution I didn't put it anywhere.

I couldn't help but mull over all the good times I'd had with my childhood youth groups and with Merida and Keith. We'd done so many things together—music festi-vals, concerts, plays, road trips, beaches, camping trips, all the things teenagers do. But the older I got, the more I noticed they required conformity and a lack of authen-ticity. I could never be my true self in front of them because, to be honest, it would've disgusted and scared them. Even if it didn't come out that way in their words, their constant sneaking around to fix me would've gotten the message across. I needed more from supposed friends, and I felt so thankful to have seemingly found it in my new friends.

The purple and pink sky on the drive back to Honors tried to force something beautiful into my mind over Merida and Keith's vexatious rambling about how pumped they were to be connected with a church so quickly, oblivious to my reluctance. I jumped out of Keith's car as soon as it came to a stop at the curb in front of Honors and jogged through the courtyard to avoid what I feared came next on their agenda.

"Hey, Monte!" Keith yelled from the car, confirming my fear the same way he had before. "We'll be here next week, same time!"

I went on without reaction, taking comfort in the fact that I would be doing everything humanly possible to keep myself out of any other church.

I couldn't wait to link back up with Imani, Ryder, and Avery. I walked into my empty room and plopped down on my bed, sending the text they wanted in the group chat, and within five minutes, my phone buzzed with a response. They discovered a spot up on the hill overlooking downtown and invited me to join them there. So, I dressed down into more casual clothes and had my phone guide me to their marker on the map.

From the spot they found, even through the light fog, I could see all of downtown Morgantown and nearly all of the downtown-adjacent neighborhoods from the riverbank to the hilltops. Across the dark Monongahela River stretched the suburb of Westover and a little further upriver rose the tall buildings of Morgantown's Wharf district. The central university halls shined in the projector lights hanging off them, and city side-walks bustled with students despite the late hour.

"Hey guys," I said, walking toward the group with a smile on my face.

"Hey bro. Smell that?" I took a big whiff, and sure enough, I could smell something really strong, something I couldn't quite recognize.

"What is that? It smells a little like a skunk... or maybe burnt coffee?"

They giggled at my guesses.

"Ryder's rolling us a joint," Avery said.

"A joint?"

Ryder sat in the gravel behind a short brick wall licking a seal along the length of a small, white paper tube. He twisted one of the ends and packed green leafy stuff further into the other end with his keys.

"Wanna spark it?" Ryder looked over at me and extended his hands with both the joint and a lighter, and I nodded. He came to me and began a tutorial on how to light a joint before biting the twisted part off with his front teeth.

I said I'd smoke it but not without pause. All the stories I'd heard about pot came rushing back to me: people getting addicted, people going crazy on it, and the worst of all, people using it as a gateway to other, more addictive drugs.

But then I remembered how everything people told as a child was starting to feel like bullshit mind games used to keep me under someone's thumb. Everyone always told me I felt miserable because my heart had a god-sized hole—a hole only he could fill. Why, then, had I spent my entire life filling the hole with him only to come up feeling empty as hell? It didn't make sense.

I brought the joint to my lips, flicked the lighter, and inhaled. I don't know what I expected, perhaps something like the cigarette that nauseated me by the road months before, but it wasn't like that. The burning started in my throat, spreading like wildfire down my esophagus and into my lungs.

I coughed harder than I ever had before, and with each cough, out came a giant, billowy cloud of smoke. Imani laughed her ass off as I nearly hacked my lungs up over the hill in front of me, the lights of Morgantown blurring below. As I stared out across the valley, what I saw and felt transformed. Small points of light scattered around me, twinkling as if the stars above had crashed into the world below to eradicate the darkness.

"Small puff this time, not like a cig," Ryder said on my next turn. "The big hits get the job done, but the small hits are good, too."

I didn't get the beginner's tolerance Ryder and Imani warned me about—my muscles relaxed after the coughing subsided, and my eyes grew severely dry over the next several minutes. I drifted away on some puffy cloud of positivity with my new friends in my new town with my new life, and I never wanted to look back.

CHAPTER 9:
DO IT, THEN

T hanks to my pretty sleepless summer at home and late nights with Imani, Ryder, and Avery, I had no problem getting to sleep early the night before class, and waking up the next morning was much easier than I expected. With my backpack loaded, my hair combed, and my cologne spritzed—the cologne I no longer left my room without—I felt ready for class and had more than enough time to spare.

I trekked across Morgantown in heavy heat and music-festival-sized crowds to every class, wondering how elitist and judgmental my new classmates and teachers might be, worried about coming off as too snobby or not snobby enough. Thousands of students walked in the same direction as me and in the opposite direction, too, wearing anything from suits and dresses to jeans and hoodies. We were everywhere: courtyards, cafes, side-walks, parks, ledges, lounges, and even parking garages. I couldn't have spit my gum out without hitting an-other student, and it didn't make me feel great.

I missed being able to walk out my back door and into

the forest. I missed waking up knowing exactly what I was going to have for breakfast, lunch, and dinner. Mama's comforting smile. School's familiar smells. My roots somewhere I could see them. I missed so many things about home.

University scared me, especially when I thought about all the strict things my high school teachers told me to expect out of professors, but all of that turned out to be, yet again, no more than some fear-mongering false information. Professor after professor laid to rest my worries with a detailed syllabus and attendance policies that matched high school in severity for the most part. Some had cell phone policies, and some didn't. Some checked attendance, and some didn't. It honestly felt more relaxed than high school in many ways, but the material covered seemed more complex and extraordinarily interesting.

I found myself absorbed in Anthropology 101 more than any of my other classes. When Professor Navarro passed around an arrowhead from a society that existed thousands of years ago, I studied each man-made chip and engraving, and a sort of smug grin crept onto my face. It took my breath away, holding something crafted by someone who lived so long ago, but the more I considered its age, the more I considered it an invalidation of the Biblical scholars who'd shaped my worldview at Old Prospects Baptist.

I held, in my hands, physical evidence of the earth and human society existing far earlier than the six thousand years they'd always sworn by, and it tasted so sweet knowing they got something else wrong. Even if that wasn't in and of itself a fatal blow to their know-it-all teachings, the fact that this arrowhead and its creator existed far before the idea of Christianity was.

How could it be, I pondered, *that everyone who lived went to hell because they were born before the fiery pits were written about?*

I could see beyond the scriptures and sermons for once. My life was mine to consider, and I was working with all new information. Drinking and smoking hadn't killed me. Giving into gay thoughts hadn't burned me. And contrary to what everyone told me to expect if I ever backslid, the guilt didn't stick.

The dawn of a new era—the Era of Monte—I chose to forget about almost everything from my old life. If something made me happy, and it didn't cause any harm, there was no reason for me not to do it. I wanted to understand the world as a member of it rather than as some half-invested tourist whose sole purpose was to pass through, too obsessed with the next stop to enjoy this one. I didn't need church anymore, and Merida and Keith seemed to have finally gotten the message and stopped asking if I was coming to church altogether. Church fell fully into my rearview mirror where it belonged.

One cool weekend in early October, when the leaves began to turn and the nights grew cold, Imani and I decided to take a walk up the Rail Trail, which followed a path created by the remnants of an old railroad through town. We hopped on the path behind her favorite Asian supermarket and walked north, winding along the broad valley carved out by the Mon River over millennia. We walked about a mile on the paved path until Imani steered us over the hill to a dirt one leading to the muddy riverbank. It forked at the river, where one way disappeared under the hazy brown waves, and the other continued along the river's edge to a stone tunnel. The deep tunnel extended underneath the Rail Trail and into the hill on which Morgantown sprawled, and a rocky creek babbled out from it, creating swirly streamers of clear water in the muddy river.

"¿El fuego?" Imani asked in an attempt to flaunt her new language skills. She sat on a loose cinderblock on the wall at the mouth of the tunnel and tapped next to her, inviting me to join her.

I reached into my front pocket and pulled out my new blue lighter for her, but she insisted I "take greens." I sat on a cold cinderblock beside her and raised the blunt to my lips, cracked my lighter, and watched the flame curl into the end when I inhaled, igniting the magic greens inside.

I got better at taking hits and came to love smoking with Imani. When we smoked, wherever we were, my body relaxed, and my mind slowed down. Music or silence, conversation or company—it simply did not matter. Good times came easy with her as we watched the worries of the world float away on clouds of smoke.

"So Monte, tell me what's going on in your world." Imani took advantage of a moment of silence to drop the conversation to a more intimate level, something she often did, something I found fascinating about her. Her "deep talks," as I came to call them, made me uncomfortable at times, but they always made me think.

"I'm loving all the independence I get living out here on my own," I said, fully aware she'd be digging to unpack that sentence.

"I feel you. It's nice calling the shots, and Morgantown's got loads of shots to call. Were you not given much independence at home?"

I couldn't believe she was just going to take it there so casually, but I didn't mind spilling my guts to her. "Not really. I had so many people telling me what to do and what not to do back home I never had the chance to sit down and figure anything out for myself."

"That must've been terrible as a teenager. Were they all religious?"

I chuckled. "Oh my god, yes. If a rule wasn't from school, it was from the church. I wasn't even allowed to read or watch Harry Potter, and Wizards of Waverly Place came into question a few times. They laid out all these rules and told me I had to follow them to find happiness, but I never found anything except more emptiness. Emptiness and loneliness." I watched as the wind whirled crunchy leaves around us, ruffling the trees overhead. "I have felt happiness before, but never in church. I think that's what I'm out here doing now—trying to find *that* happiness again."

"I hope you find it, man. Any ideas on where to look?"

Immediately, someone came to my mind. He'd been my only source of peace back home, and just the thought of him gave me butterflies like the ones I felt the day I first saw him in the hallway. I wondered for a moment if he remembered me because I remembered him so well.

His lean body and soft lips.

His golden locks and brown eyes.

His pure smile and sweet fragrance.

But he was back in Nicholas County, or even further away for all I knew. A subtle sniff of my wrist would have to suffice.

"I think I want to find someone. I've been thinking about maybe getting into dating."

"Oh yeah? Anyone specific or just dating?"

"Just dating." That was a bald-faced lie. If I had things my way, I would've run into Amias somewhere, and things would've worked out perfectly between us. Real-life didn't happen that way, though, and I needed to get something else started.

"So, I wanna talk about something, and I don't want you to take it the wrong way." She waited on me to nod. "You've been using the term 'bi-curious' to describe the way you dance at the clubs, but I've only ever seen you with guys."

Fuck me.

"Do you think maybe you're gay?"

Nobody had ever asked me such a question, not with her level of sincerity and compassion anyway. My head emptied, refilling with the insecurities people had called me out on since birth. "I don't know." That answer surprised me as it came out of my mouth. My go-to response to that question had always been "Absolutely not," but it didn't come that time.

And, to my surprise, I didn't hate myself for having admitted it.

"That's okay. I just thought I'd ask." She spoke candidly and bumped me playfully on the shoulder.

We finished our blunt and jumped back up on the trail to head back to campus. Imani handed me one of her headphones and put the other in her ear before turning on a vaporwave playlist. I couldn't help but smile because I felt like I could openly and safely get acquainted with a whole different side of myself, one I spent years running from.

Never before could I have so openly considered I might be gay, not unless I wanted preached at and prayed over, but the more I thought about what being gay meant beyond all the homophobia I internalized, the more right it felt.

A week or so later, after spending an uncountable amount of time determining whether or not I actually wanted to do it, I started making changes. I still maintained my bi-curiosity among my friends and told my family I was straight, but I downloaded a gay-specific dating app and increased the distance to as far away as Pittsburgh.

How big of a deal could it be?

Within an hour of launching my account, messages from men all over flooded my inbox. I finally worked up the courage to respond to one late one lonely weeknight right before Halloween. Relying solely on pixelated thumbnails and short message previews, I tried carefully to choose the cutest sender who hadn't started with a picture of his cock.

He went by Chris Zhao. He had impossibly perfect skin, short black hair, and a strong preference for gym clothes. But in one picture, he wore an expertly fitted suit and medical coat in front of the *WV* signage at the university hospital, so I knew he took care of himself. He was fit but not intimidating and sharp but not stuffy. He sent a nice first message.

Check, check, and check.

Shortly after my first reply, he sent another. He was eager to hear from me, made obvious by a straightforward invitation to his place. My mouth tingled, my bones rattled, and my mind splintered in a million different directions as if I'd been waiting in line for a roller coaster and finally made it to the platform.

I can't do this tonight, can I? I mean, nothing is standing in my way, but am I ready for this?

Instinctively, I walked to the little black fridge in the corner of the room and took out one of Sam's cheap beers. The chilly can cracked open under my finger, and I chugged it. I accepted the invitation before it could have any effect, though.

No backing out.

I quickly trimmed up my body hair and brushed my teeth. I wanted to wear something nice but easy to remove so I slipped into my khaki joggers and a loose, red t-shirt, but then that looked too casual, so I replaced it with a flannel that was a little too warm. I settled on a baseball tee. I was tying my shoelaces when I got a text saying he'd arrived, so I sprayed on my favorite cologne and left my room behind.

As I strode out of the shiny metal elevator, I saw him for the first time through the giant lobby windows standing beside a white BMW. He looked nothing like I'd expected—probably around the age of thirty-five, which was a solid lead on my nineteen, and wealthy as hell. He wore a handsome red blazer and a black deep V-neck with jeans, and a silver watch probably worth more than my car gleaned in the streetlights on his wrist. I stopped at the front door and considered turning back, but the liquid courage I chugged upstairs gave me the boost I needed.

Time to let go.

Chris opened the door for me as I approached his car. After a quick, "Hey," I sat down on the tan leather seat, and he gently closed the car door before walking around to the driver's seat. His cologne overpowered the air fresheners jammed in the A/C vents, but it had nothing on Amias Parker's. I took a whiff of my wrist.

We cruised along to Vivaldi, which I found a jarring ambience to set considering our agenda for the night. I only hoped it meant he liked to be romantic.

Chris grabbed the volume knob and turned it down. "I'm going to fuck you rough. I want you to know that. Your profile had you listed as a sub, right?"

That put to rest my curiosities about his levels of romanticism. "Yeah." I *had* listed on my profile I was a submissive, and he was a dominant, but I had little concept of what that truly meant. All I knew was I didn't know what I was doing. I just wanted to do it.

"And you're a virgin, right?"

"Mhm," I answered as we rolled up to a red light. He groaned at my response.

When the car came to a stop, he looked over at me, biting his bottom lip, moving his eyes up and down my body. He picked up my hand and pulled it over to his lap, glowing red in the glare of the traffic light. I thought he was going to have me hold his crotch the whole way to Cheat Lake, but he took my hand and spit in it when the light turned green again.

"Stroke." His instructions were limited, but they were very clear. With my clean hand, I pulled his pants and boxers down slightly, and an average but girthy dick stood stiff as a tree out of a thicket of black pubic hair. I started stroking his shaft with my saliva-covered hand the way I'd always stroked mine, but my arm bent awkwardly to grip his shaft from the passenger seat.

He grabbed my arm and pulled me over onto the middle console.

"Unbuckle."

I obeyed.

Chris kept me giving him a hand job through town,

only pushing me away to spit into my hand again or to keep himself from finishing all over the car. Once we got onto the highway, however, he flung my hand away and set cruise control, pulling his pants down further. He reached for the seat adjustments and rolled his seat as far back as it would go. Then, he grabbed the steering wheel with his left hand. With his right hand, he grabbed mine, sticky and slimy with drying saliva and pre-cum, and ran my fingers up and down from his groin to his neck.

"Suck me."

I knew exactly what he meant for me to do, but I had never done that before. I only knew what I'd seen in porn. He seemed to grow harder at my lack of confidence, though, and a creepy grin coiled slowly into existence under his nose. I bent over the middle console with my knees in the passenger seat and moved my mouth downward. My lips swallowed as much as they could, about three-quarters of his erect penis, but it was not enough for him. He grabbed the back of my head and pressed me further downward, triggering my gag reflex.

Every time I went down and subsequently choked, his dick pulsated larger. The occasional dry and wiry pube wiggled into my mouth and nose from his balls and the base of his shaft. A couple times I tried to pull away to keep myself from dry heaving, but he pushed me back down every time, enjoying the lubrication provided by my nauseous overproduction of saliva.

It wasn't until we got off the highway at Cheat Lake that he finally let me come back up for fresh air—only it wasn't fresh. It was heavy with the smell of his overwhelming cologne and body odor. I used my hands to wipe the sticky goop out of my mustache and beard, re-adjusted my glasses, and returned to the passenger seat.

"You're good for your first time," he said with that same creepy smile. "Let's wait until we get to the bedroom to finish, though."

Chris turned up a steep concrete driveway and pulled up to a giant brick house overlooking the lake and surrounding communities. He led me inside, and I quickly noticed how pristine everything looked. From the polished cherry floors to the black marble countertops, his house had been well-maintained in every way, more than I expected. The colored accent lights on the walls and under the furniture and aroma from the coordinated wax warmers in every room added a sense of hominess despite the barren, manufactured feel of the décor, which felt more reminiscent of a hotel lobby than of a bachelor pad.

He poured us each a glass of wine and then another. I managed to get a handle on my anxiety and trembled less after the second one. The classical music playing over the built-in speakers started to grow on me, too, and he seemed very comfortable, which made me feel like I could let my guard down. He poured us one more glass and told me he was ready. I followed him upstairs, glass in hand.

On the walk, I wondered if I was ready for this, thinking back to the life I led before. I knew what I was doing in that life, even if I didn't always love it entirely. This was new and scary. It felt foreign, as if I'd moved to a new country instead of a new town. I wanted change, though, and I reminded myself that change comes from new things.

We arrived at the end of a long hallway lined with

closed-off rooms and came up to a set of black French doors with opaque white windows. He looked back at me and pushed both doors open, pulling me in across the cherry hardwood that continued into his room. His king-sized bed rested on an area of dark red carpeting centered on the far wall, swallowed by a black comforter and red satin sheets.

A small amount of generic art hung on the white walls and stood on a few of the black tables around the room with very little to add as far as aesthetic went, and the classical music and accent lights followed us into the bedroom, too. I thought from the smell he must've washed the bedding in his cologne, too—the same tacky kind he sprayed on before picking me up.

He pulled me through the sliding glass door onto a cold concrete balcony.

"This view is stunning," I said, awestruck by the night-time views his financial stability awarded him. At the bottom of the mountain, Cheat Lake extended as far as I could see in either direction up and down the valley, reflecting the near full moon on its calm surface, and across it, lakeside bars and resorts bustled with locals and people in town for Halloween parties. Down a ways toward Morgantown, freeway bridges ran dense traffic across the dark band of water. Lights scattered sparsely around the lake, and above, the moon and stars sparkled in the sky between a few shadowy, wispy clouds.

I noticed he hadn't stopped staring at me from his spot on the brick banister.

"Enjoy the view," Chris said, slipping behind me.

He rubbed his hands around my waist from my dick to my ass, squeezing occasionally along the way, and unbuckled my belt. His fingers wriggled between my pants and underwear like fat caterpillars, and he force-fully pulled my pants down, which scared me until I reminded myself he had to if we were having sex. I had my glass raised to my lips when, without a word, his hands gripped my hips and spun me away from the view, nearly causing me to drop the glass over the wall. His gaze shot down my body to the dick growing ever so slightly through my tight boxer briefs. I licked the last of the wine off of my lips and bit my top lip teasingly at him.

"I want to fuck you so badly," he quivered.

Do it, then, I wanted to say.

"Do it, then," I said.

Chris spun me back around and bent me over the low wall, pulling down my black briefs and kicking them and my joggers out of the way. He pressed his pelvis into my ass and poked around with his warm cock to find the entrance.

When he finally found the way in, I let out a low moan and gripped the cold brick wall in front of me, knock-ing the wine glass off. I looked straight down into his sloped front yard where the glass shattered and its bits exploded down the hill, overwhelmed by the burning, stretching sensation of his dick pressing in and out of my body.

Wheezy moans graduated to vocal pleas. I couldn't control them.

"That's so hot," he struggled to say over his breathless-ness. "You're tight as fuck."

Either due to the immense pain or overconsumption of alcohol, I started to dissociate from my body. I watched myself raise my wrist to my nose and sniff, and I suddenly imagined Chris was Amias.

His face in my head, *his* scent in my nose, *his* dick inside me. Sweet escape.

Chris pulled out and led me to his bed inside, shoving me under his cool satin sheets where he kept fucking me.

"I'm cumming," he said about two minutes later. I focused on the deep red ocean of shiny sheets around me and tried to capitalize on moments when the pain dulled to a numb pressure to rub my dick, sniffing my wrist anytime he made a noise that reminded me he wasn't Amias.

Chris's thrusting intensified and then slowed rapidly. "It's happening." His semen shot all over my ass and back, some of it into my hair, and he collapsed onto the bed with closed eyes.

I didn't say anything despite being nowhere near finished. I walked to the bathroom in the corner to do my best to wipe his fluids off my back.

Chris came in and turned on the shower conveniently late enough to have missed the opportunity to help me clean up.

"Get in with me."

I stepped in.

"You're a damn good time, I hope you know that."

I don't know if I knew that, but I knew I was a better time than him.

After our shower, I hinted I needed to get back to Honors, and he shuttled me back in his BMW, praising me the whole way for my tightness, my tongue control, and my grip. He harped on the potential for fucking in hotels across Morgantown or maybe even somewhere else someday. He wanted to take me to bars and clubs in Pittsburgh.

I enjoyed feeling something, even if *something* didn't feel particularly wonderful.

When we finally got off the highway toward downtown, he made one last stop at a gas station for "A Gatorade and some smokes," and I stayed in the car. His phone's nonstop buzzing from the middle console caught my attention—and annoyed the shit out of me—so I decided to flip it over.

Several hours' worth of texts and missed calls from a contact named "Baby Girl" shined bright white on the screen. I tapped on a notification that pulled out a whole thread of messages. She sounded concerned in her texts, irate even, about not being able to reach him all night, hinting at some infidelity in the past.

Then, I read a message I wished I hadn't.

"If I'm not enough to convince you not to do it again, please think of our three beautiful, innocent children you stupid bastard."

I lost my virginity to a married father.

Even faster than I had gone up the mountain did I crash back into the valley. There was no undoing it. There was no improving it. I could only try to move on and do my best to keep regret from ruining everything else. I entered Honors silently, blocked him, and went to bed.

CHAPTER 10: WHO ELSE

I tried to forget about Chris, and due to the busyness of college setting in, I didn't have a hard time with that. The trees eventually lost their leaves and their color as Morgantown plunged deeper into the cold of autumn, and the darkening of days seemed to be reflected in the faces I passed on campus. Classwork grew more challenging, and it became nearly impossible to make it through a day without a burning hot cup of cheap coffee keeping my eyelids propped up.

I came to find most people were content to serve the purpose of a placeholder friend—somebody who talked to pass time, never making any valuable points, regurgitating the same things every day. They were more like coworkers or the friendly person who worked at the post office. I didn't necessarily think of having them in my life as a bad thing, but I got more out of people like Imani.

Imani talked to fill time—to fill it with reflection, change-making, exploration, and anything else as long as it meant something. She'd find me at a party enjoying the view on some rando's back porch and offer me a cigarette, always the Camels with the menthol beads you crack, and we'd talk about school or love or life until the lights inside went off and the door locked us out in the cold. She'd pick up where she left off as if she'd never been interrupted when we got in the Uber to head back to Honors.

She could do the same thing at a bar, in a park, or anywhere else I happened to catch her with a few minutes to spare. Time couldn't be wasted when Imani was around, and she became my favorite person ever because of it.

Actually, she was my second favorite person ever, but she reminded me of my favorite person in the way she asked questions about me and could keep a conversation going without me having to drag her along. She seemed to genuinely want to get to know me.

Imani and I liked to live sort of pricey lives, though, and with my student money drained and my parents so far away, I decided to grow up and get a front desk job at this old hotel on High Street, the Morgantown Hotel. It was a nice-looking joint for a hotel from the 1920s, and the fact that it was only a few blocks from campus made it one of the busiest hotels downtown. The sports bar in the lobby and rooftop French restaurant meant it drew in equal parts rambunctious sports fans and esteemed university guests, though the fans came in massive herds on home-game weekends. It didn't feel particularly glamorous or high-paying as far as jobs went, but it provided a steady enough income to support my new lifestyle.

I got back on my hookup profiles, but any potential candidate had to pass a social media background check thanks to Chris Zhou. Before I even read their first message, I started looking guys up and flipping through photos, searching thoroughly for any sign they might have a relationship or children or any other disqualifying baggage.

I preferred not to learn their real names, though. Knowing names meant remembering and remembering meant building a history, and I preferred not to think of it that way.

I'm making up for lost time. That's all.

Plus, nobody could live up to my standards, which, to be fair, probably wasn't so much their problem as it was mine.

When I felt let down, and I always did, I picked myself up by imagining I was meeting Amias Parker for Italian food or that he was ramming me from behind in a random bedroom. I pictured his silky, sweet lips pressed against mine as I licked the very teeth he flashed at me in every smile. I couldn't understand why I'd gotten so hung up on him when we'd only been together a handful of times, but I didn't want to question it because I didn't want to taint it. He was my one great memory, the one I wanted to hold onto for as long as possible. Someone would come to replace him eventually—or hopefully, for my sake—but until then, I didn't mind thinking of him.

I learned that marking myself as "submissive" attracted men who didn't give a rat's ass about me. Some guys would buy me dinner, some got me drinks, and some did nothing extra, but every "dominant" I met did the same things: take me, fuck me, and leave me.

"You're the best bottom I've ever banged."

"You've got a tight ass on you."

"Let's do this again kid."

I think they thought their words flattered me, but I felt like no more than a sex toy from the wall at the mall.

Then, I replied to this brown-haired boy named Braxton. He was a twenty-five-year-old guy from Pittsburgh with a cute sense of humor, the quirky kind that revolved around expertly timed memes and GIFs in text conversations, and he got my attention by doing things as simple as starting the conversation.

He probably didn't realize it, or maybe he did, but he was the first guy to do that. He'd randomly send a cute meme or a song he thought I might like and the question, "How's your day going?" and I got fuzzy feelings knowing he was thinking about me. I didn't know if he could give me what I'd been looking for, but he was already off to a better start than anybody else.

Braxton spent his days as a nurse at a hospital in the city where he seemed to spend more time than he did at home. He enjoyed "a little" BDSM on occasion, according to his profile, and I could tell from both clothed and nude pictures he was well-hung. He showed no sign of having a family and even linked me to his Instagram without me having to ask for it. Good all the way around.

It started like a dream, but one I didn't wake up from. We texted day and night, talking about anything from sex and relationships to school and work. There even came a time when we stopped sending "Goodnight" texts—the conversation continued the next morning as if it never ended.

"Hey, freak," he texted while I laid in bed thinking of him late one night. We'd let the chat fall off naturally an hour or so earlier so we could continue the next morning where we left off, but he had something else to say, obviously.

"Hey, creep. You're up late," I sent back.

"I wanna ask you something, and you're not allowed to judge me."

"Um... Okay?"

"Have you ever heard of mutual masturbation?"

"I think so," I responded, noticing a heat creeping over my body.

"How about phone sex?"

"Of course."

"Picture this: we Facetime and set our phones up so we can see one another jerking off. We can play with the lights and the music, and we can do whatever it takes to make it a good time for both of us."

I zoomed to the fridge for a can of liquid courage.

"I'm down," I replied after emptying the can.

The first time felt more like acting out a scene in the worst kind of porn than it did phone sex or mutual masturbation. I moaned at times but only because he did, and the miniature image of myself in the corner reminded me how awkward I looked. Braxton seemed to enjoy himself plenty, though, because he orgasmed rather quickly and easily.

I struggled through the second night and then again on the third and fourth nights, and Braxton seemed to be catching on, which is probably why he invited me to his duplex in Pittsburgh the first weekend of Thanksgiving break.

I picked up some shifts at the hotel to keep from having to go home over break, and it worked out perfectly because my aunt and uncle, who worked for the university, liked to spend holidays out of town and needed someone to housesit. I was thrilled to watch their brick palace over the river in Westover, and I didn't even have to tell them how big of a favor they were doing me.

Honors cleared out around noon on the first Saturday of break, and I successfully migrated across the river to meet my aunt and uncle for their housekey. They kept their home somewhat cluttered for an educated couple, but they had all the coolest things: comic book collections, antique furniture, a massive selection of V.H.S. tapes, and a functioning V.C.R. I didn't have time to play with any of their fun things, though. As soon as they left, I texted Braxton to see if he was ready for me, and he was.

I'd become a pro at meeting random strangers from the internet, but Braxton didn't feel like a stranger. He felt like someone I already knew, and I couldn't wait to get to know him more.

He stood in his dark oak doorway with his hands holding each side of the doorframe when I arrived at his bright red duplex in the middle of Squirrel Hill. He stood barefoot in a loose pair of running shorts and a paint-splattered tank top, and his floppy espresso-colored hair waved around in the breeze like feathers on his head. He wriggled his finger at me, a gesture to exit my car and join him on the porch.

"Hey, you fuckin' cutie." He set his eyes on me as I slowly came up the stairs to his front porch.

"Hey, you fuckin' cutie," I echoed.

Braxton grabbed me by my shoulders and slammed me into the wall with the most aggressive kisses I'd ever received. He acted and looked and moved unlike anyone I'd met up with. I'd always been the tallest guy in the room, but he rose a whole head taller than me, easily, forcing him to lift me when he made out with me. I wrapped my legs around his lean waist, and he no doubt felt my boner pressing into his abs because I felt his lifting up under me as he carried me into his bedroom.

Braxton hovered above the bed, sucking my face, and then he dropped me onto the plush white comforter. He lifted his tank top over his head and kicked his shorts and underwear off, giving me a good look at his long, beautiful dick. It stuck straight out, curving slightly upward in a way that made me tingle.

He slowly crawled over me and took his time unbuttoning my denim shirt and pulling it off, kissing, licking, even biting my body along the way.

Next came my chinos.

Then my underwear.

I didn't have to do anything but lie there.

A pioneer in his own right, he used his hands, his mouth, his legs, whatever he could to show me how much he wanted me. He worked his way up my torso with his warm tongue, and my head turned up toward the headboard, then out the open window at the city, then back at Braxton.

He came face-to-face with me and cracked a smile before ravaging my lips with his delicate violence. His light brown body hair tickled my chest and stomach every time his body moved, and he smelled so good— fabric softener, eucalyptus, and man.

I had to bottom pretty much exclusively no matter how badly I hated it, and Braxton intuited this like the top he was. He flipped me over and leaned down, exhaling hotly into my ear. A chill shot up the back of my neck and out through my arms, and the sight of goosebumps rippling across my skin turned him into an animal.

My body had grown used to the pressures and stretching associated with sex, so with Braxton, I felt no pain. Only heat and passion and rough, beautiful sex.

He climaxed pretty quickly and wasted no time in flipping me back over. He began at my mouth, his lips salty and dewy, and sensually licked his way through my chest hair, down my happy trail, right to my dick. With his tongue, lips, and even some teeth, he provided me with something nobody ever had. I couldn't help but let out a moan or writhe occasionally, just him and me.

No theatrics. No drama. No negligence. I never wanted it to end.

His sucking and licking went on until, at last, my favorite sensations came over me with the force of a tsunami. My toes curled, I lost my vision, every muscle burned, ecstasy. I'd never felt it that strongly before.

Come back. Please.

When I could see again, I watched out his open window as some of the first flakes of the year came early, spitting down past the window. I thought for a moment I could see Amias's face dancing around in the sparkling bits of white dust on the other side of the glass.

Suddenly, Braxton jumped off of me. I returned my attention to the bedroom to find him wiping my cloudy liquids off his cleanly shaven face at the foot of the bed.

"Time for a shower." He ran out of the bedroom ass naked. I lay there on the covers, legs like noodles, head in the clouds.

"Come on lazy bones," he said, peering around the edge of the door at me.

We didn't do much washing in the shower, though. No, it was mostly face-sucking. He pulled his steamy lips away and pressed his forehead against mine, whispering sweet nothings.

"You're so fuckin' cute."

"I'm glad you messaged me back."

"There's nobody I'd rather be with this Saturday."

Braxton turned the water off right when I started thinking he should suck my dick again, but I didn't plead for more since we had a movie to get to. I dried off and went to his room to get my clothes back on, but he disappeared. About fifteen minutes later, I heard him walking back down the hallway and peeked out the bedroom door to get a glimpse.

Braxton caught me looking and twirled down the hall as if it were a catwalk, showing off the black jeans hugging his thick ass like a second layer of skin. His bulge called my attention every time he turned in my direction, too. His hair maintained that disorganized cuteness over his boyish face I loved when I saw him in the doorway. I felt so lucky to have him.

I found on the ride to the theater that Pittsburgh was an unexpectedly beautiful city and a larger one than you'd think. I looked over at him when we stopped at the first red light, high rises sticking up behind the hill in front of us, and he grinned dorkily at me.

A beautiful city for a beautiful man, I thought.

He reached across me and cracked the windows around the car, took control of the music playing over my phone, and lit two menthols with the built-in cigarette lighter. We held hands and puffed our cigarettes the rest of the way there.

After the movie, he recommended we fool around a little more at his place, and I agreed because I wanted more of his voluptuous ass. I couldn't wait.

I didn't notice the silence much on the way back to

his place, probably because I found his music and the city lights hypnotic. The highest points along the route gave me a glimpse of the miles and miles of rolling hills scattered with lights of all colors in the suburbs of Pittsburg, and the towering skyline occasionally popped up in the distance behind them.

I pulled around a recognizable corner, and his duplex sent my heart sputtering out of control. I put the car into park, but Braxton hopped out before I could shut off the engine, jogging across the narrow street and up the steps to his door.

"I think I'm too tired," he shouted across the dark street as I closed my car door.

"What?" The chilly night air swept over me.

"Let's just call it a night." I didn't like the tone he used, but I didn't have time to tell him that. He turned around and walked inside, locking the door behind him. I checked my phone, and it was only 11:30 p.m., which wasn't too late for a nightcap back in Morgantown, but maybe in Pitt, it was.

I had a long drive back to Morgantown filled with familiar feelings, feelings I'd hoped to never feel again. I mulled restlessly over the events of the evening, searching for anything I could've said or done wrong but coming up blank every time. I stopped at a gas station about halfway back to fill my car up and decided to text Braxton.

"Had a great evening and enjoyed the movie. Can't wait to see you again." A tear inched down my cheek. I felt like screwing up was the thing I knew best and like I may never do anything else.

I got back to Westover and pulled into my aunt and uncle's garage. The gasoline stains on the floor and lumber in the back smelled surprisingly pleasant, but I much preferred the cinnamon wax warmers spilling their scent into every room of their home.

I climbed into my cold bed well past 1 a.m. for a lonely, restless night, anxious to hear from Braxton. He seemed so different from all the other guys I'd met, so I thought things would play out differently with him. But I rolled over the next morning to no response. It only sickened me for a moment before I remembered I had to get ready for my eight-hour shift at the hotel.

Nine to five. It was bound to be agonizing with such a heavy boulder in my stomach, but I threw on my dark green polo and khakis and went anyway.

The first half of my shift passed slowly, which management told me to expect on Sunday mornings when the university was closed, so I had more than enough downtime between guests to obsess over Braxton and a text that would likely never come. I balled up enough to send him one more text, hoping maybe he'd forgotten to respond and a new message might remind him. "Hey, hope I didn't say or do anything to upset you. I had a really good time yesterday. Pls hit me back."

I hesitated but sent it quickly when my manager walked in. Meghan was a kind manager so long as you didn't step out of line, and we weren't supposed to have our phones out on the clock. It was a good thing she didn't notice. I'd been working there for about a month, and the last thing I wanted to do was mess up one of the only good relationships remaining in my life.

"Hope your first morning went well." Meghan sounded oddly chipper. She was an old-fashioned lady with long, wavy gray hair and one of the most purple wardrobes I'd ever seen.

"No problems to report, ma'am."

"Good." She paused and checked the drawer and computer I'd been using. "So, listen. I know you're new, but you've picked up well. I just hired another young man who's going to be shadowing you starting tomorrow." I agreed to show the new hire the ropes, not that I had a choice.

The second half of the day passed as slowly as the first, and the fact that I couldn't get out of my head about Braxton only made it worse. It wasn't until the end of the day when I was parking my car back in my aunt and uncle's garage that my phone finally lit up with a response.

"There is something. When I was using your phone last night, you got at least two messages from other guys on dating apps. Why do you still have those?"

My heart fell out of my chest, and a sloppy layer of wetness spread across my eyes—too much of any emotion tended to have that effect on me. I could've told the truth: that I didn't think we were exclusive yet; that I'd been on the app just in case things didn't pan out; that I kept those apps going in the background in case he wasn't able to make me feel the way I needed to feel.

But none of that felt right.

"I don't know Braxton. I'm sorry. I'll delete them." I did immediately.

"It hurt me to see that, Monte. I don't know how I feel."

I couldn't come up with a reply. We'd only been talking for a couple weeks and only met each other in person one time. If I'd known we were exclusive, I never would've been unfaithful to Braxton. I just needed to *know* first.

"I just need a day. Let me think things over. I'll text you

in the morning."

I felt so glad Imani and I decided to split half an ounce of weed for break. I didn't even mind that smoking forced me to confront the bitter wind of a dying autumn. I needed to feel anything but normal.

I must've decided to lay my head back in my uncle's recliner when I got back inside because I woke up with a stiff neck to my alarm and the sun beaming through the bay window in the dining room at me.

I once again rolled over to a blank phone—not what I wanted. I wanted happy and fun, fiery and passionate, the way things were supposed to be.

Whatever, I thought. *Maybe my new coworker will be able to help me keep my mind off it.*

It was a sunny, crisp autumn morning in Morgantown. A slight fog shrouded what downtown buildings didn't stand a few stories high as I rounded the knob across the river. It was a still morning, too, and the rich scent of dead leaves and wood smoke hung heavily in the air. The streets were nearly empty, but one car zoomed in behind me, a dark blue Dodge Charger, and followed me the whole way to the hotel. I parked in the alley behind the building, where employees normally parked, but this car pulled into the gravel lot across the street. I surmised it must've been my trainee.

I sat in my car to see if I could get a glance at the new guy so I could mentally prepare to meet him, but thanks to the university's extensive sidewalk signage downtown, I could only see bits of him as he made his way to the front entrance. He seemed like a sort of tall fellow, just an inch or two shorter than me, with floppy golden locks blowing freely in the breeze and khakis skinnier than mine. I gave it a few minutes before heading inside to avoid looking suspicious.

Meghan came out of the office behind me when I was logging in on my computer. "New guy's doing his on-boarding paperwork and training videos. Show him the ropes when he's finished, okay?" I could tell she'd had a long night at the hotel, circles under her eyes and frizzy hair and all. Then again, I think you'd be hard-pressed to find someone who didn't have those qualities in Morgantown.

"Sure thing, Meghan. I'll do my best." She grinned slightly and clacked across the black marble floor, out the door, and she was gone for the day.

I threw up the *Be right back* sign and left for my lunch around noon. I strolled up to this quaint Japanese restaurant on Fayette Street, just off of High, and returned to the hotel to eat my lunch in the lobby bar in hopes of getting some pre-training face time with the new hire.

When I was slurping down my miso soup, I heard him come out of the office and greet the head housekeeper. He spoke politely but confidently and let her know he couldn't wait to shadow me—like me, specifically. There was something about the way he said my name. It was almost as if he knew me very well. I cut my break a few minutes short and threw my takeout containers in the trash can by the exit before returning to the front desk where I was hit with a scent I had come to love, or outright depend on.

Holy fuck.

There, behind the front desk, stood Amias Parker.

I stopped dead in my tracks, shaking my head back a little. I didn't want to stare, but I had to for a couple seconds. I pinched myself to make sure I wasn't dreaming. I wasn't. He looked as handsome as ever, and he still doused himself in that same cologne.

"Well, hello." He spoke first, gracing me with his most glorious half-grin.

"Hey," I said with an involuntary gulp.

"You remember me, don't you? Because I remember you."

Those words would've killed me had my heart been a weak one or even a not-very-strong one. I thought I might pass out, and then I thought I might cry, and then I thought I might laugh. "Of course, I do."

"Good." He chuckled assuredly.

We had so much to catch up on I forgot about everything else. I watched as he talked, the muscles in his jaws flexing with the same sexy definition they had months earlier. I admired his glossy lips and for a moment fantasized about throwing everything off the front desk and sucking them right there, but I couldn't.

Amias moved to Morgantown a month before I got there so he could save for his real estate licensing classes. He'd seen on Facebook that I moved to Morgantown and hoped he might run into me at some point, but when I asked him where he was staying, his answer put a lump in my throat.

He was living in a townhouse out Van Voorhis Road—with his damned boyfriend.

I would have to settle for being friends, which was okay with me, but even if it wasn't, I was just happy to have him back in my life. The rest of the day flew by uncharacteristically. I normally would've loved that, but I found myself slightly sad at the end of my shift.

"Thanks for letting me follow you around today," Amias said, brushing his hair back with his fingers as the wind blew past us on the sidewalk.

"That's what they pay me for. Thanks for being good company." I sounded so lame, but he smiled anyway. "I'll see you in the morning."

"Have a good night, Monte."

Wrapped in cold, detergent-scented bedsheets, I stared at the bumpy popcorn ceiling in my aunt and uncle's spare bedroom from the warmth of my covers, but I wasn't obsessing over whether or not I'd done something wrong or crying about always ending up alone.

I felt excited—excited about working with Amias, excited about seeing, smelling, and hearing him every day, excited that in some way, even if it wasn't my preferred way, we could be together.

CHAPTER 11: GHOSTS

My phone buzzed Tuesday morning with a pages-long text from Braxton about how he couldn't trust me and likely wouldn't be able to for a while, but he was open to trying if I could prove my commitment to him. He demanded proof, and although it made me feel about six inches tall, I sent him a screen recording of my phone's entire app list.

I'll just have to prove how good I can be, I thought, suddenly feeling as if I'd fallen back into my last summer at home. I didn't want to lose him, but I also didn't want to live in fear of losing him. I hated how out-of-my-control everything was turning out to be.

I hurried out the door, eager to get to work. Meghan switched to night shifts to focus on more of the "behind the scenes" aspects of managing the hotel as she liked to put it, so from nine to five, it was just Amias and me. I couldn't help but wonder if he had an agenda as I showed him for the tenth time how to check in third-party reservations and for the twentieth time how to use his fingerprint to log on to the computers. I certainly would've taken my sweet time learning had he been showing me how to learn, and the fingerprint scanner was a clever ruse to get our hands to touch.

But it was probably all in my head since I'd been thinking about him for so long.

Amias had just gone upstairs to help a guest when a tall guy in jeans and a polo approached the front desk with a takeout bag full of food containers, scanning the receipt stapled to it. "Hey, is Amias here?"

I kept working on the computer after realizing he wasn't checking in. "Sure is. He'll be right back. You can leave that on the desk, and I'll make sure he gets it."

His eyebrows arched in the middle. "Um, no. That's okay. I can wait."

I pointed to the sofa near the fireplace in the corner of the lobby. "Have a seat over there."

Ten or so minutes later, the elevator pinged and opened for Amias. He noticed the delivery guy on the sofa and approached him rather quickly, almost as if the bags he held contained the first food he'd seen in days. The delivery guy stood up to greet him, and their lips met in the middle with a kiss lasting longer than I cared to look.

"Hey Monte, is it alright if I go on lunch?"

No. Stay here and hang out with me. Fuck that guy, but not that way.

"Sure, enjoy your break." Bullets of sweat ran down my back and chest, vibrating every time my heart thudded, and I suddenly didn't want to be at work anymore. I'd never had him, yet I felt like he'd been taken away from me again.

Without any introduction or mention of my name or his, they left the hotel holding hands. I thought about how if I'd been raised by a "worldly" family, I'd have been able to go for Amias the first time. I'd have been the one bringing him lunch. I'd be going home with him after work. I'd have lost my virginity to him. I could imagine it so well, but that was all I could do.

When he got back, I didn't say anything, and I didn't bring it up for the rest of the week. I wanted to know more about them, to know how he felt about this guy who brought him lunch, to understand the version of their future he told people about, but I couldn't bring myself to ask. I preferred to imagine they didn't have much together.

At least I had something with Braxton. We Facetimed Friday night about our plans, or rather his plans for us, for the next day: a late afternoon pizza date in Squirrel Hill followed by a tour at the Andy Warhol Museum.

Saturday afternoon came, and I found myself feeling less excited and more nervous about seeing him again. I pulled up to the curb on Murray Avenue in Pittsburgh at 4:30 p.m., right on time for our date, and texted Braxton to let him know I'd arrived.

The pizza place was right across from my parking spot, half-covered in vines and fully-covered in decorative lights, but Braxton was nowhere in sight. I looked down the bustling street and up it, too. Not there. The benches scattered along the sidewalk? Not there either.

I gave him five minutes before texting to get his E.T.A. No response. Ten minutes later, I decided to send another text. Still, no response.

I sent a few more, and each one was met with radio silence. I started to worry when, finally, forty-five minutes late for our date, Braxton came strolling down the sidewalk, his head towering over everyone else. He looked over his stiff shoulder and stepped through the front door. My phone buzzed with a call from him once he'd been inside for a few seconds.

"Hello."

"Hey Monte, where are you?"

"Waiting in my car on Murray Ave. Where are you?"

He paused for a moment. "I've been waiting inside for almost an hour. Can you hurry?"

I swallowed.

"Monte, are you coming? I've got a table, but they want it back if my date doesn't show."

I hesitated but took a whiff of my wrist and spoke briefly before hanging up. "Be right there."

I took my time putting change in the meter—a couple hours' worth of nickels, even though I had plenty of quarters and dimes—and walking across the street. I pulled the door open, but before stepping in, I held it for the elderly couple meandering out. The mouthwatering aroma of fresh tomato sauce, baked bread, and roasted garlic had my stomach growling ferociously as I admired the cracked brick walls and seemingly random Italian city maps hanging on them. Behind the short brick wall separating the dining room and kitchen, freshly grated cheeses, crisp veggies, spices, and even bits of fish sat in shiny silver trays embedded in a layer of crystal-clear ice, and cobblestone-lined holes in the back wall contained pizzas browning in front of open flames. A wooden door marked "Cellar" swung to and fro as workers in white button-downs went in empty-handed and came out with bottles of wine.

And then there was Braxton, sitting at a table in the back corner. I slipped my hands into my pockets and took a seat across from him.

"Hey." He didn't look up from his phone.

"Hey, Braxton. How was your week?"

"You talked to me all week. Shouldn't you know?"

I wanted to keep the conversation light for my sake if not his, so I played every game he insisted on. I answered his question. I didn't ask him to put his phone down. I didn't ask him to treat me like a human being. I just wanted to feel happy again.

I suggested we scrap the museum and go someplace he could get drinks after we finished our pizza. He suggested a quaint pub a short walk from the pizza place.

"I *am* glad you came to see me again." Braxton kicked a pebble ahead with his foot and kept kicking it with every step.

"It doesn't feel like it. Are you still mad at me?"

"I'm alright." He kept his eyes on the pebble as it bounced off his shoe.

We turned down a dark alley with a few dumpsters and a dirty metal door. The words "Redd's Place" glowed yellow on a red sign over the pub, which looked like no more than a door and a small, grated window shoved into the back of a vintage movie store.

He walked me right in, and inside, the place looked different from the clubs and bars I'd been to in Morgantown. It was one long, narrow room with a bar on the right side and two bartenders behind it: a red-headed young man with a curled handlebar mustache and an older woman with green hair.

On the left, a row of booths ended on one side at a unisex bathroom and the other at a pool table with rainbow felt. A live band, performing from a small stage near the door, serenaded a humble audience spread across several round tables with Amy Winehouse covers, and the smell of fried food and beer filled the air overwhelmingly, more overwhelmingly than the wood and leather everywhere.

Something else caught my attention when my eyes adjusted to the dim lighting. Men on men, women on women, people on people—I'd come to a place where people like me outnumbered people like everyone else, and I loved it.

Braxton pointed me to a booth by the abandoned pool table and walked up to the bar. He spent a few minutes schmoozing the mustachioed bartender as if he knew him and returned with two massive glasses of foamy Guinness. He sat one on the coaster in front of me and started swigging the other one.

"You pissed me off, but I'm into you." I couldn't tell if a few sips of Guinness already loosened his tongue or if he just felt bold.

"I'm sorry. I didn't mean to hurt you."

"I know. That's why I'm glad you're here. I can tell."

I did my best to spend a few seconds chugging the thick beverage. He was already halfway finished.

"You know, Monte—" He belched. "—you are so adorable." He finished off his beer. "Hurry and finish yours and I'll get us a couple shots before we go."

I didn't know where we were going, but I did as he said and handed him my empty glass. He came back with four shots of something clear, reaching two in my direction. "These are for you, good sir."

Braxton raised a shot glass to me, a tip to raise mine back. "A toast, to you realizing how special I am and deleting those stupid apps."

I huffed but took the shot anyway. Strong, buttery, burning whiskey—it forced me into a cringe and finished like cream.

"I hope you're down for anything," he said.

"I'm down for anything with you."

Absent of my usual crippling inhibitions, I grabbed the second one and downed it, too. Braxton looked at me astonishedly and threw back his last shot, pulling me up from the leather-wrapped bench and out the door by my forearm. We stumbled down block after block of crowded sidewalks to an area where homes began to mix with businesses. The mess of buildings blended into one concrete, brick, and vinyl-sided blob, but his bright red duplex stood where it had when he sent me away.

Braxton dragged me to his bedroom and pushed me back on the bed, the place I thought we weren't going to end up. He crawled over me, sucking on my body and face the way he had before. His body froze solid when he noticed my hardened dick, and he leapt out of bed and pulled the curtains together, leaving the sliver of sunlight between them to fight the darkness alone.

Braxton flipped me onto my stomach and pressed my face into the mattress so far I thought he may have broken my nose. "You've been awfully naughty, Monte."

The sound of metal clanking sent a familiar pang of fear through me, one that made me want to run as far away as I could. I'd heard that sound only on the worst days at home—the days Dad made sure not to spare the rod.

The crack of a leather belt pounded through the silent room, and a moment later, my ass burned from the whip of one. His hand forcefully pressed my head back to the mattress when I raised it to look back. My lungs pumped so quickly I thought they may explode.

I needed to focus on anything else, and the things I had to choose from didn't help much: the gray stains forming on his white comforter where my leaking eyes had been forced against it, the echo of my moaning off the walls, the salty taste of sweat, the burning sensation growing across my backside, or his aroma wafting over me every few seconds.

Or, briefly, something wonderful: a wavy bush of caramel-colored hair and a precious half-grin with the power to send evil away. I raised my wrist to my nose and decided to focus on nothing else until it was over.

It seemed like days passed before Braxton finally dropped the belt on the floor, and my body sank further into his bed than I thought possible. Stripes of pain stung intensely across my ass, thighs, and lower back as if a million hornets dug their stingers in and left them there, but I could only rest for a moment before Braxton's throbbing dick pressed uncomfortably into me. He clapped his thighs against mine a few times with loud, bearish moans and violent slaps on my ass.

He finished stridently, running out of the room after, and the squeaking of metal knobs followed by the hiss of his crappy shower head down the hall let me know I had a minute to myself.

I slurped myself to a state of control and rolled over, peeling my face off of the damp comforter. I grabbed a tissue from his bedside table and wiped the thin layer of sticky saliva and tears from my fuzzy chin.

Everything felt so familiar. I screwed up. Someone punished me. They ran off scot-free, leaving me to deal with the damage alone.

The axe forgets what the tree remembers.

Mama always said that. She told me she picked it

up on one of her trips to Zimbabwe when she was younger, and it helped make sense of my self-worth in the moments after a harsh punishment from Dad or any other leader or a run-in with a bully. I'd get sick thinking about how Jonathan or Delilah or Dad or Meri or anybody could take whacks at me and walk away unscathed. "A tree, with many purposes yet to be determined, shouldn't waste time with axes, who have only one purpose," she'd say.

Her words helped me make sense of traumatic situations after the fact, but they didn't erase anything. I knew how few people saw anything worth a damn when they looked at me. The rest saw someone moldable, someone they needed to make adjustments to, someone to take their anger out on.

I thought of staying. I thought I deserved it. I thought it was normal.

But then I remembered Amias.

I stood up and was carefully pulling my shirt down my sore back when Braxton returned, smelling of Dove and Garnier Fructis, humming a tune I thought I recognized to be a hymn.

"I guess I'll see you next time." I grabbed my phone from the bed.

"I guess you will." He chuckled.

I paused and looked at him, but he said nothing else. "Can we talk about wh—"

"No. We don't talk about it, Montgomery. We can never talk about these encounters." He looked at me sternly and smiled. "Want to stay for a bottle of wine?"

"I'm good." It was in the way he said *encounters*, letting me know to expect more in the future. I grabbed my jacket, tied up my shoelaces, and hurried out the front door.

Every exhale created a cloud in front of me on the long walk back to Murray where I left my car. I didn't mind the walk so much because the sky oozed purple and orange onto the city around me, and in places, I got to forget about everything as I stared out over an ocean of tie-dyed suburban hills.

With my hands firmly on the steering wheel, I could no longer hold back my tears, but I drove off anyway. The glittering glass high rises of downtown Pittsburgh rose around me on my way home, and the way they reflected the last splashes of evening light reminded me of that night in City Park with Amias and the way his eyes seemed to contain their very own sunsets when he looked at me. His warm embrace gave me something I didn't know existed, and no matter how much I wished, every other person I met lacked the ability to inspire it.

I tucked Braxton to the back of my mind, safe in the fact that no matter how things ended up with him, I had work with Amias to look forward to.

When I got to my aunt and uncle's house, I went upstairs and gently pulled my clothes off, careful not to drag them across any of the new tender spots. The pain had weakened from a sharp sting to a sensitive soreness, but it persisted so agonizingly I worried I wouldn't be able to sleep.

I waddled to the full-body mirror in the bathroom, underwear around my ankles, and gave my reflection a long look. Several bruises extended across my back like lines, scattered from the middle of my back to the tops of my legs but mostly concentrated on my ass. Some of the welts, the ones he inflicted earlier, were a gnarly shade of blue or purple and hurt like hell even when

I wasn't touching them while others were yellow or slightly brown and only hurt if I applied a lot of pressure.

I couldn't sit or lie down. I couldn't wear tight clothing. I couldn't even scrub my back in the shower. I took two allergy pills, slipped face-down into bed, and ended up sleeping through my alarm.

When I did eventually get up and motivated, I got to work moving back to Honors. Braxton texted me around 4 a.m., but I was reluctant to open it. It was either an apology, an explanation, or a normal message, and I didn't feel like reading any of those.

And I didn't have to, thanks to the reawakening of the group chat I was in with Imani, Avery, and Ryder. The chat was less active over Thanksgiving break, but it picked back up on Sunday when everyone wanted to make plans—well, by plans I mean for me to pick them up at the bus station, and by everyone I mean almost everyone. Ryder's family came into some "serious issues" over the holiday, and all he would share with us was that it kept him from returning to campus.

I picked Imani and Avery up late Sunday afternoon, and we matched on a blunt for a short welcome-back road trip around Morgantown. I was just thankful to be back out doing things with normal people. Imani plopped in up front with a playful punch on my shoulder while Avery slid quietly into the backseat.

"So, how'd you handle Morgantown without us?" Imani looked at me with a scrunched face, probably because she was so damned observant.

"I didn't."

"What does that mean?"

"Remember the guy I told you I was talking to, Braxton?" I took my first hit and turned onto West Run Road from Van Voorhis.

"Yup."

"I saw him over break… Twice." Avery leaned forward eagerly and squeezed my shoulder from the backseat, congratulating me kindheartedly.

"How'd that go?" Imani asked.

I took my next puff and told them everything that had happened between us—the good first date, my dating apps, his reaction, his terrible reaction.

"What a shithole. I can tell it's stuck in there, though." She pointed to my head. "Wanna talk about it?"

"I don't know, Imani. It's not always easy for me to know how I feel." I paused, but she left the pauses. "I really like Braxton, ya know. He's the closest thing I've had to a boyfriend, but I saw something awful in him over break."

She still didn't speak. I grabbed the blunt from her and took my next hit, turning up Riddle Avenue—the steepest, bumpiest road in the universe.

"I guess I consented, though. He asked me at the pub if I was down, and I told him I was down for anything." The realization made me feel queasy.

"Don't think like that, Monte. You always have the right to back out if things go where you don't want them to go. You don't have to do shit if you don't want to."

"He texted me this morning."

"He did? The fuckin' nerve. What'd he say? What're you going to say?"

"I have no idea."

"Well, it's your life, but if it were mine, I'd cut him off. Deleted and blocked. Nobody should have to put up with shit like that, and if he's doing it this early, imagine how bad it could get later on." She briefly grabbed my forearm. "I'm sure there's someone a thousand times better out there you could focus your energy and time on."

I watched the road bend over hills and weave between buildings and parking lots on the way to downtown, thinking the whole time about what Imani said. I knew exactly who was a thousand times better, but I couldn't have him. And for some stupid reason, I couldn't find another person who even came close.

Finding people who didn't deserve the time and energy I wanted to invest in them was pretty easy. I could've walked down any sidewalk in Morgantown or Pittsburgh or anywhere else and found a dozen or more undeserving people, but finding someone who wanted to match my passion and see my emotions seemed impossible, like something I only had one shot at. I felt like I may never find another person, even just one more, who deserved everything I wanted to give them. I'd already met my quota on happiness-giving people.

I knew leaving Braxton's message unread was the right thing to do in the long run, but I climbed into bed and wondered if it was too late to read it and send him a message. I cured that right up by spraying some of my favorite cologne on my pillow, and I fell to sleep soundly with fantasies about a future with Amias playing in my head.

The first week back to class after Thanksgiving break, I spent my evenings at work, training Amias and squeezing in study time whenever I could. Finals were creeping up in the distance and so was the busy holiday travel season at the hotel. His mere presence in the background made work less work and more getaway, though, even when I had a billion things to do.

I'd stand at the desk, checking in guests who thought they belonged to a more advanced class of human than me or flipping through a dense article about the Olmec colossal heads, and he'd lean back on the counter and watch me. I'd glance over and catch his eyes darting away, pointing nervously at the artwork on the wall or the wavy flames in the fireplace. The way his thick ass curved over the edge of the countertop in his tight khakis caused my heart to palpitate and my palms to grow uncomfortably damp. Then, he'd glance back at me, and I'd go back to serving the guest I'd zoned out on or skimming the article I needed to reread.

I loved it every time, but the injustice of it all made me so sick. I couldn't stand thinking about how I could've—how I should've been the one he called "Boyfriend."

If only, I thought.

Dreams of Amias grew too powerful to be contained within the pathetically tiny amounts of sleep I managed to suck from the nighttime and began to crowd into the daytime. I fantasized about him in class, on lonely drives across town, on walks with Imani, everywhere I went. I'd go to sleep and wake up drenched in sweat with a cold wetness in the crotch of my underwear and his face fresh in my memory.

Imani told me she was sick of me zoning out in the middle of our deep talks, but I couldn't help imagining biting Amias's lips as he ran his fingers through my hair. He had become something I both wanted to escape to and escape from.

Right there he stood at the front desk with me almost every day, within reach and still unreachable. I went home thinking about him. He went home thinking about his roommate, or *Boyfriend* as he liked to call him.

On the last Friday of fall semester—the one before I'd be separated from my friends again, this time for a month—Imani texted me with the offer of a blunt and lunch, both on her. Our destination was the same stone tunnel we smoked at on many occasions, which had become one of the only places we smoked when it was just the two of us. She sparked the blunt as soon as we started over the hill toward it, the cold wind blowing across the river and nibbling at my nose and cheeks. The creek, much muddier this time than last, gushed out of the tunnel with bits of leaves and the occasional plastic bottle.

She took another hit and handed the blunt to me. "So, how were finals?"

"Eh." I took a long hit. "Time will tell."

There was a pause, one that seemed to suggest I should brace myself.

"You haven't been to a party with us in weeks, and you haven't been off campus since coming back after Thanksgiving break. I'm not hearing from you as often as I used to, and when I am, you sound closed off. It's like you're distracted by something. Everything alright?"

"Yeah, I'm good. Just exhausted." But I was also distracted. I just didn't want to have to explain why.

"I get that. Was it the partying or the sexing?"

"Both. I'm not cut out for all that stuff constantly, especially hooking up with a different guy every weekend. I start to think I'm finding someone who makes me happy and then they're gone."

"I'm the same way man. It's not for everybody. You think you'd be happy in something more committed, maybe not with an abusive shit bag this time?"

I chuckled, hoping my nervousness wasn't seeping out.

"All jokes aside, you do deserve something amazing, Monte. Don't give up. You'll have your chance with the right person."

The corners of my mouth curled upward when she said that. I hoped she was right.

"So, listen Monte. I know you said you're partied out, but I'm having my annual Christmas party in Chapmanville next Friday, and I think you should come. Everyone's gonna be there. Avery, possibly Ryder if he can make it from Connecticut, lots of people from my high school. It's gonna be our one last hoorah before the new year, a sick-ass party, the best one of the semester. Not sure how else I can make it sound fun. What do ya say?"

I took a big, resiny hit and watched the blunt turn to smoke on the other end, inching closer and closer to my fingers. "Of course I'll be there."

WINTER

It is the life of the crystal, the architect of the flake, the fire of the frost, the soul of the sunbeam. This crisp winter air is full of it.

–JOHN BURROUGHS.

CHAPTER 12: ESCAPE

Winter break kicked off with me rolling out of bed at my aunt and uncle's empty house and planting my feet on the brutally cold floor. A hot, dry breeze rattled out of the vents on its way to fight the cold air back to the fogged-up windows as white flakes fell outside, and the branches of the bare, brown tree in the yard wobbled as if dancing with one another.

For a moment, I regretted asking Meghan to keep me on the schedule over break. It would've been nice to lay back down and pull the warm covers over me, roll over on my side and face the wall, and close my eyes—safe from the cold, harsh world. But work provided the excuse I needed to justify returning home for only one night over winter break, so I didn't mind.

I asked Meghan for an extra day off for Imani's party as soon as I got to the hotel, and she, of course, had no problem giving it to me. She told me she appreciated my commitment to the hotel, but I already knew that. She never asked questions when I asked for an extended lunch or a day off.

The best part was she hadn't the slightest idea why I looked around eagerly every time I walked through the front door or why I always volunteered to pick up shifts if they happened to coincide with Amias's. To her, I was the worker bee who cared too much about my job, the kind of worker a manager can love, but it wasn't about work.

It was about *him*.

Walking into the lobby to smell his cologne or knowing I'd be greeted by it if he came in after me soothed my soul like no drink or Bible verse ever had. I stopped spraying it on before work because the living, breathing source worked behind the desk with me several hours a day, and the spritzes fading on my wrist took away from the magic of standing next to him. I looked forward to his smile shining on me more brightly than the sun reflecting off the small piles of snow outside, lopsided and gloriously beautiful, and his eyes sparkling like the icy puddles across the street. I felt as though I'd fallen into Dreamland, and I never wanted to leave.

Maybe Dreamland will follow me into reality. I crossed my fingers and clocked in.

Amias came in late for his shift that morning, something he'd never done, but I felt it best not to talk about it. He hung his head low, eyes reddened and beard a little less perfect than usual, and he didn't say much as he slunk back to the office to clock in.

He actually didn't say anything all morning, just that he'd been having issues with Matt all night, so I didn't ask any more questions. I knew what it felt like to have something pried out of your cold, lifeless fingers when all you needed was a little time to process and someone to listen when the time was right.

He'll come to me, if and when he's ready.

Sometime in the afternoon, a guest called the front desk to report a water leak on the fourth floor. Meghan wouldn't be in for several more hours, and maintenance was out for the week on vacation, leaving us with only one option: to handle the issue ourselves or at least check its severity.

Since the front desk was nearly guestless between checkout at 11 a.m. and check-in at 4 p.m., we put the *Be right back* sign up, let the bartender know we were going upstairs, and pressed the button on the wall to call an elevator.

Ping.

I motioned for him to go first, and at the same time, he motioned for me to go first. Then, we tried to squeeze in together, bumping shoulders.

"After you." The words stumbled from our mouths simultaneously.

Amias finally ran in. "Beat you." He smiled for the first time that day, knocking the breath right out of me. I stepped in.

Ping.

I turned to face the doors as they closed and suddenly didn't know where to look.

Up, down, left, right, directly into his eyes? I had no idea what was right, but I wanted to look at him.

I did, briefly. He was watching the number on the screen climb as we did with a faint grin. I decided to watch it, too.

Ping.

He was looking at me from the corner of his eye now. Even when I looked away from him, I could feel his gaze. I looked over in time to catch his eyes jolting forward again, so I did the same. I forgot what to do with my hands, my sweaty ass hands. I tucked them into my pockets.

Ping.

My heart pounded at a volume similar to the grinding of the elevator machinery. He looked at me again, but this time with more directness. I turned to see him, and he stood facing me now with the smile I loved more than any other glowing under his nose. I smiled back.

Ping.

God, I wanted to ravage him right there in the elevator. I wanted to rip his clothes off and turn him against the wall. I wanted to get so close I could hear his secrets, know his flaws, be wholly his and he mine.

Ping.

I let out a deep breath and stepped through the now-open metal doors, carefully inspecting the blue river of carpet in the hallway for any evidence of a leak. I wanted to avoid initiating anything other than professional encounters with Amias, so I kept my distance. Then he found a dark patch in the carpeting and called me over to help investigate.

Sure enough, water trickled out from underneath the door to room 416, so I pulled out my master key card and swiped us in. The water overflowed into the hallway, but due to the raised lip between the carpet by the door and the tile in the suite's kitchen, it hadn't gone very far into the room.

I tiptoed across the saturated floor and opened the bathroom door, revealing several streams of water dripping off the stone counter and into the pond on the floor. Someone, probably a disgruntled housekeeper or maintenance worker, had clogged the sink with toilet paper and left the faucet barely running, probably intending to damage the hotel by slowly flooding the fourth floor.

Meghan ran a tight ship, and as a result, she tended to rub employees the wrong way pretty frequently. She treated most of us disposably because, to be honest, in a college town with an entirely new pool of people to hire from every four years, we were disposable. She knew many of us wouldn't be able to work there for more than a few years, and it made her unwilling to invest very much effort in people. I was lucky because I'd been schmoozing people my entire life, and I knew the best way to butter the toast, so to speak.

Amias maneuvered across the wet tile floor, careful to avoid the biggest puddles of water, and toward the tap.

"Oh my god." With his hands in the running stream of water, he called out, "This is insane! Monte, come here and look at this." I approached cautiously as he filled his cupped hands with water, examining closely. "Do you see those tiny things floating around in the water?"

"See what?" I leaned in to check. "No, I don't see—" Before I could finish my sentence, his hands catapulted cold water at me, soaking me from head to toe.

Such juvenile behavior would've probably pissed me off from anybody else, but Amias looked so happy for a moment I didn't even think to react angrily. The mirror vibrated with his victorious bellow for a more-than-generous amount of time before he cracked his undeniably cute half-grin at me. I laughed it off and patted myself dry, and I laid the rest of the towels on the floor to sop up the water.

When I arose from laying the last towel, Amias's face

was so close to mine I could feel the heat in his breath. I noticed he had on much more makeup than usual, but he managed to keep it natural-looking. His glossy pink lips shimmered in the bright white light coming from the four bulbs over the sink, and his eyes looked bigger than ever.

He reached his hand up and wiped a drop of water off the tip of my nose, flicking it to the ground, and white-hot electricity surged through my veins, painting my cheeks a darker red with every heartbeat. A toothy smile was all I could muster in response to his persistent half-grin.

I kicked one of the towels around to sop up a different puddle and sent Amias to set the suite's climate control unit to dehumidify and to start looking for a fan. I knew full-well the rooms didn't have fans, but it bought me enough time to set my trap.

I quickly grabbed one of the complimentary cups from the toiletry tray on the bathroom counter and pulled the plastic packaging off. I had just enough time to fill it with water when the sound of his footsteps nearing the bathroom startled me into position behind the bathroom door.

"Hey Monte, I can't—" He came through the doorway, and I launched my cup of cold water over him, covering him from head to toe the same way he covered me.

Triggered by my quick and sarcastic laugh, he zoomed across the narrow bathroom and pressed his fingers firmly into my sides, backing me into the corner. His body pressed against mine, and we cachinnated until my cheeks ached and the muscles in my sides felt like they might rip away from my body. I leaned forward to soothe the pain and pressed my forehead into his tight stomach where his mouthwatering, spine-tingling aroma overwhelmed me.

Amias grabbed one of the white washrags from the rack behind the toilet and began wiping the water away, and with each scrape of the dry, brittle rag went a strip of his makeup. Emerging from behind the thick layers of cream and powder were patches of bare skin, but I began to notice something that didn't belong, something left by a vile and wicked person.

Two large purple bruises caught my attention: one under his left eye and one on the back of his right cheek. The slight swollenness of his left eye suddenly became apparent and faint red scratches crisscrossed his face like roads in an atlas. I tried not to let my concern and despair leak out as he continued wiping his face, but it was an exercise in futility.

It was impossible to understand. Nothing he could have possibly done would have made him *deserve* something like that. Nobody deserved that garbage, but he was especially undeserving, and the fact Matt was too fucking stupid to see it enraged me. I hoped he'd say something about a wrestling match gone wrong or clumsy trip down the stairs and that those marks hadn't been caused by a swinging fist, but I didn't think I'd believe him even if he did.

I recognized those wounds. They weren't the kind left by an accidental bump against the corner of a coffee table or an elbow in bed. They were the intentional kind, the kind left by people who couldn't control their emotions and who thought other people were responsible for their own misery.

Amias's eyes grew wide as he noticed my crumpled eyebrows and empathetic half-frown. He stopped wiping and looked past me, into the mirrors hanging on the wall behind the tub, and the corners of his mouth drooped lower than I'd ever seen them. I couldn't think of anything to say to make him feel better, so I said nothing. I gave him what nobody ever gave me: silence, a shoulder to cry on, and an ear to vent to.

With quivering lips, he said, "He's really a good guy... Matt is. He just gets so caught up in his feelings. He..." He grabbed at the air in front of him, unable to squeeze any more words from it, tears rolling down his cheeks.

"We don't have to talk." I picked up the damp rag on the counter and continued gently wiping off his makeup. Every scratch, every welt, and every dark spot, even the traces of red where tears had chapped his cheeks over several hours, it all came to light. I wished with everything in me the rag would fill with magic and wipe the marks away, but it didn't.

I wanted to cry and scream and curse into the sky, but I couldn't.

I wanted to commit a murder and a kidnapping, but I couldn't.

It wasn't about me, and I couldn't make it about me.

When the last of the makeup ran down the sink drain with steamy water, Amias lowered his head as if he'd done something wrong, his body shivering between sobs. All of a sudden, it felt as if I'd known him for eons—like we were kindred spirits destined to be intertwined for eternity. I knew exactly how he felt and where he stood. He didn't deserve to feel that way any longer. I didn't want to feel the way I had been feeling any longer. We both needed something new.

I wanted him. I had for so long, but now I had no reason to keep it concealed.

Amias turned wistfully to face me. His makeup was gone except for the few places where waterproof layers only smeared, but his resilient beauty shimmered through anyway.

Overtaken, my eyelids slid shut, and I leaned in slowly. His lips met mine with a flaming passion, one I remembered from the first time they met at City Park. His strawberry lip gloss tingled my lips as I sucked it off of his, and his breath warmed my upper lip every time he exhaled, each one seemingly louder than the last. He pulled away regretfully once, but only for a second before coming back in with more passion.

I popped out to make absolutely certain the deadbolt and chain on the door were locked.

"Follow me," I said.

I grabbed Amias by the hand, and we ran to the bedroom. He climbed onto the king-sized bed while I pulled the drapes together, leaving them cracked enough that his fit body remained in a resplendent rectangle of golden light from the afternoon Appalachian sun, the only source of beauty in the mostly-gray room.

I watched longingly from the window as he stripped naked and heaved his clothes off the bed. I stripped down, too, though I stopped at my boxer briefs. I still couldn't believe what was happening was actually happening, and I didn't want to blow it by coming off as too presumptuous. The heat from the overhead vents drizzled down on us like a dry cloud, chasing the cold away and blowing the hair on his head ever so slightly. He raised his kind eyes to mine, pupils constricting in the intense sunlight, and patted the bed next to him, his heartbeat as visible as his growing dick.

My heart nearly flopped right out of my ribcage. Everything I wished for, everything I felt I missed out on, everything I wanted but could never have—it was all only a few steps away.

I lumbered across the room and wriggled into bed so that we were lying face-to-face, knees interlaced, fuzzy and warm. Amias took the back of his hand and caressed my cheek, using his other index finger to scratch me from my neck to my belly button slowly and erotically. His hands were cozy and soft like sunbathed leather and their touch electrified me while also somehow calming me. I felt like I could sense his energy, and his thoughts bled through his skin and into my bloodstream. He was everything I'd dreamed of and more.

Come closer, I heard him thinking.

I lifted my body off the bed, and Amias grabbed my underwear by the waistband before looking at me with a hopeful smile, as if for the go-ahead. I gave him a nod, and he yanked them off and threw them on the floor behind me.

We scooted impossibly close to each other and pressed our heads together. It felt as if his forehead was made to be smooshed against mine. With his strawberry-flavored lips, he began to suck on mine again, and the motion metamorphosed from smooth and manufactured to rough and unadulterated in a matter of seconds.

So unrehearsed, so natural, so exhilarating, he was unlike anything I had ever experienced. We made no plans and declared no roles. There were no unrealistic expectations established or false hopes set up beforehand. We fell into the moment with grace—completely together.

Amias shifted over me, rotating his body so that his dick was in my face and my dick in his. He stretched his neck down and began to suck my dick, and fighting moans that threatened to rattle the headboard, I slipped my mouth up between his thighs and began to suck him. Our rhythms came together, and we thrust to one cadence. The sun beamed through the crack in the drapes, illuminating the beads of sticky sweat scattered across our skin like golden glitter, and I got lost in the smell of deodorant melting under his arms and the cologne seemingly coming from his pores.

I never wanted it to end. I'd waited so long for exactly this, and to not have savored every last second would have been the romantic tragedy of the century. This was for more than the moment I lived in. It was for the future I wanted to live in. I needed to remember him in all his glory and to be left with no questions or regrets.

Everything that wasn't Amias became bokeh. My back cracked upward, arching off of the bed, and his muscles juddered like an old car at a stoplight. Euphoria like ocean waves crashed over me, and his exclamations seemed victorious, too. Suddenly, we finished all over each other.

Amias rolled over and laid next to me on the crispy hotel comforter, reorienting himself so that his head was next to mine again. He grabbed a couple tissues from the built-in dispenser on the nightstand and wiped the evidence off my face before cleaning his own.

Steamy and naked, we lay with our sides pressed together, hypnotized by the silence in the room and the smooth whiteness of the ceiling, and my heart began to beat faster with joy and concern and hope and fear. Amias turned and flashed me my favorite half-grin, temporarily clearing my mind of everything.

I didn't even notice his wounds. I didn't remember a thing outside of the four walls around us. There were no words between us. There was only happiness, only peace.

But it couldn't go on for eternity.

I happened to glance down past the foot of the bed, and a hotel-branded card urging guests to reuse bath towels and bedsheets stood centered and framed on the dresser. Reality hit me like a bag of bricks. Work was hardly the place I dreamed of having sex with Amias for the first time, and regardless of who the piece of shit on the other end was, I felt like a dumbass for doing it while Amias was in a relationship. The last thing I ever wanted to be in his life was a regret, a mistake, the reason he'd have to say, "It will never happen again." I never wanted to run the risk of being no more than a rebound or a wake-up call.

And yet, I'd fallen weak again, as if I expected anything else from myself at that point.

But then again, he seemed to have fallen into my arms as quickly as I fell into his. Had he been as committed to his relationship as I thought he was, he wouldn't have let it go so far with me, and it wouldn't have been so effortless—like putting the last piece of the puzzle in its place. What happened between us felt like more than the shallow sex I had become accustomed to. There wasn't only flesh and bone but a connection that evoked thoughts and sensations I'd have been willing to walk around the world for.

I hated to just walk away from it, but I rolled out of my spot next to Amias to check my phone. What felt like minutes had been an hour or more, and Meghan was scheduled to show up any minute. I shot out of bed and started recomposing myself.

"We're screwed. We've got to get back to the desk.

Check-in started forever ago." I looked over at him and slid my phone back into my pocket.

He hadn't stopped staring at the ceiling, but his face conveyed a much different message now. His brows had grown uncharacteristically straight, and the busy eyes of someone who'd made a terrible mistake waned beneath them. He looked as though he'd just been in a terrible car accident, and I hated to think I caused him more stress. I wanted to believe what had him so stressed out was our irresponsible absence from the desk, but I knew deep down work had nothing to do with it.

He regrets me.

His eyes drifted to the floor and remained there when we spoke, which all of a sudden wasn't very often, and he seemingly struggled to utter more than one or two words at a time. The elevator pinged, and the doors glided open for us, but he told me he forgot his badge back in the suite and dashed down the hall, encouraging me not to hold the elevator for him.

"I don't mind holding it for you."

"No, really. It's okay. I don't know how long I'll be."

He ran back down the hall, and the elevator door slid closed. The void of loneliness I'd grown up in began to feel like the one I was meant to die in. It became more and more obvious by the day I was meant to be alone, wandering the world by myself because I couldn't figure out how to make anything work.

A line of irate guests greeted me with sarcastic sighs and muffled curses as soon as the elevator opened in the lobby. The sun had fallen below the hill behind the hotel a while ago, and in its absence, the windows around the lobby sucked light out rather than letting it pour in. I rushed across the expanse of polished flooring in the lobby and around the desk, yanking the *Be right back* sign off it and greeting the first angry guest.

There, tucked safely under the counter, sat Amias's badge. My heart stopped, and the red-faced guests on the other side of the counter turned to smoke. The lobby grew dark around me and the winter cold broke through the walls, chilling me to the bone in seconds. Something undeniably real had transpired between the two of us upstairs, but it didn't seem to matter to him as much as it did to me. His emotions clouded his judgment as much as mine clouded mine, only he had a lot more to lose over it.

The elevator pinged several minutes after the last of the guests had been checked in and out came Amias, eyes inflamed and cheeks puffy. He looked at me again a few times, but not for long and always with an empty gaze.

The sparkle was gone from his eyes. No smile perched upon his lips. He spoke very little for the rest of his shift, over forty-five minutes long—once to help me report the water damage to Meghan and again to say he'd see me after Christmas. I wanted to scream my apologies at him, but then, what was I sorry for? I wasn't sorry. A craving so strong it couldn't have been tucked away burned within me since the moment I met him, a craving for the exact thing we'd just done, and I couldn't possibly have regretted it. You can't easily regret a dream come true.

I did regret how things played out between us, though. Amias's feelings slipped through the cracks of my mind when the opportunity to make my dreams a reality came along.

My stomach began to churn sourly as I realized who I'd become and what role I'd taken on in his life. I was to Amias what all those men had been to me: inconsiderate, self-centered, a mere bump in the road of life, and one you'd prefer to see in your rearview mirror. I had surely become a "Dude" to him, guided only by the feelings of my dick. Gone were any chances I had with him.

He vanished quietly out the glass doors and into the inky darkness gobbling up the street.

CHAPTER 13: TRIPPING

My car's engine grumbled to life, sharing its energy with the dash, and Michael Bublé's version of Jingle Bells played fuzzily over the radio. I grabbed the ice-cold knobs marked "TEMP" and "FAN" and turned them all the way up before shifting into reverse and backing out of my aunt and uncle's dark garage and onto the icy driveway. The garage door banged and clattered once I got out, sliding back down and slamming against the weathered concrete pad. I thought about backing into the street and getting straight on the road to Chapmanville, but I preferred driving my car when it had time to warm up.

I couldn't wait to get back inside. Frosty blades of grass felt sturdy beneath my shoes, crunching with every step I took toward the door, and the bare branches on the tree in my aunt and uncle's front yard knocked about in the never-ending gusts of bitter wind.

Waves of heat exploded from behind the heavy front door when I shoved it open and stepped through to wait. I'd been feeling like my weekend off for Christmas

—and Imani's "sick ass party"—might never come, but when it did, I was more than ready.

Work hadn't been bad per se, but shifts certainly passed by more slowly than they ever had, and holiday travelers tended to be needy guests. Instead of focusing all my energy on normal front desk tasks like checking guests in, recording reservations, or tidying up the lobby, I spent most of my pre-Christmas shifts fetching cranky vacationers whatever toiletries they forgot at home or rollaway beds or the wi-fi password or anything they called to complain about. It never ended.

And to make things worse, Amias hadn't been back to work. He returned to Nicholas County and wouldn't be back until after the holidays, but the way we left things made the time apart feel more permanent than temporary.

Things will never be the same, I thought, watching the white clouds puffing out of my car's exhaust in the driveway.

The white layer of frost covering my windshield eventually melted, and the road beckoned. I grabbed my backpack for the long weekend and headed out into the cold once again, pulling the door shut and locking it behind me. Imani invited me to spend the night before the party at her uncle's place, which was actually her place, too, to keep from having to drive all day the day of the party, and of course, I accepted it.

Imani's party was set to be the best party I'd ever been to, according to her, and it couldn't have come at a better time. Guilt ate at me like a life-sucking parasite all week over the way shit played out with Amias, but I couldn't help enjoying the memory a little bit, too.

The taste of him glazed my tongue with unmatched

sweetness, and his fragrance danced around my nose with arousing strength even though it had been days since I last touched him. I could still feel his warm hands pressing my face further into his prickly beard, his lips on mine, our noses rubbing. A perfect moment in time played over and over again in my head behind the clouds of wrongdoing and worry.

Thoughts of how Matt might react to Amias if he ever found out sent me to some of the darkest corners of the universe. I thought of him taking swings at Amias's beautiful face, leaving more bruises and scrapes as he screamed the most heartless things imaginable at him.

My heart raced. My grip on the steering wheel tightened. I had to stop thinking about it.

So, I looked around.

It was my first time out of Mon County since class started in August, aside from my trips to visit Braxton in Pittsburgh, so I sparked my blunt, pulled back the sunroof cover, and enjoyed the road trip across the old, weathered mountains of West Virginia. Northerly, dense Morgantown was a solid three-and-a-half-hour highway drive and an entire culture away from southerly, quaint Chapmanville, and once you passed through a few towns around Morgantown, I-79 became a highway through the middle of Nowhere, Appalachia. The forests, bejeweled with bright yellow, orange, and red trees just a couple weeks ago, were now a fuzzy gray and brown entanglement of wiry branches swallowing hill after hill against the cloudy sky. Bleak December air seeped in my cracked sunroof with heavily filtered sunlight, which struggled to heat the atmosphere through thick clouds and seemed to disappear when I drove through the occasional snow shower.

The stout high-rises of Charleston towered distantly over the suburbs in the valley, and the road bloated to six lanes and filled with traffic. My mind grew similarly crowded with flashbacks of the summer before moving to Morgantown, a few long months earlier, when I had come to the Town Center Mall and found the striking cologne I'd been emboldened by, or rather the cologne that reminded me of the striking individual I'd been emboldened by.

He'd become so much more than some guy to me. To remember him and to know he remembered me made me feel superhuman. I wanted to live in those moments in room 416 forever, locked away on a bed made neon in the sunlight, staring into the starry eyes of my eternity. But reality prevented it, and I'd have to settle for living in my memories.

Out of the blue, tears trickled down my cheeks and my lungs couldn't seem to take in enough air. My pulse pounded loudly and erratically, rippling through my muscles and across my skin like an earthquake.

I wanted easy, and life never gave me easy. If I thought about that fact for too long, it always sent me someplace dark, someplace I didn't like to dwell. I looked at others in my life who didn't seem to have such a hard time finding their spot and wondered why I couldn't have it that way, but I had to remind myself of something Mama told me growing up:

"Your feet move independently from everybody else's, Monte, so there's no sense in looking sideways."

I continued out of Charleston and got back on a road through the middle of nowhere. Immaculate churches clad in white vinyl siding or sturdy masonry stood proudly every mile or so, some only a hundred yards from one another, and between them, cottages, modern suburban homes, and trailers lined the highway, each with a chimney adding to the heavy layer of smoke hanging between mountaintops like a clothesline.

In the mountains south of Charleston, West Virginia tended to be a little *more* West Virginian. Accents were thicker, mountains rose more sharply around narrower valleys, and people took pride in doing small things like holding the door for the next person or waving at strangers as they drove by. Words like "fire" and "tire" came out like "far" and "tar," and people gave directions relative to landmarks like the holler, the creek, or the big oak tree. It annoyed me as a kid, but it felt nice to be back in a place that felt like home again.

Around three in the afternoon, my car struggled over one more hill before beginning its final descent into the valley in which Chapmanville was nestled. The tallest building in town, rising to a mere eight stories among the twenty-five-plus story mountains, stood prominently in the center of the cozy town straddling the Guyandotte River.

After a five-minute drive down busy Main Street, my phone directed me onto a steep concrete driveway up the hillside. At the top of the long ramp, Imani's family dug into the mountain to level off a platform large enough for two sturdy brick homes and a huge backyard, which all sharply contrasted with what I expected when Imani described her homestead as "a couple of shacks on the hill" before.

One of the homes, the larger of the two, sat on the edge of the earthen platform with a spacious front porch overlooking the community in the gorge. Its chimney smoked slightly, and the white shutters dripped with water from the melting ice on the roof but looked as though they'd been painted recently. The other home, smaller but one story higher, sat between the larger one and the heavily wooded hill. The lights inside were off, and no smoke billowed from its chimney.

I rolled my car into the flat parking area behind the houses and jumped out, stretching my legs and cracking my back. I was grabbing my backpack from the trunk when a thump on the shoulder startled me so much I banged my head off the car trunk.

Imani laughed with a snort. "Scared ya, did I? Come on, wuss."

She took me inside the home on the ledge and led me to my temporary bedroom, which was really her uncle's home office. A large, green air mattress took up most of the floorspace and a corner desk loaded with boxes took up whatever floorspace would've been left. The room had obviously fallen into disuse years ago given the layer of hazy dust covering everything and the calendar on the wall from July 2008. I hated the way it all made me feel.

Loneliness was one of my least favorite feelings and one of the ones I'd been plagued with the most in my life. It swallowed me whole sometime in my childhood and never spit me back out in the way a turbulent sea swallows inexperienced sailors, and that room was like a maelstrom threatening to take me straight to the depths. I had no problem not spending much time there.

Imani led me on a short hike down a wooded path after I dropped my bag off. We marched along the side of the mountain until we came to a clear-cut alleyway following a powerline on its way out of the valley, and Imani approached a giant stone covered in moss and lichen resting directly in the center of the clearing.

"Come on. It's easier to get on from the back."

I followed her around the stone to a couple small ledges leading to the top and climbed up behind her, the stingingly cold mountain air penetrating my lungs with every deep breath.

A few blocks of Chapmanville became visible at the bottom of the clearing when I reached the top and took a seat on the edge with Imani. She reached around a bump in the rock and pulled out a metal Scooby-Doo lunchbox filled with pot-smoking paraphernalia and some dank-smelling bud. She reached into the clanky, rusted lunchbox and raised a fat blunt, ready for toking.

"Care to do the honors, my good sir?"

"Don't have to ask me twice, madame." A quick inhalation sucked the flame in through the tip and dragged the thick smoke from its burning contents down my throat and into my lungs. I took a normal-sized hit but broke into a coughing fit, my lungs desperate for the clean air around us, my esophagus stinging as if it had been sliced all the way down. The world blurred with tints of blue and purple as if I stood up too quickly. The blunt slipped between my fingers, and I almost dropped it over the edge. It was all I could do to keep from rolling over myself.

"Oh yeah," Imani barely got out through her laughter. "I loaded this one with kief, so you're welcome. I wanted us to be nice and stony when some other people get here in a few."

Ah, kief. The glorious pollen-like crystals gathering in the bottom of Imani's grinder packed a particularly harsh punch and could knock a person off their ass if they didn't expect it, and I didn't. *You're welcome* was right. I took my next hit and passed it back.

"Thanks for that," I said, halfway genuinely. I grinned wide, and my drying eyes squinted. "By the way—who all is gonna be here?"

"Tonight? Just a couple of my friends from high school. Uncle Tommy's gone until Monday, and Avery and Ryder are coming at some point tomorrow I think." She took her hits with much more grace than I had taken mine.

"Hell yeah. How many people do you think'll be here tomorrow night?"

"Probably a couple dozen. I'm just glad the weather's gonna be halfway decent most of the night so people can go outside. Being locked inside a hot house with everyone all night sounds like actual hell. And they'll have no excuse not to walk home at the end of the night."

Three loud thuds in the distance cut our conversation off before it could get anywhere.

"Sounds like someone just got here. Wanna finish this later?" She held the half blunt we didn't get to smoke up to my glassy eyes and I nodded with a grin. An outburst of laughter from the direction of the houses prompted Imani to take off like a giddy child to see who had arrived. I followed behind at my own pace, climbing off the stone carefully and taking in the numbing air and untouched nature like exhibits in a museum.

The path, worn in from years of walking, ran flat along the hillside from the powerline to the backyard, littered with crumbly leaves and brittle branches. The long dirt trail cut through dense evergreen rhododendron thickets and meandered across the open forest floor. It broke only once to cross a small creek, but a conveniently downed tree provided a stable enough bridge to get across to the backyard.

I sauntered across the vast lawn to the driveway. Behind an open passenger door on a car I didn't recognize, Avery and Imani reunited with a tight hug and claps of laughter, both probably eager to be back together a day earlier than expected, and two guys, brown-haired and heavy-set, stood closely on the other side of the car.

Imani focused on me as I neared. "Guys, this is Monte, my best friend from Morgantown."

Best friend? I mean, I guess I knew that, but hearing her say it first validated it, especially with Avery right next to her when she said it. I smiled a dorky smile.

"Yummy, a snack," the taller of the two guys said with a gross look on his face before I could so much as wave. My hand shot up instinctively to cover my flushed cheeks. "Aw, I didn't mean to embarrass you, sweetie. You've gone red as a tomato."

"Ignore him," the shorter guy offered, punching his partner on the back. "Shech likes to see how much he can get away with."

Shech? I scratched my head on that one, afraid to repeat it because I didn't want to sound stupid. Imani later informed me it was short for "Shechem Hamor," pronounced sheek-em ha-more, and he was indeed the complicated love partner of Michael, the guy who sort of defended me from him.

"Y'all have a good weekend and take a few extra shots for me." Michael gave Shech a peck on the lips and looked me in the eye before getting back in his silver car. "And *you*—don't take his shit, you hear me?"

I didn't know what he meant, but it didn't me take long

to figure out. As soon as his boyfriend was far enough down the driveway to be out of sight, he joined me on the porch and leaned against the railing. Imani and Avery were too distracted with one another inside to notice I'd essentially been trapped.

"So, what's your deal?"

I scrunched my eyebrows. "Excuse me? My deal?"

"Yeah. Your deal. You seem uptight." He came closer to me, and I pulled away. "Loosen up."

"I'm sorry. I'm just a little nervous. It's been a rough couple weeks."

"Oh yeah? I'm sorry to hear that. The shrooms I got for tomorrow will do you a world of good."

I stopped, speechless. Nobody had informed me about shrooms or told me I needed to know what they were.

"Oh, sweet Jesus. Did Imani not tell you about the shrooms?"

"Uh, no. What's a shroom?"

An obnoxious laugh exploded out of him like an air horn. "'What's a shroom?' Are you serious? Imani!"

"Yeah?" She came out onto the porch.

"Did you not tell this boy we were tripping before the party?"

"I thought I did." She looked at me. "We're tripping before the party, but you don't have to if you don't want to."

Everyone stared at me. My chest grew tight as I considered the possibility of actually tripping on a drug I'd only learned about seconds ago. The closest I'd ever been to "tripping" at all was getting cross-faded on weekends through first semester, and to be honest, I didn't like the idea of being in a state where my emotions controlled my perception. My emotions tended to be particularly unpredictable, reversing direction at the drop of a hat, and it scared me even when I was sober. I hated to risk exposing everyone to that.

To take them, to hate them, to love them, to trip on them for six hours—it all scared the shit out of me. My tongue prickled, and a sour taste spread across it.

"I'm down. Let's trip."

The sun had fallen below the ridge on the western end of the valley, and we were gathered around the kitchen island sharing a massive dinner from Tudor's Biscuit World when Shech started going off about how good the shrooms he got for everybody were again. Imani begged to see them, and Shech, a self-proclaimed person of the people, had to keep his fans appeased.

He walked into the living room and returned a few moments later with a grody, worn-out backpack, plopping it on the counter, unzipping it slowly. The pungent smell of weed and fruity cigarillos assaulted my senses far before I could see any trace of shrooms. He reached in and dug for several seconds through what looked like clutter and trash before finally pulling out a wad of sandwich bags and laying them next to his backpack. Shriveled brown, tan, and white pieces of dehydrated mushrooms filled the bags, each labeled "3 gs."

According to his self-report, Shech had enough shrooms there to "send eight to ten people to the moon and back." He planned to hold onto them until we were ready to take them, but he seemed to enjoy jumping on every opportunity to remind us how lucky we were he only charged five dollars per bag. "Close friend discount," he'd say, over and over. He made it so hard to feel thankful. He actually made it so hard to like him or to ever want to be in the same room as him, but I had to deal with it.

That night, when everyone was winding down and conversations ran shorter, Imani and I finally found some alone time on the front porch. She pulled the half-blunt that remained from our earlier smoke sesh out of her pocket with both hands, trying hard not to bend it any more than her pocket already had, and raised it to her mouth, and her face glowed bright orange as she flipped her lighter at the tip, inhaling slowly.

The lights of Chapmanville illuminated the floodplain below us like a mini-metropolis with stray veins of light shooting up the occasional hillside street or out a densely packed holler. A tiny sliver of the moon peeked through fast-vanishing holes in the clouds, providing little escape from the darkness eating the colorless, giant mountains looming all around. The branches on the trees surrounding her family's property clacked about like wooden wind chimes, growing louder in the gusty wind.

"You don't have to do anything you don't want to do tomorrow," Imani reminded me as the woodsmoke scented air blowing up the hill rattled the empty flowerpots hanging from the front porch.

"I'm ready," I shot back. "I can handle myself."

CHAPTER 14: BAPTISM

The room's dreary decor lacked color except for the dark green air mattress and red window treatments, neither of which did the place any favors, and the faint yet unmistakable scent of mothballs lingered in the air, clinging to my blankets and pillows like a bad memory. Fingers of morning light poked through the sheer curtains over the home office's large window, turning the clouds of dust floating around me a thick red color. I wriggled out from under the quilt and crawled out of my squeaky vinyl bed, reaching for my phone.

11:38 a.m.

I stepped over to the full-body mirror, blotchy with smudges and a thick gray film, and primped my hair, pressing the stiff spikes formed on the back of my head by my pillow down to my scalp, before leaving the quiet privacy of the office to see what a morning at Imani's would be like.

Shech, who had a half-empty handle of spiced rum in his hand, bopped happily to Imani's jazzhop coming from the speaker on the kitchen island, pausing to flip the cinnamon-coated French toast in the crackling skillet every so often.

The kitchen looked surprisingly grand with bright white tile floors and cabinets made of reclaimed planks, which Imani said were pulled from her late grandpa's barn, and the skylight overhead served as a spotlight for the sun. The silver granite countertops, reflecting light around the room like mirrors, played against the black appliances and brick accent wall in a rather expensive-looking way. Across the large island, an octagonal archway opened up to a large living room with vaulted ceilings and a ceiling fan circulating the mouthwatering, Christmassy smell of cinnamon and vanilla around the massive room. A dark, unlit Christmas tree covered in ornaments and tinsel sparkled slightly in the corner.

"Good morning adorable." Shech giggled at himself as I stepped onto the cold tile. "I see someone likes going commando."

Annoyed, I readjusted myself through my basketball shorts. Shech seemed mostly harmless, mostly because he had been friends with Imani for so long. Annoying was probably the worst he was going to get.

A burst of energy shot through my veins. "You sure do like to hear yourself talk, don't you?"

"Sure do. Everyone else is on the porch smokin' baby doll. Breakfast will be ready shortly."

I looked out the large panoramic windows facing town and saw Avery and Imani passing a bong filled with green water around on the porch swing. I strode across the living room, stepping through the white French doors and onto the concrete porch.

The valley was still as a painting despite the cars rushing by on the blacktop and some large birds circling above, scanning for something to eat. A gentle breeze blew the ceiling fan on the porch in slow circles and jangled the wooden wind chime, and a few songbirds could be heard singing their songs in the distance.

Imani and Avery let me join them for the last few hits on their bowl, and then I packed another one. Within minutes, the world felt less unnerving again, just the way I liked it. We cashed the bowl, and Shech sprang through the doors onto the porch with a serving plate piled high with French toast, a stack of plastic cups, and a bottle of maple syrup. In the other hand, he carried a frosty gallon of whole milk.

"Eat up, bitches. Long day ahead for our bodies." At once, the plate and milk jug banged onto the glass table in the center of the porch, and like a pack of hungry arctic wolves, we tore into them.

Back inside we trudged after devouring breakfast, kicking back on the pleather sectional in the living room for what Shech called the "pre-trip charge." He told Google to play Bob's Burgers over the T.V. and went to clean the mountain of dirty dishes breakfast created. Imani and Avery sat pressed against each other in the corner of the couch, scrolling on their phones, every blink slower than the last, and I sat on the end, halfway watching T.V. and halfway thinking about Amias.

Consumed was my mind—consumed with worry, with lust, with a wild hunger for more of him and a painful awareness of the fact that I couldn't have him.

I hated the bruises on his face, the hands that put them there, and that they would be the same hands holding him in every Christmas picture I would inevitably see on his profile. Those filthy hands would get to do all the things mine should've been doing: keeping *his* hands warm, eating *his* grandmother's homecooked food, ripping open a gift picked out especially by *him*. But those hands—those stupid fucking hands—would surely leave new bruises and fresh scratches across his face as if that were the purpose of their relationship.

Maybe he'll end up in the hospital. It'd be nice if he got caught drinking and driving. I wouldn't mind seeing him framed for murder.

Amias deserved so much more.

I hated myself so much I decided to pull up his profile just to get it over with, scanning the "Photos" section for new pictures. There weren't any, though. He hadn't posted anything in several days. Not seeing him dressed up in a cute Christmas outfit or an ugly sweater saddened me, but not as much as seeing Matt's arms around him would have. I tossed my phone onto the couch next to me and kicked back, hoping whatever was happening on the T.V. might be enough to distract me or lull me to sleep.

Ryder came through the door a couple hours later, weary from the three-and-a-half-hour drive from Morgantown. It was something like an eleven-hour drive from his home in Farmington, Connecticut to Chapmanville, so he broke the trip up over two days and could hardly hold his eyes open when he arrived. I was so glad I chose to stay the night before the party at Imani's because I would've been in his shape had I not.

Shech disappeared into the master bedroom down the hall where he set up shop for the weekend and returned a few minutes later, arms loaded with stacks of colorful things. He set a wad of plastic bags down on the square coffee table with a few coloring books, a ninety-six pack of Crayola crayons, snacks, a fruity candle, and several bottles of water.

"Trip time is upon us!" he sang as he lunged forward, squawking slightly.

Imani pumped her fist with a few masculine woofs.

We each took a bottle of water and a plastic bag containing three grams of shrooms. I watched everyone take the dehydrated, dirty-looking bits of mushroom out and eat them dry—the entire three grams.

I stuck my hand into the bag and scooped several out, tossing them back into my mouth and chewing them up. Rubbery in texture and earthy in flavor, I couldn't wait to swallow. So I did, despite every instinct in my naïve little body. I turned the bag upward over my mouth, and the remaining crumbs of magic mushroom tumbled past my tongue, shooting to the back of my throat where I had to force them down.

I spent most of the first hour in my head, heart racing as I thought about what this new drug was going to do to my body. It came on subtly, and the world began to look as if somebody turned up the vivid settings on my eyes. I could feel it and not feel it simultaneously as time seemed to slow down and speed up all at once.

An abrupt movement startled me from the corner of the couch. Imani and Avery straightened their backs at the same time and turned to face each other with undiscernible expressions, eyes wide and swirly like the Milky Way and mouths agape.

They released a cacophony of deafening cackles and concerning wheezes. Shech, who lay stretched out on the plush maroon rug around the coffee table, turned away from the T.V. to laugh with them. A serious look gripped Ryder's face on the other end of the sectional, and he suddenly appeared spellbound by the antics of the colors dancing around on the sixty-inch flatscreen.

Frustrated that everyone's trips were beginning earlier than mine, I rose, bound for the kitchen to get something to drink. As I neared the kitchen, though, the room disappeared around me, and my feet searched desperately for something solid to land on.

"Imani," I called out from the kitchen, unaware or uncaring that she didn't respond, panicking over my sudden loss of hearing. I couldn't recall what I needed from her in the first place when sharp lines of light began flopping around on the brick wall in the kitchen as if a sun-beaten river flowed upward over it. I reached out to touch it and nearly had a heart attack when it felt wet.

I placed my dry hand on the kitchen counter gently to avoid breaking it, a notion which had never occurred to me before, and tapped my ears to make sure they were turned on. Then, before I could call out again, a cold surge from the polished stone countertop shot through my hand and up my arm as powerfully as high-voltage electricity. I pulled it away, and my hand suddenly alternated between different shades of red and blue.

I blinked, and everything returned to normal. The river on the wall dried up, my hand was its normal shade again, and the counter no longer felt shockingly frozen. The knots returned to my stomach, and the commotion in the living room once again pounded my eardrums.

Fuh-uh-uck, I thought, taking advantage of the return of clear-headedness to pour a glass of orange juice.

The chilly glass ate into my fingers on the walk back into the living room, where I found several trips well underway. Ryder stepped outside with bare feet and combed through the yard with his toes as if he were being paid to document every single lifeform on the property. He bent over to touch the ground and reached up to pull on tree branches every few seconds, seemingly unbothered by the cold.

Imani and Avery, howling like a couple of excited coyotes, turned the living room into a nightclub of sorts. Trippy music videos played one after the other and dots of light shined in every direction. Colorful strands twinkled along the edges of the fireplace, in the evergreen garland on the mantle, over the archway between the kitchen and living room, and, of course, throughout the Christmas tree. Shech stood bent over at the fridge stuffing his face with a pile of leftover French toast he apparently hid in the back.

I sat back on the couch and decided to take a sip of my juice. Something normal. Something controllable. I closed my eyes, raised the glass, and nearly vomited when a thick liquid gushed from the cup and over my tongue with a neutral taste more reminiscent of cardboard than of tangy orange juice. My eyes darted downward to find a white liquid frothing about like a stormy sea beneath my nose.

Milk.

It was at that moment I realized I was in for one hell of an interesting evening.

The aroma from the candle, now visible like heat over an open road, filled every room with the scent of fresh apples, and the dormers in the ceiling zeroed the sun's rays in on me like a beam from a U.F.O. I grabbed some coloring books and spent a while trying to choose a picture to fill in, but my focus couldn't be directed for more than a few minutes at a time. There was too much happening.

The maroon rug under the coffee table shifted around like sand in a desert, and I jumped to my feet. I stood there for a long while, enjoying the feeling of the hot sandy rug sliding around underneath my toes and curling up over them when a feeling like a snake slithering up the back of my soft shorts scared me lifeless.

I dizzied myself spinning around to see what it was, and I found Shech with a dark black cloud around him, running his fingers up my thigh and licking his lips the way I imagined a cannibal might. I pulled away and backed over the coffee table, grabbing the attention of everyone in the room.

I had two options: stay embarrassed or run away.

I turned and ran out the back entrance, a solid, cold metal door that spat out directly into the backyard, and my bones turned to taffy. The cold, wet grass caught me, and I fell right through the ground and to the middle of space.

In front of me, a black hole at the center of a spinning disc of gray swirls threatened to absorb anything that drifted too close, and I noticed my vulnerability as I bobbed uncontrollably, drifting closer and closer to the oblivion-maker. It possessed inescapable gravity, pulling abstract pieces of myself through my skin and dragging them in ahead of me.

I watched as everything I'd been chasing from sex and boys to drinks and blunts were spaghettified into nothingness in front of me as long strands of light, each a different color.

I could feel it overtaking

And rising around me like a storm surge.

No matter how hard I fought, I couldn't escape the

swells.

I could think of no way to save myself, but then a number flashed in my mind: 416.

The ugliness turned to Dreamland, the one I loved visiting.

A figure stood distantly, worth a lifetime.

I needed to wait for him.

His warmth enveloped me. His fragrance aroused me. The touch of his skin set my soul ablaze. I needed him. Nothing else would do, and it was time I stopped kidding myself.

But he's going to think I'm not worth it, I saw myself thinking, giving in to the malevolent appetite of the darkness around me. *I've blown it more than once.*

I fell back into my body. A thick, heavy queasiness bubbled at the back of my throat, pushing and pulling on my stomach with every breath. Rocks and twigs scraped and ripped the skin on my knees as I fell to the ground, convulsing and crying.

There was a gurgle, a cough, and then I threw up.

I wiped the sour liquid from my lips with the back of my hand and looked around. Imani's house was nowhere in sight—only gray trees and the decaying log I leaned against. My eyes followed the thick, blackish log up the hill and watched as it suddenly reformed, growing branches and sprouting black leaves, and the forest followed it, blooming in the winter cold.

The world was the same, but now it was absent of color and feeling, of hope and fear, leaving only shades of black and white to blend on surfaces bouncing around like a rubber hose cartoon. Time, the only colorful thing I could see, seemed to take on a physical form as if it were water rushing around my shins in a swift river, unstoppable no matter how hard I kicked and stomped. The unnaturally blue liquid swirled around me at a consistent pace, uncaring of the colorless world behind or the deep ocean ahead. I looked down at its surface, and the longer I stared into it, the more the blurry reflection of me felt like reality and I felt like the reflection.

A different version of my life came to the surface—The Anti-Me. I saw a version where I hadn't been taught to repress my feelings and to assimilate to a crowd who blindly followed The Stupid Rule Book, where I was able to say "Yes" more than I was told to say "No," and where my life, one full of my own handpicked priorities, was full of color and vibrancy. There were no obstacles for The Anti-Me because I grabbed opportunities by the shoulders and kissed them until they were mine. There was no heartbreak because The Anti-Me admitted to falling in love forever ago and got to him first.

My reflection smiled without me.

It loved without me.

It grew and aged and died without me, and even in death, my reflection looked happier than I did in life. I felt sick, like I was missing something, someone.

Love yourself, I heard in *his* voice.

My eyes grew misty as a tight sensation over my ribcage made it increasingly harder for me to take full breaths. I sat down in the rushing currents of time, letting its cold waves break over my lap, and leaned back in the flow. It washed over my stomach, my chest, and then my neck.

I held my head above the surface and watched as the colorful liquid around me faded to black with the impurities pulled out through my skin. The black cloud expanded downstream, crashing over rocks and bubbling

BECAUSE I REMEMBER YOU

around debris on its way out of my life for good. My head sank beneath the shallow ripples, eyes open, and it felt as though time washed away every wrong thing I'd ever done. The sins and guilt were gone, sent to the past where they could be of little concern to me—forever a part of the flow but not in control of what was to come.

I peeked back above the waves and wiped my eyes. Color returned to the world, and the black leaves that bloomed on the trees now exploded with color and life.

I watched upstream in awe as the creek brought with it the color of life and sparkle of joy I'd always wished to experience. It felt unreal soaking in it, taking in its power to inspire a smile more genuine than any I'd ever known.

I crawled up on the bank, soaking wet and feeling revived, and rolled over in the dirt, legs still in the colorful stream. I watched the sun overhead, and I finally felt happy, or like I could finally reach happiness. Utterly enveloped in a sensation I'd only ever thought could come from heaven, I lay there, cheeks burning, eyes closed, and enjoyed the relief of forgetting.

* * *

I woke up on the frozen bank of a creek in the middle of the woods. Just downhill from me, a log connected one bank with the other, and I realized where I was: a few feet from the trail Imani led me down before. When I arose, the shade of the earth itself had overtaken the land and cooled the atmosphere off considerably, forcing me to retreat to the dry warmth of the house on the ledge, windows aglow with yellow lights and the shadows of my friends inside.

Between the driveway and backdoor, a bright red inflatable shaped like Santa Claus I'd never noticed bobbled in the wind, and a fake-frosted, bushy wreath hung on the door. The smell of garlic from the pizza and breadsticks Shech prepared in the kitchen welcomed me back inside well before the fruity candle, now halfway gone, and the light from the silver bar over the kitchen island overflowed into the dark living room, competing with the strings of blinking lights everywhere.

Avery was recovering from a bad trip in an essential oil bubble bath prepared by Imani, who was sitting propped against the coffee table watching Steven Universe. She'd wrapped herself in a bright green and blue tapestry she pulled off the wall, enthralled like a child: hands on her knees, mouth open, eyes fixed on the beautifully animated cartoon. The soundtrack playing over the soundbar vibrated my thoughts away, too, and I slid to a slump when I joined her on the plush rug.

"Yo bro. You disappeared. How's... your trip going?" she asked in an awkward rhythm without breaking focus on the T.V., unaware of my dampness, or rather soaking wetness.

"I think I'm coming down. My feet feel like they're still covered in running water, but something happened to me in the woods. I don't remember it all."

"What happened in the woods? Any epiphanies or awakenings or—" We looked out the window at the headlights whooshing across the hill by the driveway, signifying the arrival of party guests. "—anything you wanna talk about?"

"Well, that's kinda broad."

After a long pause, I added, "I think I've been living haphazardly, not growing or doing anything meaningful, not like I wanted anyway. Looking back, it honestly just feels like a bunch of clueless exploration. I think I've gotta prioritize my own needs a little more, ya know?'

She nodded.

"Not in a selfish way or anything, but I've learned when it comes to getting that *actually happy* feeling, the only person who really cares is me."

"I don't think exploring is pointless, but I get what you're saying. What's the plan then? Going forward, I mean."

"I'm not entirely sure. My next goal is to find someone I can connect with."

"Have you not been doing that? I mean, it was wild when you first started having different guys over every week, but you tried to slow things down with Braxton, didn't you? Tell me what it's gonna take to make Montgomery Lee happy."

My head, still influenced by magic mushrooms, took me to the last time I felt genuine happiness and the first time I was with a person who showed me the affection my heart and soul demanded.

416.

His scent.

His humor.

His individuality.

His insane dick-sucking skills.

My happiness.

"Yeah," I replied, lowering my head bashfully. "There's this one guy. He's only ever made me feel good, even when he shouldn't have, and I think I'd make him feel good, too, if things weren't so complicated."

I believed that, too. Sure, he looked reserved and maybe even a little regretful after our lovemaking—and that was absolutely what it was—but he was probably just worried. He had a boyfriend, albeit a piece of shit excuse for one, and he had just been making love to another guy. But it wasn't just any guy. It was me, and it wasn't the first time we'd gotten close.

I didn't know what to expect out of the future given the messiness of the past, but I knew a few things. I would've only touched him tenderly. I would've only yelled his name with explosive pleasure. I would've only made him cry from laughing too hard. I knew I'd cherish his soul if ever I could, and no amount of time, space, or circumstance could take away from my memory of him even if they did force me to practice my patience.

I thought he'd been put in my life for a reason the moment I saw him in high school, and I knew it the moment I saw him waiting for me on the bed, drenched in gold, inviting me over with a smile as real as any. And one of the many best parts about everything that happened between us was that he wanted me, too—I heard it in the way he said he remembered me and saw it in his glistening brown eyes.

I hated that I'd have to live through every second alone until fate led us together officially, but I didn't mind that we'd be a couple with a long backstory. I liked the thought of having a long, drawn-out story to tell our friends or, and I got pleasantly lightheaded thinking about this, our future grandchildren. Of course I'd have never said that out loud, but it was one of my happiest thoughts.

"I guess now all I can do is I wait until things line up between us."

CHAPTER 15: FIRE

By 10 p.m., the house was overflowing with people from Imani's high school, people she met in Morgantown, and probably a few extras. Everywhere I looked, foreign eyes glowed over hollow smiles in the glare of the Christmas lights, bouncing up and down with no rhythm to music they probably weren't even listening to. The shrooms were still in my system because everything dripped with color, and any patterned surface appeared to ripple and bend. But I was well into the coming-down phase by that time, which was more subtle and easier to control than when I'd been knocked on my ass outside.

The Christmas tree, flickering brightly with multicolor lights and a fiber optic star topper, illuminated the darkness nearly on its own, and its inconsistent blotches of light splattered across walls and bodies in everchanging ways. The T.V. was no longer painted with colorful animations echoing peaceful music; instead, it rumbled the subwoofer to the beat of the same club music I'd heard a million times before. The bass of every song exploded out from the small black box beside the entertainment stand, through the floorboards, and up into my bones, and a seemingly endless stream of people with red plastic cups poured into the living room to dance their cares away on one another. I forgot for a moment I wasn't at a frat party in Morgantown.

"These are for y'all," Shech yelled after emerging from the crowd, reaching two plastic cups in our direction.

Imani and I peeled ourselves away from the rug under the coffee table for the first time to fill our cups with jungle juice from the storage tote on the front porch, which I didn't expect to like but did. The dangerous concoction fell somewhere between green and blue on the color spectrum, and it tasted so sugary I couldn't pin down what liquor was in it. I'd never had a drink at a party that tasted so non-alcoholic before.

We went back inside with full cups, and Shech had returned to the kitchen with his friends, all seemingly over the age of twenty-five, to guard several bottles of straight liquor. Imani and I fell back into our spots on the floor, leaned against the coffee table, and tried to get through our drinks as quickly as possible.

No matter how I tried to shift around, Shech seemingly made a way to stay where we could see one another. His shameless attempts at getting my attention and trying to make eye contact with me from a whole room away would've probably given me the creeps if Imani and Avery hadn't assured and reassured me all weekend that he was harmless—"all bark and no bite," as they put it. He sure liked to fucking bark, though.

I was almost finished with my drink when I noticed a ball of white in the corner of my eye. My head turned instinctively to see what it was, and it was Shech, way too close to me to have such a hungry smile ripping through his puffy cheeks. His left eye fell closed and dragged his right eyelid halfway down with it in what I assumed was a shit-faced attempt at a wink.

Had he caught me a couple weeks earlier, or perhaps even a few days earlier, he may have gotten a wink back out of me, but not now. My heart belonged to someone else, even if he didn't know it yet, and I preferred being alone over being with another guy I knew I had no future with. I'd wait however long I had to for my forever with Amias, and nobody would be given the opportunity to drag me off track, especially not some garlicky-vodka-scented, horny, cheating asshole I'd hopefully never see again.

A couple guys conveniently broke his chilling gaze when they stepped between us and grabbed different corners of the coffee table, pulling it away from my back without warning. People stumbled around on the floor erratically once it was out of the way, filling in the new makeshift dancefloor behind us, so it was either jump up and join them or be trampled down by them.

Imani seemed to bounce into another headspace as effortlessly as ever, probably to fulfill her duties as hostess of the "party of the year," but I had a harder time adjusting. I watched as she bopped up and down with everyone else, chugging what was left in her cup, while I sort of fell into the unsteady mob. It wasn't a bad place, though, because the effects of the acid were colorful and energetic still, and I wanted to milk it for all I could.

I danced and thought about the future, and I saw Amias in it, in some capacity, in a romantic capacity hopefully. I felt like I might never outrun the thoughts of him that ate at my brain all day every day, and I didn't mind that. I knew what I wanted from him now.

It felt wrong to believe a drug like shrooms could've

provided me with any amount of clarity, but I'd seen things on my trip that felt as real as life. I watched my reflection live a life I dreamt of living, felt the inky blackness of the past ooze out through my skin with the thickness of blood, and watched as everything I hated about myself and the world was swept away by the never-ending flow of time.

But still, I felt that pesky self-loathing lurking in the background, telling me I screwed myself over and made everything more time-consuming than it needed to be.

Christ, I thought. *What'd I have to go and do something so damned stupid for?*

I hadn't asked him on a date. I hadn't hinted I was interested in him. I hadn't even waited until he was single first. I went straight for dirty, sweaty sex, but it felt like so much more than that.

It felt like a connection to the only person I knew I belonged around and the only spirit in the universe with the ability to make mine feel whole. Something about him felt unrealistic—almost magical in a way. He made me feel as though I'd been born again and taken those first precious breaths of life, and I needed to keep on taking them to survive. His mere presence put the two of us in a bubble, and everything outside our bubble stopped existing. I loved our bubble so much that I never wanted to leave it for fear that it might pop and be gone forever, but I had to, at least for a little while longer.

I couldn't do anything except wait—wait for Amias to wake up and see he didn't need Matt's abusive hands providing anything for him, wait for him to realize how much he was worth, wait for my opportunity to take him by the hand and show him the worst in me was better than the best in Matt. He'd come to those conclusions in his own time. I was all but certain it would happen for him because it happened for me, and I was determined to be there for him with open arms and no distracting commitments when it did.

I wanted to stop obsessing over the whole situation even if only for a few hours, so I decided to play a risky little game with Shech to hopefully get my hands on some of his booze. My head still felt a little cloudy, cloudy enough to keep me captive in a place I couldn't live all night, and he stood between me and the one thing with the power to make me stop thinking. I surmised what everyone told me about how harmless he was had to have been true because the only thing he had done all weekend was act like an obnoxious little shit, but so had plenty of other people.

Creepy? Maybe. Threatening? Not really.

I turned to see if he was still watching me and caught him staring from the kitchen again.

"Well, howdy doody to you beautiful. How can I help ya, darlin'?" Shech said as soon as he noticed I got close enough to hear him, cutting his friends' conversation off.

I walked up to the kitchen island and stood underneath the harsh light hanging above it, trying desperately to conceal how giddy his hyped-up reception made me. "I hear you're the guy with all the liquor."

A barrage of laughter nearly deafened me, and Shech and three other members of the large group raised a half-empty bottle, each one a different brand of liquor.

"Take your pick."

I opted for the Fireball whiskey in Shech's hand. Another member of the group, a slender girl with blonde and blue hair, reached below the island and pulled out an unopened fifth of the amber, cinnamony liquor.

"Oh, that's the last one, and since it's just a couple days until Christmas, we wanted it." He reached out to prevent the girl from sliding the glass bottle across to me, and another menacing smile pushed into his chubby, stubbly cheeks. "But I guess I could let you have the whole thing if you stay here and get drunk with me."

I hesitated, entirely aware of who I'd be committed to hanging out with, but I came to the kitchen for one thing and wasn't leaving without it. "Sure, I'm down."

The kitchen erupted with a few "Ahalrights" and "Hell yeahs" from different directions, and the bottle screeched across the counter to me. Shech passed around a container with enough shot glasses for each drinker to get one. They weren't average shot glasses, though. They were the size of teacups and had "FOR THE BIG SHOTS" written across the side.

I filled mine a quarter of the way full and began twisting the cap back on my bottle.

"Nah. That shot glass is not even close to full, sweetie. I said drunk, not tipsy."

I did as I was told.

Shech raised his glass. "On three, bottoms up. Three!"

We clanked our glasses together over the island, tapped them off the counter, and then raised them again, this time to our mouths. My dry lips cradled the startlingly cold rim of the clear glass, and the blazing, syrupy liquid poured into my mouth, burning my tongue and esophagus on the way to my stomach like battery acid. The liquor I thought tasted the way Christmas would—spicy and smooth like a liquid graham cracker—left an aftertaste that built in intensity the more I swallowed, and the glass was so damned huge it took several gulps to finish it off. I almost couldn't finish it but finally did and realized I was the last to raise my empty shot glass bottom-up.

Following a deep-throated gag, a hot, convulsive chill crept up my back and out through my limbs. I found myself warming up from the effects of the Fireball within minutes, and with my inhibitions vanishing, I craved another.

Before anybody else could refill theirs, I squeezed my nose and threw another glass back for the second round. The bottle on the counter grew increasingly enticing, now just under three-quarters of the way full, and I stared into the orange liquor until an idea formed in the back of my mind.

Shech had specified I couldn't leave the kitchen with my bottle unless I was noticeably drunk, so I concluded the best course of action would be to take care of that as quickly as possible. I raised the bottle to my lips and tipped it upward, and Fireball bubbled furiously into my mouth.

A pressure building in the back of my throat forced me to put the bottle back down on the counter. Drool began to pool under my tongue, flowing from every surface like water flowing from a bloated mountain after weeks of heavy rain, and I could taste the drops of stomach acid accumulating behind my uvula. Swallowing became harder but more essential as I struggled to contain what threatened to explode onto the kitchen counter.

"I need a minute," I uttered, heading quickly for the bathroom with one hand over my mouth and the other gripping my half-bottle of cinnamon whiskey.

I dug through the crowded living room and swayed past the family pictures in the hallway, staggering past doorway after doorway until finally coming to an open one that led into a bright white, narrow bathroom. I threw the door closed behind me and fell to my knees in front of the toilet. With barely enough awareness to notice skidding across the tile skinned my knee up pretty badly, I dipped my head straight into the white bowl, hacking up nothing but drool. The ammonia-backed stench of urine forced my throat and stomach into a more violent dance to appease my nausea, but still, I only dry-heaved and drooled.

I rolled back into the floor, every muscle in my body aching from the dry heaving, but the coldness of the tile provided some sort of weird relief as I lay there feeling the Fireball shut down my senses. I struggled to see what was right in front of me and couldn't find the will to stand up on my own.

I'll call Imani.

I stretched out my body so I could reach my arm into my tight pants pocket and pulled out my phone. I typed in my passcode. It didn't work. I tried again. It still didn't work. It took multiple tries before I finally got my phone unlocked, and by then, I had forgotten why I pulled it out in the first place.

I decided to scroll around on Facebook to pass time, hopefully enough time for my stomach to settle and for me to regain enough strength to climb out of the floor.

I scrolled—someone got engaged.

I scrolled again—terribly-designed meme.

I scrolled one more time—heart-stopping post.

It was an update from Amias, but it wasn't any old update. It was an update to his relationship status, and it said he was newly single.

I wanted so desperately to feel sad or heartbroken for

him. I wanted to feel remorse for the things I'd done to lead to their breakup. But I couldn't. He finally got away from the person I wanted him away from, and an opportunity for us to be together was so close I could taste the strawberry lip gloss.

I considered he may have been too burdened by the truth to keep up the lie, which seemed likely considering his angelic character. He had cheated on the boyfriend he lived with, and he had done it with me.

A rock formed in the back of my throat when I thought about how Matt may have reacted to finding out he had been cheated on. I could only hope Amias had told him everything over the phone or that he hadn't told the truth at all.

Matt could've come after me, too. He knew where I worked, and he could've very easily figured out what car I drove and followed me home. My aunt and uncle's house was a big one with many doors and windows, and I was typically there by myself. We could've both been in danger.

Matt faded to nothingness, though, as I looked back toward the future. Amias wasn't going to be tied up in a relationship anymore. He was single, and he would eventually be looking for somebody to spend forever with.

All I had to do was, still, wait.

After tapping around on his profile for a few blurry minutes, Imani busted through the bathroom door to check on me.

"You alright, man?"

"Totally good," I slurred, locking my phone and taking another swig.

"Okay. I was just wondering because most people who

are 'totally good' aren't lying in front of the toilet drinking Fireball alone."

"Hey ugly, I'm doing alright, especially now."

"I'll act like you didn't call me that and help you anyway." She grabbed me by the arm and lifted me out of the floor like a rag doll. "I need a cigarette, and you need fresh air."

I followed her off the front porch and over to a quiet place at the edge of the yard, hardly able to keep myself upright. We stood facing the drop, once again looking down on the town below, and Imani pulled out two cigarettes and lit them simultaneously.

She reached one to me. "Here."

Cigarettes never hit the spot like they did when I was smashed. The smoke didn't hurt, the shitty taste was less noticeable, and the nicotine hit more intensely. We stood quietly and watched the valley, which I had grown fond of doing, as the breeze blew off the mountain, whipping our smoke trails out over the steep front yard in front of us. Near the house, a loud bunch of folks around my age roared around a bonfire, reacting to each other's stories of adventures and plans for the future, but there, where we stood alone on the ledge, I felt more peace than I had all night.

"Whadaya think?" Imani asked.

"I'm having a blast. I—" A hiccup cut me off. "—don't think I've ever had this much to drink before." I had to sit down to keep from falling over the hill, and cold water seeped up through the pointy tufts of grass and into the ass of my pants.

Imani laughed and sat next to me. "Glad to hear it. I've been pacing myself so I can keep up with everything that's happening, and I'm pretty sure everyone else is in your shape right now."

I reached out my half-empty bottle of Fireball, and she grabbed it.

"Thanks, man." She took a few swigs and sat it on the grass between us. "I'm having a blast, too, but honestly, I'd rather be stoned watching some cartoons."

"Oh man, amen to that. That sounds pretty nice right now. This view is killer, though."

The lights of Chapmanville flickered around below us like fireflies. A clear patch in the cloudy sky gave way to a moon surrounded by thousands of stars, casting a dim bluish hue over the hillside and valley directly below us. Far off in the distance, a storm flashed bright lightning around the valley, cracking low rumbles of thunder that went unheard if you couldn't tune the drunks and the music out. It was as good a place as any to smoke and talk with Imani, and it would've been a great place to wind down for the end of the night.

Then, the sound of the most repellent person in Chapmanville stomping off the porch and down to the bonfire made me miss my aunt and uncle's house back in Westover. I turned my shoulders slightly, hoping he wouldn't see me.

"Imani! Monte! Get your asses over here!" Shech shouted from a log he settled on by the fire.

"Duty calls." Imani took off across the yard, slightly drunker but still obligated to make sure everyone enjoyed themselves.

I sat there for a while longer, riding the wave of substance-inspired peace for as long as I could.

"Monte! You, too, sexy thing!"

I wished I could start dry heaving again, but I could never be so lucky. I grabbed what was left of my whiskey, took another swig, and waddled across the yard to the bonfire. The giant orange and yellow bush of light radiated a hotness that reminded me how cold the night was. I suddenly understood why everyone who came outside gathered around it.

I took a seat next to Imani and Avery on a patio swing next to the flaming firepit, but Shech's gaze was inescapable, even across the tall blaze from him. The fire whipped up between us, sheltering me from his gaping eyes, but when the high flames devolved into smaller ones, those frozen eyes continued to glisten hungrily in my direction. He called out to me anytime he sensed I was zoning out and wouldn't dare let me wander back inside alone, and the half-liter of whiskey I'd downed didn't make resisting any easier.

I dropped the empty bottle on the ground, and the crowd hushed.

"Hey man, you're not looking so good," Imani said.

"I'm—"

The ground got closer and closer until everything went black.

I couldn't have been asleep for more than two hours when I heard the door behind the desk creak open slowly and suspiciously. The total darkness, swallowing every bit of light trying to bounce around in the office, kept the person's identity concealed. I couldn't tell if my eyes were even open anymore. All I could do was lie there.

My eyes fell shut again, but only for a second when I felt the air mattress growing tighter and larger beneath me. Someone else had climbed into bed with me.

Outside the closed office door, the house had grown quiet, and the thin lines of light that had been peeking between the door and frame were gone. Whispers of rain and ice pellets blowing around on the roof and the occasional boom of thunder were the only sounds I could make out anymore.

A few silent minutes later, I heard the mystery guest squeaking across the queen-sized air bed in my direction, seemingly out of breath. Suddenly, the smell of whiskey and woodsmoke overtook me. My unknown and uninvited bedmate sat there for only a few more minutes before reaching across my torso, their cold, greasy skin rubbing against my warm flesh. I felt a hand grip my thigh, which was pressed into the air mattress, and I was flipped over—face-up.

My heart juddered like a dryer with a cinderblock in it and within seconds, the world was black again.

CHAPTER 16: AFTERMATH

Most of my memories were hidden behind walls built by a vengeful hangover when I woke up alone the next morning with my back pressing through the mattress and into the floor. I looked around the dingy old room, dizzying myself, and noticed the pillow on the other side of the bed had been smashed and the blanket dragged halfway into the floor.

What the hell?

The hands on the clock above the desk showed the time to be just after 10 a.m., and someone, probably Imani, left a bottle of water on an ottoman next to the air mattress. I grabbed it and twisted the cap off, chugging the whole thing in a matter of seconds. The worst bits of the night started coming back to me.

The liquor. The nausea. The bedmate.

It felt mostly like harmless drunken party antics except for that last part. I had no memory of what happened between us, if anything, or who they were. I couldn't remember if I'd said anything to invite the person in or if they'd intruded and acted maliciously, if it was someone I knew or a stranger from town, if anything sexual happened between us or if someone just came in to make sure I hadn't choked on my vomit—I hadn't a clue. But it wasn't just the bedmate I couldn't remember. I struggled to remember anything about the whole night, good or bad.

The house seemed to mirror my disquietude with dozens of red plastic cups and glass bottles scattered about in the way you'd expect rusted cars to be scattered about a junkyard. The Christmas tree stood, still shining, but the lights on the mantle had been pulled off to one side and dangled above the floor. A small fire burned in the corner fireplace, filling the room with a scent that should've comforted me but didn't.

My body felt sore and heavy, almost glum, as if it remembered something I couldn't. Nobody saw anybody come into the office with me after Imani carried me in there, so I thought I'd ask her.

I scratched my throat with a dry bagel from the box on the island and downed a glass of water before joining her on the porch where she was enjoying her morning smoke.

"How ya feelin', Monte?"

"Rough this morning." The cold concrete porch shocked my bare feet, and Old Man Winter had no problem blowing through the thin fabric of my hoodie.

"I'll bet. You were pretty messed up when I brought you that bottle of water last night on my way to bed, but you seemed like you were on cloud nine, man, giggling and going on about some guy you couldn't wait to see again." I didn't remember that, but I did suddenly recall what I'd been so happy about.

Amias is single. I felt the corners of my mouth turn upward into a smile, the first one I hadn't had to force all morning.

Imani handed me a cig and a box of matches before tapping hers out under the railing and flicking it into the garbage can in the corner. "Enjoy, my dude."

I stood on the porch by myself, taking in the morning air and a dose of nicotine I knew I didn't need. The temperature dropped considerably overnight, and every blade of grass in the yard now glistened with ice and snow. All around me, trees cracked in the breeze, dropping their light dusting to the forest floor where it melted on wet ice, but the flakes falling from the sky would soon have their branches covered once more. The grinding of the metal scraper of a snowplow came and went on the street below, and the four-lane cutting through town resembled a line of black ink cutting across a clean piece of paper.

The freezing air felt so refreshing on my skin and in my lungs. I took in a deep breath and held it for a few seconds, allowing the cold to dig its way into the deepest parts of me.

It may turn out to be an okay morning, after all, I thought to myself.

I let it out, and Shech busted through the door and onto the front porch.

"Good morning sexy." He slapped my ass as if it belonged to him.

I felt like the earth might open up and swallow me whole, or maybe I hoped it would, as the memories suddenly came rushing back to me.

* * *

BECAUSE I REMEMBER YOU

*Through the consuming darkness and drunken groggi-
ness, I started to make out who had climbed into bed
with me. Shechem Hamor sat up on his knees next to
me, fidgeting on the air mattress to keep his balance,
rubbing his hands around on my cold, limp thighs.*

*"Hey, beautiful. It's cute that you fell asleep with your
glasses on."*

I didn't realize I had.

*One of his hands landed on my crotch. "You don't even
have to move. Just lay there."*

"Wha—"

"Shh. It's okay."

*I lay there, soothed by the caressing of his hands for a
brief second before I remembered Amias. I didn't want
anyone else. I tried to roll myself back over but failed
under the weight of his body, now suddenly leaning over
me.*

"I wanna go back to sleep."

"We'd have more fun doing it my way."

*I grabbed his hand to stop it from getting any further
down my pants.*

"Shechem. Stop. Please."

*He tried to press on, wiggling his greasy hands around
mine. "Are ya sure baby doll? I can make it worth your
time."*

"Please don't do this."

*He pulled his hands away from me and rolled to the
other side of the bed. "The tasty ones are always so difficult. Wake me up if you change your mind. I'd hate to let
a pretty little thing like you slip through my fingers."*

*He rolled over and fell asleep on his back, snoring
within a few minutes. I rolled back over to face the wall,
and thankfully, my drunkenness grew too strong to con-*

trol once again, and I passed out.

* * *

"Ya know, Monte…" Hearing my name slither off his tongue made me physically sick. "…I'm sorry."

I expected some slimy defense for the bullshit he tried to pull or a horny-ass joke about it, but an apology seemed like a step in the right direction.

"Sorry for what?"

"I'm sorry to have missed out on you after all the work I put in. I don't let many pretty, young things like you off the hook so easy."

Like the corner of a page into a fleshy finger, his words sliced through my eardrum and straight into my brain. The bastard spent the night filling me with liquor, probably intending to catch me in bed drunk out of my mind.

I dabbed my cigarette out on the bottom of the railing and dropped it in the trash can before going back inside without a sound, and I went straight to the office to get my things together.

"Hey Imani, I'm gonna get an early start on the drive back to Nicholas County." I couldn't look at anybody as I walked through the living room to put on my shoes.

"You sure? You're welcome to chill for a while, shake off the hangover. I know you've gotta be suffering from a gnarly one."

"I'm good. Mom hit me and told me it's supposed to get bad that way, so she wants me to head out A.S.A.P." I hadn't heard from Mama, but I needed an easy departure. "Thanks for everything."

"No prob, Bob. Thanks for coming. Watch for deer and

let me know when you make it home."

The last thing I should've allowed myself to do in that condition was drive halfway across a frozen, mountainous state to a home where my sins would've certainly spawned animosity should they have come out, but I needed out of Chapmanville. I started the engine, turned on the heated seat and defroster, and pulled out of Imani's steep driveway.

I had never hoped for a Christmas to pass quickly, but I did that Christmas. I wanted to skip ahead to where I could see *him*, lie with *him*, be with *him*. I felt selfish thinking about those things with a guy dealing with a fresh breakup, but I couldn't help it. A glimpse of him and the goodness he possessed drove me wild with desire, and the only thing standing between me and his peace-bringing face was a night at home.

I distracted myself with Sylvan Esso and the scenery, and I didn't mind that. The highway twisted and curved like a river through the valleys, and the mountains rose like Titans all around me, disappearing into clouds that dropped white flakes to the earth.

When I crested the top of the mountain I grew up on, driving became less automatic. Snowbanks rose several inches on either side of the road, which had become much more snow-covered in the absence of warming sunlight. I shifted my car into a low gear and coasted slowly off the mountain and into the driveway I never wanted to ride up again.

Don't get me wrong—I was excited to see my family. I hadn't seen them in months. I kept in touch with Mama by text or phone call whenever she wanted to check in, and there wasn't much of an expectation for keeping in touch with Juliet and Remi. But Dad and I hadn't shared a word since August, and here I was about to stroll up on Christmas Eve as if I never missed a beat.

I could only imagine the lecture I'd get when he found out I hadn't been to church since August or that I'd been spending weekends on High Street. It had to have been him who ordered Merida and Keith to spy on me at the start of the semester, and I wasn't ready to face the wrath he'd likely been cooking up.

With my backpack hanging lazily from one shoulder, I plodded across the snow-covered backyard to the backdoor and stood there for a moment, considering whether or not to get back in my car and head back to Morgantown early.

I could tell them Meghan called me in for a shift at the hotel, I thought, staring at the rimy doorknob.

The backdoor swung open before I could make a decision, and a wall of heat pummeled me from inside. Mama greeted me with the warmth I'd been longing for, wrapping me in the tightest embrace of my life before I could lock winter outside with the backdoor. I felt the sting of a newly-formed tear in the corner of my eye and realized the reunion I tried to skip out on was exactly the thing I needed. Or exactly one of the things I needed. Dad shut the door behind me, and I grew tense knowing he stood between me and the exit.

"Hey son," he said with a straight face. "We've missed you around here." He opened his arms for a hug, a quick one, but still a hug. I thought maybe he didn't know what all I had been up to or didn't care since I wasn't soiling his good name in a church somewhere anymore. It didn't seem likely, though. It seemed more likely he was setting up a trap to get me to open up, and he would strike when my defenses were down, ready to exorcise me of the imaginary gay demon again.

I gritted my teeth, waiting for an underhanded comment that never came. He only hugged me and led us to the kitchen.

Mama baked two trays of cookies for my arrival: one tray of sugar and one tray of chocolate chip. A fluffy faux tree as wide as a couch stood in the fully decked-out dining room, drenched in colorful lights and the occasional, flickering white one. New baubles and handmade ornaments from my childhood adorned its branches and sparkled in the millions of lights like tiny disco balls, and packages cloaked in different patterns of wrapping paper crowded around its base, covering the flannel tree skirt. It was actually starting to feel like Christmas.

My bedroom looked the way I remembered it, though —cold and gray, lacking any sign of a comfortable personality or a life worth living.

"So, how was your first semester?" Mama asked, helping me settle into my bedroom.

"It was great. Lots of ups, a few downs. Mostly the stuff I filled you in on when you messaged me."

She laughed for a second before looking as serious as could be. "Ya know, Monte, your dad noticed you didn't talk to him all semester. Not even one message. That's four months without a single word from you."

"I know, Mom, but you don't understand." I didn't want to do this now, but I guess I had no choice. "The damage he di—"

"I do understand, Monte. Or I know it if I don't understand it. We all know it. That's not what I'm saying." She hesitated, frustrated her point wasn't coming across clearly. "He's been seeing a therapist, and he quit his pastorship at Old Prospects. Did you know that?"

"Well, no, I didn't." Dad had been a pastor at Old Prospects for years, since before I started middle school, and he *always* harped on people who saw therapists, insisting they were crazy or lacked the faith in god necessary to get through life. I couldn't believe she wasn't lying to me or trying to guilt me into apologizing, but that wasn't like her.

"I know you didn't. You couldn't have possibly known it. He's missed you. He knows he messed up big time and constantly. I do, too."

"Yeah. Both of you did, but he did way more, mom. Growing up here was fun and we had our good times and all, but I felt like I was living in a prison. All I ever wanted to do was please you and Dad, to please the church, to please everyone. I gave up so much of myself to make it here, but that didn't matter when I needed it to. Not to any of you." She dissolved into tears. "Love was not the first thing I felt here. I felt alone here. I felt judged and condemned here. And when I needed someone to be my rock, you all turned against me. Every single one of you. I had the worst night of my life here, and trust me, Mom, I have had a lot of terrible nights since then."

"Damn it, Montgomery he kn— I know it." She froze and looked to the floor. "Our priorities were so messed up, and I never had the backbone to speak my mind, even for you kids." Her sniffling graduated to steady sobbing. "I don't know how I could ever make it right. I guess I can't. And I know it's not worth a thing to you now, not after all that, but I'm so sorry. You were my son, and you should've always come first in my life. I know that, and now, so does your father. We wasted so much time trying to change and control you when all we were really doing was setting ourselves up to lose you and causing damage you may never heal from, and that is the absolute last thing I want for one of my babies."

Instantly, my face went red hot, and I could feel my lower lip quivering. A tear rolled down my cheek and crashed into my collarbone, and Mama pulled me in for another hug, a hug so tight it cracked my back, a hug so tight it seemed to heal every wound, or at least numb them.

"A mother knows her children, Monte, and son, I love you to death *exactly* the way you are," she said as we backed away from one another.

She wiped her tears away with the scrunched-up tissue from her pocket and smiled at me. "We're making gingerbread houses and having snacks in the kitchen when you're ready."

She left me with a lot to process, but my favorite thing she said was she loved me *exactly* the way I was. She couldn't have known anything about who I had become for certain, but it felt like she did when she said those words, the words she'd written on the back of the painting she gave me the day I moved out. She'd probably always known who I was. Looking back, I could see it in the way she defended me dyeing my hair blonde in middle school or in the way she let me wear plaid shoes even when others said they looked too girly. It all made so much sense now.

But the fact Dad quit pastoring and started seeing a therapist didn't make any sense. I supposed it was good, but it still felt like a little too much. I needed time to think about it or to consider if it was part of a convincing trap. It was Christmas Eve, though, and I had things to do.

Once we completed the gingerbread houses, Dad asked me to help him by the woodstove. He made every effort to keep the smoke from escaping into the living room as he shoved the last few pieces of dry wood from his rack into the hot cast iron stove, but it was inevitable. I don't think anybody minded the smell, though. Christmas wouldn't have felt like Christmas without the smell of Mama's cinnamon candy and cookies and the faint smell of Dad's woodsmoke.

"Would you help me carry some more wood down, son?"

I predicted this request when I saw him picking up the last pieces of firewood, so I had the empty bronze rack in my hands by the time he finished his sentence.

The trail to the fallen tree that had become this year's firewood supply was little more than a thin stripe of mashed mud, ice, and dead leaves through a forest floor of pristine, snow-covered brush. The muddy, chunky mixture gushed around beneath me, splashing onto the white snow around me, and with every step, more of it clung to the bottom of my boots, making them heavier the further we went.

Dad had already sliced the downed trunk of the tree into wooden cylinders, ready to be chopped. He took his calloused, leathery hands out of their gloves and pulled the axe from the tree stump, preparing to hack the cylinders into usable pieces of firewood.

"Monte, uh, listen." Dad faltered with the axe now over his shoulder. "I need to talk to you about something." He slammed it down into a piece of wood.

"Sure dad." I instantly started sweating inside my

hoodie and jeans despite the penetrating wind piercing through them.

"It's about what happened last summer." Dad paused briefly, leaning against the handle of his axe. "It's about how I treated you your whole life." He threw his gaze in my direction as if expecting me to say something back, but I couldn't. "You've always been a pretty good kid, but that never kept me from being hard on you. I, uh, well you, your mom, Remi, and Juliet helped me see that I effed up on that commitment pretty bad.

"I'm only human Monte, and while that's no excuse for the mistakes I've made, I do hope it helps you hate me a little less. I fall into these tracks where I throw up blinders, making it hard to see anything I don't want to see. It's not your fault or your problem, but I want you to know I'm aware and working on it.

"I just... I'd hate for you to make the same mistakes I made in my life, but I guess I have to let you grow up as freely as I did. You deserve that much. You deserve a father who loves you." He started to whimper before choking it back like a shot of cheap vodka, chopping more firewood.

"Now, help me get this wood down to the house."

Together, we loaded ten or fifteen splintery pieces of wood onto the carrier and took turns lugging it back down the slippery hill to the house, catching up on the high points of the last four months as we went. He filled me in on how he left the church because he felt the wrath of its congregation after Deacon Sorek caught him buying a can of snuff at a gas station outside of Richwood. He reiterated several times he wanted nothing more to do with the "dogma of the people" and had moved on to focus on the "love of the spirit."

I filled him in on my classes, my rough grades, and my intention to bring them back up, and I gave him the slightest hint I'd taken a dip into the world of alcoholic parties. A tiny, stupid thought blipped into my head to share with him I'd had sex, maybe even to go as far as telling him it was with a guy, but that had no chance of ever happening. I still felt I couldn't let my guard down entirely, not until I knew for sure it was unconditional love I was in the presence of. For now, I enjoyed not having to force myself through my time at home like I thought I was going to have to.

We celebrated Christmas Eve without our usual Bible readings and church service, and instead, we spent the evening playing Monopoly and Crash Bandicoot, which we hadn't done in years. We called it a night after Dad realized it was 2:30 in the morning.

Christmas came early, like pre-sunrise early, and we opened the multitude of gifts picked out for us, mostly clothes chosen by Mama. The day seemed to have been arranged to make up for lost time—we spent a lot of it sitting around talking, laughing, and watching Christmas classics. Delicious food in dozens of colorful glass dishes sat in the center of the dining room table at dinnertime, and I enjoyed my first homecooked meal in months. Mama's steamy, fluffy rolls were best slathered in butter and dipped in her mashed potatoes and gravy, and to spice things up, I liked to rip the roll open in the middle and slide in a thick slice of sugared ham and some green beans.

I sat back after dinner with a full belly and heart and enjoyed my last few hours at home relaxing on the couch. I almost wished I hadn't asked to be put on the schedule the day after Christmas, but alas, duty called.

Christmas night saw me exhaustedly driving down another road, this time two and a half hours north to Morgantown, and my stomach tied itself in knots over my eventual reunion with Amias at the hotel. The timing of his change in relationship status aligned so amazingly with what we had done in the hotel I couldn't shake the feeling that I was the cause of their breakup. I didn't need to shake the feeling, though, because in less than twenty-four hours, I'd know the truth. He'd either come in dreadfully depressed and sorrowful about losing Matt over a mistake or perhaps he wouldn't come in at all because he was too disappointed and disgusted to see me ever again. And I'd go on depressed, knowing I squandered the best chance I'd ever been given.

I didn't want it to go that way. I begged the universe or god or whoever would listen for it to go any way but that way. I preferred the scenario where he came back to work smiling and ready to find something good with someone better. I wanted him to see me and know I was the one for him the same way I knew he was the one for me. I wanted to find out he spent the holiday thinking about a future with me.

Orange and yellow lights scattered across Morgantown and its surrounding communities as they came into view sometime after midnight. The air over the sprawling town was thick with a heavy orange haze as snow fell as in sheets over bright streetlights, but the streets were as quiet as could be. I loved the sight of my aunt and uncle's suburban home more than I thought possible. Their automatic Santa inflatable was the first thing to greet me, followed by the strings of frosty blue LED lights lining every straight edge on the street-facing side of their house. Electronic candles flickered faintly in each window, and the Christmas tree lights sparkled bright white, just as they were scheduled to.

I knew I'd be out for the count as soon as I got inside and lay down, so I rolled a blunt and hotboxed the car before going in. I sat and scrolled around on Facebook, puffing and puffing until my car was full of smoke. I bullshitted around on my feed, telling myself Amias wasn't the reason I was online, but his name ended up in the search bar, and his profile came up under it.

His updated relationship status still sat prominently as the top update on his profile, and he hadn't posted any new pictures since the last time I checked. I opened his pictures and scrolled through the ones I'd already seen.

A picture of him eating a hotdog at Milan Puskar Stadium.

A picture of him throwing a frisbee at Babcock State Park.

A picture of him without a shirt on by Split Rock Pools on Snowshoe Mountain.

My dick began to grow in my pants, and I readjusted myself to give it room. When I looked back at my phone, I noticed the symbol resembling a thumbs up on the bottom of the screen had turned blue.

I accidentally liked the picture, which he posted over a year ago.

Feelings of panic danced with pleasure as I considered what exactly I'd done. Whether I chose to save face and unlike his picture or to stand my ground and leave things unchanged, he would still see the notification. I could unlike it and show him it was an accident, that I didn't mean to tell him I was there, that I was embarrassed to like his picture. Or I could show him that I liked his picture, that I loved it, that I was proud to have been looking at it and to have my name under it.

I chose to show him what he meant to me.

The house wasn't as warm as I'd hoped because my aunt and uncle, in all their environmental consciousness, liked to program the thermostat to set itself at sixty-two degrees when nobody was home. I tapped the temperature on the digital display up to seventy-two, and the heat shuttered on, dimming the lights for a second. I crawled into bed and picked my phone up off the nightstand one last time, opening Facebook in search of another distraction. The bell at the bottom of the app was illuminated and highlighted in blue.

My heart nearly beat out of my chest, across the floor, and out the window into the cold for a night run when I saw the notification. It was Amias—he had liked one of my pictures. It was a picture of me doing yoga on the beach on my senior trip, one I'd posted nearly ten months earlier.

I locked my phone, and for the first time I could remember ever doing so, I went to sleep with a smile on my face.

CHAPTER 17: MEMORIES

I prepared for work the morning after Christmas with what felt like jagged rocks grinding in my stomach, my jaw sore from gnashing my teeth together all night. I couldn't predict with any confidence whether Amias was going to make my year or break it, but I'd know in less than an hour. Regardless, I felt pretty comfortable assuming he'd be mine someday, and I hoped that day had already begun.

My shoes dug through the deep white blanket of airy flakes from the front porch to the garage, and a few bony trees across the street broke the rays of the sun rising behind them, casting shadows that danced like wooden puppets in the snow. Though only a couple houses sat between my aunt and uncle's home and the main road, not a sound could be heard, and the only clouds in the sky spewed from my mouth on every exhale. I wished I could let my car warm up, but I had no time. Amias might've already been at the hotel, waiting for me.

He wasn't, though. The lot across the street where he

usually parked was empty, and I couldn't find him hiding anywhere in the hotel with a cup full of cold water.

The schedule in the manager's office revealed Amias wouldn't be in until noon, meaning I had to spend the morning alone and without an answer to my question. And to make matters worse, the day after Christmas was infamously slow at the Morgantown Hotel, so I had nobody to need me, to pull me out of the trenches zigzagging across my mind. The bar and French restaurant were closed until New Year's Eve, and nobody would be back in town for university business until January. I suddenly missed the calamity of the pre-Christmas rush when I had no time to overthink and too many people demanding my attention.

I dusted the desk for the fifteenth time and cleaned the monitors for the twentieth time. The windows by the front doors were so clear it looked as though they'd been removed. Even the elevator got a nice polishing. I would've done it all to pass the minutes keeping me from seeing him again.

It was almost noon when I ran out of busy work to do, but clocks seemed to be ticking at one-tenth their normal speed and showed no sign of speeding up. My clenched fists hung by sides as I leaned against the table behind the front desk in the same spot he'd been leaning before, dreaming of dragging him in and pulling him so close our bodies might become attached.

Amias Parker and Monte Lee. Amias and Monte. Monte and Amias.

The combination sounded so smooth in my head, like words destined to be together forever—sand and the beach, burgers and fries, the moon and stars, Amias and Monte.

I began scrolling around on my phone to find some way to divert my attention to something besides waiting, and a great surprise greeted me at the top of my feed. He'd just posted a selfie.

"Big day today!" he wrote over the picture. He was in his car in his green work polo, white teeth gleaming between two half-curled lips I longed to suck on. Nobody had liked it yet. I tapped on the thumbs-up icon and made myself the first one, and my heart skipped a beat when my name appeared under his picture as I fantasized about being under him in room 416 again.

It skipped another beat when the front door opened, and Amias straight-facedly schlepped into the lobby with Ray-Bans guarding his eyes. He filled his eyebrows in as sharply as ever, and he wore the rainbow pins he always had on symmetrically under the collar of his polo.

Amias walked around the desk as mysteriously as he'd come through the front door, and the titillating cloud of fragrance that followed him everywhere consumed me, making all the organs in my chest pump faster than I thought possible.

He threw me a foreign smile that said something like, *This is for you but only because I want to be polite,* and stepped into the office to clock in. His fingers clicked the mouse a few times and tapped around on the keyboard, but not one word came out of him as he prepared for the day. I heard him slide a drawer open on the filing cabinet. Then, he closed it. Suddenly, his footsteps started toward the lobby, and I jumped to a computer to act like I'd been checking my email.

"Hey." His sunglasses hung crookedly from the placket of his polo. I loved the way he always left one button undone as if to say, *Here, world. See my chest hair or maybe even bury your face in it.*

"Hey. Did you have a nice Christmas?" I hoped to sound confident, but my voice cracked anyway.

"I guess. It's always nice having time off, isn't it?" He glanced over at me. "Could've been better, though. I had to end things with Matt. Or they ended on their own, I guess?"

I could see him struggling to explain the situation, but he eventually worked up the nerve. "I don't know where he got the fucking idea, but he proposed to me. Big ring and one knee and everything—I guess he thought it would be romantic, but we aren't, or weren't I guess, ready for that. I never really believed he was the one for me anyway." His arms crossed themselves on his chest as his words rumbled out apathetically. "How was yours? The party at your friend's house?"

"Oh shit, man. I'm sorry to hear that about you and Matt. And as for the party—eh, it was a mixed bag, but Christmas with my folks was actually pretty nice. Nicer than I expected. I kinda hated coming back last night."

"Really?" He paused for a moment and looked down before looking back at me, lights flickering like fire in his eyes. "I was kind of excited to get back."

I didn't know what to say. I mean, I was beyond excited to get back and see him, but there was no way in hell I could let him know that, especially with him being freshly single. I would not blow it for myself this time. "All I meant to say was that I enjoyed reconnecting with my family, but I have to admit, something here kept me wanting to come back the whole time."

"Oh yeah? What?"

You, I wanted to say but couldn't.

A late checkout saved me from having to come up with a lie. I had essentially been thinking about the opportunity to spill my guts to Amias since his updated relationship status sent me to dreamland a few days earlier, but several things stood in the way of it happening now.

For starters, there was the fact he was fresh off a hot relationship, one so committed they lived together and one of them had so much invested in it he proposed. I didn't want to serve as his rebound. I wanted to have a real shot at something special with him if I was going to have anything at all.

Then there was the fact I wouldn't have known what to say or how to say it to him. To come on too strong or to disappoint him in the very beginning would've soured our roots, and I couldn't be the one who ruined everything again. I'd wait for him to make the move, or at least to drop more obvious hints.

We spent about half the afternoon trying to lure out as many smiles as possible from one another. It felt like the first day I saw him back in high school.

"Hey bro, your shirt is unbuttoned," I said sarcastically when he walked back into the lobby after his break. I received the open-mouth smile I hoped for.

"Oh really?" he asked, yanking his collar apart, unbuttoning a couple more buttons. "How's this?"

Everything we said to each other all afternoon was shrouded in sarcasm, but when I came back from my last fifteen-minute break of the day, Amias seemed to have gobbled down a can of Popeye's magic spinach.

He looked at me with wide eyes. "Why don't you come to my place after work today? Matt moved out before I got back this morning, so it'll just be the two of us. We're off at the same time, and I happen to know you don't have plans tonight."

I loved his big goofy smile and scrunched-up brown eyes.

Unable to think of anything preventing me from going —not that I wanted to be prevented—I obliged.

My nerves were mangled and my mind broken. I couldn't fathom a world in which something so precious could just fall into my lap. But then again, it hadn't necessarily fallen into my lap. It had slowly and teasingly been dangled over my head, held up by closed-mindedness or existing relationships or time, only to land in my lap after many nights of regret and misguided attempts at creating happiness out of thin air.

This was my opportunity, and I wouldn't let it pass me by.

When our shift finally ended, and it felt like it may never, I followed Amias back to his place on West Run Road, trying to imagine what we'd do when we got inside. I wanted to believe we'd go in, talk for a while, and end up in his bed and that we'd walk away knowing who we wanted to spend the rest of our lives with, but my desires didn't have the power to forge reality. And my life had this funny way of always working out terribly. I couldn't bear the thought of losing him for good, so my hopes had to remain suppressed. I settled for expecting a glass of wine or a quick bowl pack and some Netflix on his couch.

His couch. Ugh. I smiled.

Amias led me halfway down the valley to a quaint townhouse on a gated street, probably something he qualified to lease with Matt's nursing income. The last fleck of the sun was dissolving over the mountain behind the row of stucco townhouses, coating the world and everything on it in splashes of indigo, when Amias pulled his Charger into the garage underneath the pinkish home. My car struggled up the short, steep driveway, and I set the parking brake and stepped out.

I looked up at his townhouse and noticed a bird, a beautiful blue one, perched on a bare branch on a small birch tree in the front yard. It sat there for the longest time, singing its beautiful song fearlessly for the world to hear. Not the punishing winter cold nor the roaring of the garage door motor nor the slamming of car doors could hamper its carols.

"Are ya coming or what?" Amias caught my attention from the front door.

When I looked back at the birch tree, the bird had flown away.

I followed Amias inside and found his home was well decorated and mostly clean but with a comfortable lack of pretension. There were a couple dishes in the sink, but the counters and floors were spotless. On his brown sectional, a few hoodies draped here and there and a blanket spread sloppily across the back gave the impression one could kick their feet up and relax. He placed a Styrofoam tray of gourmet cheeses and two glasses of red wine on the coffee table and lit the vanilla candle in the center before taking a seat next to me.

"Forgive the mess. I just got back into town this morning," he informed me, throwing his feet up on the coffee table.

"No, it looks good. Cleaner than my aunt and uncle's place in Westover and just as nice."

"Aw, thank you. So, what shows do you like to watch?" He flipped on the giant television hanging on the wall across from us.

"I'm cool with whatever."

Small talk was all I seemed to be able to squeeze out as he clicked around the apps onscreen for something to turn on. At least it was small talk with him, though. It felt better than any deep talk I'd ever had with Imani or Mama or anyone else, and I savored every sweet second we sat together on his couch.

He turned on The Office and snuggled back, nudging so close his head pressed against my arm. Every surface in my mouth grew slick with saliva when his aroma became the only thing I could smell. The tension between us grew undeniably thick, and I knew he had to feel it, too.

"I said no because of you." He sat up and looked over at me with glassy eyes.

"Excuse me?" I straightened my back and leaned in to make sure I heard him correctly.

"When Matt asked me to marry him, I said no because I remembered you, because I remembered what we did at the hotel. I remembered the way being with you in that bed made me feel. I remembered the way seeing the smile on your face made me feel. I remembered the way I felt the night you walked away from me in City Park. I won't bullshit you—there were plenty of reasons Matt and I weren't going to work out, but you were the reason on my mind when I turned him down."

I placed my hand over my right ear to make sure it was working properly and then my left one, too. They were both working loud and clear. He said all of these things, all of these perfect things, and my mushy brain struggled to process it all.

"I thought it was just a crush until we met up at City Park that night. I wanted to do more than talk you through your feelings, but I chose to bury it after you pulled away. I hated myself for letting you go and for trying to move on after you were gone, but you needed to find yourself, and life goes on.

"I tried to find bits of you in Matt, and I thought I found them and that I'd just have to work really hard if I wanted to see them. But you... you, Monte... you wrecked all of that. You showed me what good feels like and what being with someone should feel like. It's because of you that I know what it's like to fall asleep thinking about someone every night and wake up dreaming about them every morning, and I couldn't go on without telling you."

My lungs stopped working, and a faint feeling grew behind my eyes. I felt like a child who thought the gift I'd asked Santa for would never come only to find it lodged behind the tree the day after Christmas. His words slaked my thirst for something real, something mutual, something new and old and written in the stars.

He worded it perfectly: he showed me what it meant to be with someone, too. No power dynamic existed between us, and he didn't make me feel beneath him the way other guys had.

I suddenly realized I'd spent too much time fantasizing about this exact moment and not enough time planning what I'd say if it ever actually came. I opened my mouth, hoping the perfect words might drip out, but they didn't.

"Monte, please say something... anything to let me know I'm not as lame as I feel."

The world paused.

My head soared into the clouds.

My heart fluttered like the wings of a young butterfly.

The back of my tongue burned as I considered how I could cure his worrying.

Words couldn't come close to explaining my feelings.

I had to do something to show him.

He deserved to know.

Sliding my legs onto the couch so I could face him, I cupped my hands around the back of his head and pulled him as close as I could. Our lips came together like two stars that'd been chasing each other in circles for millions of years—fierce and fiery. His prickly mustache, warm from every deep breath of his, brushed against mine as his lips curled up on my face. He wasted no time turning his entire body to face mine, pulling his legs up over mine, and without stopping his warm kisses, he gently lowered me onto my back, taking position over me.

There was nothing I could do to mess it up. I was living my destiny, and it was the best moment of my life.

He pulled away and began to undress me, starting with my pants, then my shirt, then my socks and underwear. He dropped his khakis and flung his shirt to the floor when every square inch of me was visible.

With his black boxer briefs still on, his dick bulging through them, he leaned back over me and pressed his lips to mine once more. This time, however, he worked his way down my body, sucking his way through my chest hair, across my belly button with his tongue, and finally, between my legs. His lips, sheeny in the faint glow of the table lamp and television, wrapped around the head of my dick and moved downward toward the base. Up and down he went, using his tongue, his cheeks, even his teeth to turn my world upside down. The heat that'd been building in my legs since the last time we were together spread through my body like a fever from my head to my feet.

A surge of endorphins flooded my system, and the living room swirled with colors and emotions I'd only experienced because of Amias. The world and all its worries vanished with his skin on mine. I wanted to be there on his couch with him for all of eternity. His kisses healed me. His dick-sucking exhilarated me. His spirit felt profound in some way as if I lay in the presence of more than just another person.

Then, all the familiar physical sensations came over me: my back arched, my toes curled up, my vision faded, and finally, I came, ejaculating all over his face and chest. Amias loomed sexily over me with the power and grace of a wildcat, watching my face flicker with euphoria, wiping his face with his hand, licking some of it up.

Filled to the brim with adrenaline, I jumped up and over him, flipping him back onto the couch. I had only begun to return the favor when a metal-on-metal sound at the front door clanked us away from one another.

The deadbolt twisted.

The solid red door creaked open and let in the December cold, along with the startled glare of an upset Matt. He looked around the room, paying special attention to the scrambled couch cushions and half-empty wine glasses on the coffee table, then at our tousled hair and inside-out pieces of clothing, and finally at the remnants of my pleasure in Amias's beard and mustache.

"What the fuck, Amias?"

He couldn't find a word to say, and I wouldn't have dared.

"I'm not even fully moved out yet and you have some

fuckin' little ass boy in here already?"

"Hey, Matt, he's not just some—"

"Shut the fuck up!" He threw his keys forcefully at the television, cracking the screen on impact. "I'm sure I know who this is. This is Monte, isn't it, Amias?"

He confused me, but he also flattered me in some ass-backward way I didn't want to think too long about.

"You're right, though. He's not just some boy, is he? This is the guy you ended shit with me for, isn't it?" He looked at me and chuckled. "Some tiny ass twink in a cheap hotel uniform? Really?"

Amias trembled violently, but he stepped forward to speak straightforwardly with Matt. "There's more to life than that shit Ma—"

"Fuck off, trash."

"Hey now, let's calm down," I blurted out. Regret replaced courage instantly when Matt, easily five years older and with seventy-five pounds more muscle than me, turned his attention to me.

"Fuck off, dickhead. Do you even know what you've caused here?"

"Um… I—" I backed up a little.

"Yeah, that's what I thought, pussy ass. You broke up what could've been a decent marriage for me. Get back behind this pussy ass where you belong." He motioned to Amias.

"Matt, you need to leave. Now."

"I'll leave when I'm damned ready. I'm here for the rest of my shit."

Matt stormed upstairs to the bedroom, kicking over a potted plant on his way. I had never seen Amias so shaken or seen anybody vibrate with rage the way he was.

"I'm sorry you had to—" Something glass fell to the floor and busted upstairs. "—that this is happening while you're here." Amias couldn't seem to look at me as Matt audibly rummaged through drawers and cabinets for his things.

"No, Amias, please don't worry about this. If anything, I'm glad I was here when he came back." I handed him a tissue to wipe off with.

We sat back down together on the couch. I wanted to do whatever it took to avoid any type of physical confrontation with Matt, so I sat on the opposite end of the sectional, leaving enough space between my thigh and Amias's to keep from provoking him, but Amias didn't care. He almost instantly scooted down, pressing his thigh firmly against mine. My anxiety eased up with him so close to me, and after a few seconds, I noticed he wasn't shaking so badly anymore.

Matt stomped back down the stairs and stepped into the center of the living room, standing between us and the now busted T.V., throwing the nastiest glare humanly possible at Amias.

"Fuck you. I hope you rot in—"

"Enough Matthew! I'm begging you. I get it, okay? We all get it. You hate me. Now can you please leave or at least let us do this later?"

"You don't get to talk to me that way, dickhead."

Matt grabbed the succulent off of the entertainment stand and chucked it at Amias, but he ducked in time to avoid a busted face. Amias's body hardened like someone who'd just looked into the eyes of Medusa, so stiff and lifeless I could see damage had been done even if he hadn't been hit. He stood up and looked at Matt as if he wanted to say something but walked quietly to the door

BECAUSE I REMEMBER YOU

and opened it.

"Matthew, please. Leave."

"Sure," Matt said, slinging his bag over his shoulder. He made his way toward the exit quickly, and as he stepped into the doorframe, his fist wound up and slammed into Amias's face, knocking him back onto the tile flooring around the front door.

A dark red patch on the wall where Amias's head hit caught my attention, and Matt ran out into the darkness without taking time to make sure he hadn't just committed a murder. I rushed over and fell to my knees next to Amias, checking to make sure he was still conscious and aware of the date. The back of his head bled profusely from a gash carved out by the corner and a slight bruise flared up around his left eye, but he insisted repeatedly that aside from a headache, he was fine.

Matt walked back up to the open doorway and glowered at me next to Amias before saying, "I don't know what type of guys you normally fuck around with, but I assure you that even you are above this unfaithful, ungrateful prick. You don't look like much, but you can definitely do better than him." He spat at Amias.

And then, he disappeared into the darkness again, and the sound of his tires squealing away signaled we were safe.

CHAPTER 18: GO

A mias flat out refused an emergency room visit, supposedly because he didn't want to be slapped with a massive bill after being given "a couple ibuprofen for a bump and a scrape," but I think it was because we would've gone to Ruby Memorial, the hospital where Matt worked.

Though he didn't say it outright, I could tell Amias still had confusing feelings about Matt, feelings I didn't have any interest in talking about. I had a hard time being as gentle and understanding as Amias needed me to be, especially because words like *dickhead, asswipe,* and *douchebag* came to mind every time Matt's name came up, but I bit my tongue because it wasn't about me.

It was about Amias.

There was so much blood splattered on the wall and dripping from the gash in his head I worried he might have a concussion and fall into a seizure or something worse in the night, but I couldn't force him to see a doctor no matter how badly I wanted to. I let him know I'd be available if he needed anything no matter what time he needed it and left him to recuperate.

I stretched out on my bed covers back in Westover and

watched the blades on the ceiling fan chop the air to bits and spit it down on me, trying to wrap my mind around how somebody could've treated someone they loved with so much hatred.

Matt couldn't have been thinking about Amias as a person. He had to have forgotten Amias was a living, breathing human being or he wouldn't have been capable of what he did. Amias, like me, seemed to have a hard time being more than a label, but to me, he was so much more than that. He was kind and understanding, energetic and funny, beautiful and intelligent, the missing piece and the feeling I'd been craving and the soul that never left my mind.

And best of all, he dreamt of me.

He dreamt of me.

He dreamt of *me.*

Blue moonlight poured in the window on the other side of the room, shining on the rocking chair where I left my work clothes, the same ones I wore when I learned he dreamt of me. If he had laid his lovely little head down and fallen asleep, he was most certainly dreaming of me, or if he was lying in bed unable to sleep, he was surely thinking of me. I never wanted it to leave my mind.

I don't know if I believed everything between us fell out of the moment we first laid eyes on one another like some *love at first sight* fairytale shit, but that moment led to many other moments that led to these ones. I remembered so many of those precious moments: the very first time I saw Amias in the hall at Richwood High, unwittingly hypnotizing me with his half-grin and expensive cologne; the rough night after the rally where he opened my eyes to the church's underhanded pushes for assimilation; the evening in City Park when he became the only solid ground in my shifting world; the day in room 416 when he showed me the value in having someone and being had by someone; and then today, the day he made me feel good enough to run around in his Dreamland.

By 4 a.m., my eyes grew gritty, and my eyelids bounced up and down a few times before falling shut for the night when the buzzing of my phone sent them flapping back open like a spring roller map.

I reached over to my bedside table and grabbed my bright phone, staring at the screen until my eyes adjusted.

It was a text from Amias.

"Hey, not sure if you're even awake or when you'll see this, but I wish you were still here. I wish you never left."

I blinked quickly, hoping my bloodshot eyes weren't playing tricks on me. They weren't.

"I'm up. Can't stop thinking about you."

"Can we go somewhere?"

"Now?"

"Yes."

"On my way."

My brakes squealed to a stop in front of his place minutes later. He ran up in his pajamas and slippers and slumped into the passenger seat, filling the cabin up with his wonderful aroma. I tried not to fixate on his wounds from earlier, but even in the dim light of the radio, the darkened circle around his eye refused to let go of my gaze. The way he propped his arm on the center console to nonchalantly cover the mark left by Matt's fist sucked more empathy out of me than I thought possible.

"Thank you, Monte. I'm really glad you came to get me."

"Don't mention it. I couldn't sleep either. So, where are we going?"

"No clue. Let's just go."

With that, I shifted the car into drive and pulled away from the curb. Down West Run we went until we hit a red light and neither of us could make a decision on which direction to go.

"Do you have a coin?" he asked.

"What?"

"Do you have any coins in here? We'll flip one at the intersections. Heads we go left. Tails we go right. If I drop it, we go straight."

I pulled a cold quarter out of the ashtray and dropped it into his hand, smiling at him. It landed on heads, so when the light turned green, we turned left out of town. Heads again. Left again, and seemingly no more intersections.

Thick clouds kept the moon from lighting the way, leaving my headlights and the occasional streetlight to split the curtains of darkness around us alone. Somewhere in the gloomy sea of mountains, the road unnoticeably cut across the line from West Virginia into Pennsylvania, and sparse houses beneath towers of woodsmoke dotted the forest along the way, some still with Christmas lights glowing in the front yard.

Within fifteen minutes, we were welcomed to Point Marion by a seemingly endless field of stones, each presumably labeled with the birth and death of a different person. The road continued off the hill to another intersection at the confluence of the Cheat and Monongahela

Rivers. The coin sent us right up a one-lane backroad following the Cheat River further into the mountains.

A sniffling sound pulled me out of the trance the blurry road passing under my headlights lulled me into.

"Everything alright?" I asked, placing my hand gently over his on the middle console.

Amias melted into a river of tears as if the heat from the defroster suddenly thawed him. I, once again, couldn't think of the right thing to say, but that didn't feel like a problem. I quietly pulled off into a parking lot at the base of a giant concrete dam and steered across the expanse of gravel, coming to stop near the guardrail over the river.

"I, uh— I never imagined my life would turn out this way," he finally responded, shifting uncomfortably in his seat.

"What do you mean?"

"Don't act like you don't see it. I live with a piece of shit man I pretty much depend on, fresh out of high school, too broke and too dumb for college, one inconvenience from an actual emotional breakdown, just... worthless."

I wanted to cry hearing him say that. "You are not worthless, Amias." My heart thumped like a flat tire on a country road. "You have no idea what you mean to me or how our little encounters, however brief they may have been, have affected me. You made my life so much better the day we met just by being you. Do you know that? Of course you don't, because you're too good to know how perfect you are. I've wanted to be with you so badly it hurt me, so badly I couldn't be with anybody else, so badly I began to think I was losing my mind."

Fuck, this isn't about me. Keep it about him.

"I haven't met a lot of people, but I've met a few, and Amias, you stand far above any of them. I mean it. No-body has ever compared to you, and nobody ever will. Fuck Matt. Fuck Braxton. Fuck bullies and churches and families. Fuck anyone who tells you you can't be and love whoever you want." I suddenly felt like I might've been addressing myself as much as I was addressing him. "You and me—we deserve to be happy, and you make me so happy."

He stared at me, tears evaporating from his cheeks, but he didn't say anything. His straight eyebrows and inter-laced fingers didn't say anything either. I hoped I hadn't crossed a line by cursing Matt, but I meant every word I said.

Maybe he needs time to process like I did.

"You make me happy, too. Fuck 'em. You're right. Fuck 'em all."

His tiniest-ever smile brightened the car, encouraging me to stop second-guessing myself, but I wanted to change the subject away from uncomfortable shit more than anything. The past would forever remain in the past, and now felt like the time to look forward.

"You smoke? Weed, I mean."

His voice stabilized, and he sat up in his seat. "I've smelled the dank in here since you picked me up, but I thought you weren't going to share."

That earned a chuckle from me, which triggered an-other slightly larger grin from him. It was nice to see it again, even if just for a second. I passed him the bowl and my lighter so he could take greens, and he sucked it in the way I had my first time and coughed so intensely he had to recline the seat. His adorable, fuzzy little face wrinkled up as he choked on the smoke spurting out of his mouth and nose. I was able to take two or three hits before he finally stopped coughing.

"Can we get out— finish this— in the fresh air?" He gasped for air.

I wanted more than anything to make him happy, so I began unbuckling my seatbelt despite how badly I hated the idea of being out in the dangerous winter cold when the safe, warm car was just as available.

We shoved the heavy car doors open and stepped out into the frosty night air. The dam, which only let a creek's worth of water spill from Cheat Lake out of its one open gate on top, towered into the night sky like the Iron Giant, walling the valley off from mountain to mountain. Giant sheets of ice shined down the side of the dam, growing wider as they neared the water.

We slid onto the car hood, and my skin nearly froze solid against the frigid metal surface on the other side of my thin joggers. I was lucky to be downwind from Amias, though, shielded from the seemingly infinite, angry gusts.

"I'm really happy you were still up," he said.

I took my hit and passed the chillum and lighter to Amias. "I was happy to hear from you. I was so worried."

"You don't have to worry about me." He looked into the dark forest rising on either side of the river.

"I'm sorry Am—"

"You're fine. Just please don't pity me. I'm done with him now. There are better things in my future." We turned our heads just in time to lock eyes.

Am I a better thing?

We hadn't discussed what exactly we were doing, and I didn't want to kill it before it began by asking questions. I was pretty sure I knew the answer anyway. He'd shown me time after time that if I was thinking of him, he was probably thinking of me, too.

"Was he like that often?" My insensitivity made me feel stupid and a little heartless, but I wanted to try to understand what he'd been through—as much as I could, anyway. "I'm sorry. We don't have to talk about it."

"No, it's fine." He pressed against my side more firmly and stared with glassy eyes at the shallow black river below. "Not to begin with. Matthew was this sweet, caring, charming guy when we met, way back before I knew you. We split up a month or so before graduation and then got back together shortly after. Honestly, I saw a little of you in him when we got back together. Or maybe I just really wanted to? I don't know.

"Either way, at some point something changed. I don't know what happened. It was like a switch flipped in him, like all of a sudden he was comfortable enough around me to let himself feel what he wanted to feel and however much of it he wanted to feel. And, fuck, he felt so angry all the time. He told me over and over again it was a stress issue and that it would stop, but it never did. It kept getting worse, and I never left, but it wasn't because I feared him or because I had nowhere to go."

Alarms sounded with flashing red lights below the dam, and we watched as more of the dam's gates rattled open along the top, sending water and chunks of ice cascading over the wall and into the gorge.

"When you're with someone the way I was with Matthew, you feel like you know them even if you don't. Outsiders may see partners as good or bad, but it's so much more complicated than that on the inside." He chuckled, and the water began to rise on the other side of the guard rail. "It's so fucking complicated. I don't think good or bad people exist. I think we are all people. Period. We all do good things, and we all do bad things. The goal for most of us is to do as little bad and as much good as possible, but our problem is that some people are content to do more bad things than good.

"Matthew is one of those people, but I still saw some good in him as much as I loathe myself for thinking it. It came through in the way he would smile at me when he first woke up or stop and get me a Coke and a bag of Skittles on his way home from work. I could see it in the way he'd ask me how my day was and truly listen when I told him or in the way he apologized after losing control. He'd beg me not to leave and promise he would be better, and I believed him for a while."

"What changed?"

"You showed up. You made me realize I could still find the things I'd been searching for and that I didn't have to endure black eyes and broken furniture to find them." He plopped down off the hood and onto the gravel lot. "I need someone who wants to do the good for me that I want to do for them."

Amias reached out his hand to grab mine and pulled me off the hood in front of him, where the pervasive darkness fled the beam of my hot headlights and his bright eyes. Our lips met for a moment before he turned to face the river, now a silky mess of bloated gray and black rapids, and I wrapped my arms around his waist and gently pulled him back onto me. Our bodies became like one pressed against the grille and bumper, and we watched time pass us by.

The headlights faded off, and we stood in the night with one another because we had nowhere else to go

—or perhaps more accurately because we had nowhere else we wanted to go.

Jack Frost had nearly frozen me to death when Amias turned to say he was ready to go home. With heavy eyes, I stumbled back and crawled into the driver's seat, reaching for and twisting the keys in the ignition with my numb fingers. Amias did the same, but instead of reaching for the ignition, he reached for the aux cord.

The car rumbled to life, and the green digital clock in the center of the dash revealed we had spent almost two hours by the river, some of the most valuable time I'd ever spent anywhere. It hardly felt like ten minutes to me.

I started up the road to Morgantown as the sound system vibrated with the early strumming of Dreams by Fleetwood Mac. The drive was quiet but rather reflective, definitely for me but probably for both of us.

I couldn't stop thinking about how unusually eventful the day ended up being. In a twenty-four-hour period, I went from hoping Amias didn't hate me to knowing he cared for me and from hating the person he spent time with to being the person he spent time with. I went into his home and sat on his couch, and he told me about dreaming of me.

I floated away on cloud nine and never wanted to return to earth, or maybe I died and went to heaven, or maybe I was dreaming a dream I never wanted to wake up from. I couldn't figure it out for sure, but that didn't matter. It was real life now.

My peace only seemed to grow as the night sky matured to dawn and the overcrowded hills of Morgantown rolled into view in the distance. We both had to be at the hotel at noon, but I don't think either of us cared.

This was too important.

"I'm dreading going into the house I used to share and walking up to the bedroom I used to share and sleeping in the bed I used to share all by myself." Amias unbuckled his seatbelt as we drove between the pine trees on the corner of his street.

"It's a big place to have all to yourself, that's for sure," I replied awkwardly. I still slightly feared rejection and coming off as selfish or opportunistic, but I still asked, "Would you want me to come in for a while, maybe stay and keep you company?"

"I'd love that more than anything."

Amias led me inside, making sure to fasten the chain lock on the door while neglecting to turn on any lights, and I noticed he scrubbed the blood off the wall and some of the paint with it. We walked upstairs to a small living space outside the bedroom and stripped to our underwear, dropping our clothes onto the leather chaise in the corner, and just then, when he turned on a small table lamp, a scratch I hadn't yet noticed revealed itself on Amias's lower back—a long, fine, red parenthesis-shaped line.

He looked like the victim of a mugging. The amount of strength he had to have had to display the level of collectedness he did during such a brutal confrontation astonished me. I thought of him as empowered or quite possibly heroic at first, but it rapidly morphed into a sort of mournfulness when I considered not he nor anyone else should ever need to muster that much strength.

While he was spending a few minutes "getting the bedroom ready" for me, which I assumed meant removing every last trace of Matt, I popped into the hallway bathroom to get him a cup of water and some ibuprofen.

I offered to clean his wounds with a warm, soapy rag once he finally opened the bedroom door for me, and he was reluctant at first but thought it necessary since he hadn't had a shower yet. He sat on the ground in front of the chaise we sat our clothes on, and I sat down in it and started gently dabbing the fleshy wound on his scalp. It cut so deep I couldn't look without feeling squeamish, fearing I might catch a much more literal glimpse into him than I preferred. He winced at the gentlest of touches, though, so I felt the need to comfort him with a lie.

"It doesn't look that bad." I moved down and cleaned the area around the scrape on his back before stepping around and examining his shiner. The large oval of busted blood vessels encircled his eye socket completely, and it had the blue and purple tie-dye color only left behind by strong, intentional blows to the eye. It wasn't the kind you could write off as a sleepwalking accident or stumbling into the corner of the coffee table.

It screamed hatred. I could hear the pop of Matt's fist as it slammed into his face and sent him flying backward again, and I nearly lost it there in the hallway. I lightly pressed my thumb to the puffy skin around his eye, sending Amias's head jolting back, and decided it would be best to let that wound heal in its own time.

We slipped into the bedroom and crawled onto the king-sized memory foam plateau and under the soft blue sheets. For the longest time, we lay in bed face to face, staring into each other's eyes in the silent bedroom. The pink corners of his mouth pressed his peachy cheeks upward and wrinkled the skin around his eyes, my favorite eyes in the whole world. Nobody in the history of humankind had ever looked more perfect than he did at that moment with his teeth aglow in the soft morning light oozing in around the blackout drapes over the window, hair messy and eyes set on me.

Amias turned over on his side and faced the wall, reaching his hand back to pull me in closer. I slid across to him and pulled myself in as closely as I could. The curves of my body aligned quickly with his as I pressed my stomach and legs firmly against his back and legs, big spooning him until we both fell asleep there—in absolute bliss.

Surely all of that took place in a dream, I thought as I woke up and looked at the blurry room in front of me, one that appeared foreign and not like mine. I grabbed my glasses off the nightstand and shoved them onto my face, and suddenly, I could see whose bedroom I was in and remembered what led me there. I couldn't wait to see him again. I rolled over to see if he was awake. He was, but he wasn't there.

Had he left? Had Matt come back? Had he run away from this life to pursue another? I didn't know, but I wondered.

My feet landed softly on the white carpet around his bed, and I rose to them, stretching in a way that made my muscles tingle. I threw on my work shirt and pushed the bedroom door open. A hissing sound emanated from the end of the hall and then down the stairs, becoming identifiable as soon as the savory scent of frying bacon began to accompany it.

The sound and smell both led me to the kitchen, where my stomach growled so loudly I thought Amias had to have heard it from the other side of the room. He stood over the stove tending two skillets: one with bacon and one with scrambled eggs.

He looked over his shoulder at me, keeping his hands on the skillets' handles. "Good morning, Monte. Did you sleep well?"

"Better than I ever have. You?"

He smiled. "Best sleep of my life. I hope you're hungry." The toaster sprung up with two pieces of toast, and I noticed a plate with several buttered slices and a shaker labeled *Cin. Sugar.*

"Starved."

"Good because breakfast is ready." He dumped some eggs onto the two empty plates by the stove. Then, he tonged a couple slices of bacon onto each one and handed one to me. "Toast is by the toaster. Glasses in the cabinet. Milk, O.J., and water in the fridge. Help yourself, handsome."

Fuck, I'm in Dreamland. But I wasn't. Dreamland was real, and I could finally stop doubting everything.

I ate the best breakfast I'd ever had that morning, but it wasn't necessarily because his food tasted especially good. It was the best breakfast I'd ever had because he made it for me.

I got to eat it across the table from him. I got to watch him rip into a slice of bacon and stare at his bobbing Adam's apple every time he took a drink of orange juice. I felt like the luckiest man alive, to have been given a chance with the very person who'd infected my brain since day one, and I decided I'd never let him slip away from me again.

SPRING

Keep your face to the sun and you will never see the shadows.

–HELEN KELLER.

CHAPTER 19: NEW FAVORITE WORD

C hristmas break just about wiped school from my mind entirely, but when I got back on campus late the last Friday of break, it all came back to me. Sam sat in front of my T.V. shit-facedly watching South Park in the dark, howling anytime a character did something stupid—which in South Park was every few seconds—and I instantly missed my quiet bedroom in Westover.

Sam was the only reason I didn't like spending time in my room, but I luckily had other places to hang out. I reunited with Imani and Avery over sushi downtown, and I was so eager to see them again, especially Imani, but my mind was glued to one very special thing.

Whether I was hanging out with my friends, up late drinking cheap beer and trying to fall asleep in the middle of a dangerously masculine conversation with Sam, or reading an enthralling novel in the library, it didn't matter. The only thing I ever did was imagine an evening or a weekend or a future with Amias.

Taking him on road trips to places we've never been so we can experience the thrill of something new together.

Renting a cabin and spending a weekend in some town where nobody knows us enough to give a shit if we kiss in public.

Taking him to carve pumpkins, on drives to view Christmas lights, or to see Hairspray at the Morgantown Met.

My efforts at easing into things with him were futile in the face of so much pent-up passion, but it wasn't like that mattered to either of us. Easing into things with him felt sinful or irreverent as if I was depriving my body of something valuable, something it desperately needed and had been forced to go without since birth.

I saw no need to prolong our time apart any more than the world already had. I'd been through so much to get to this point, and I certainly didn't mind rewarding myself by leaning in.

I did come to see Amias less once classes started back, though, and the time apart only strengthened my already insatiable thirst for more of him. I worked irregular shifts between classes and on busy weekends while he stayed on the same Monday to Friday day shift we'd been on over break, cutting into our time together at work and on days off.

I didn't mind having to find other ways to spend time

with him, though. We had a night at the movies but only once before we decided a movie was about the least fun way to spend time with one another. The only benefit of the movie theater was the cover of the darkness it provided. We couldn't talk through the film, and we couldn't kiss or bang through it either.

So we had to find something else to do the next time, which wasn't easy. The keeping-it-under-wraps gig—since my family didn't and couldn't know who'd captured my heart—made it feel as if we lived in a storybook about our forbidden romance, but constantly having to make sure Merida and Keith weren't around quickly became more work than it was fantasy.

I couldn't reach out and grab his hand with the mindlessness I wanted to or clear our table at dinner and lean across it to shove my lips into his. I couldn't post the pictures I took of him or us, no matter how dashingly handsome he looked in them or how happy I looked to have him resting his head on my shoulder, and I took special care not to let us end up in the backgrounds of other people's photos. No sign of the life I made for myself in Morgantown could exist online or in any place other than between Amias and me.

Though my family had expressed their love for me—and if not support then at least tolerance—in ways they never had, the last thing I wanted to do was ruin it all by shocking them with such big news. I didn't want to ruin Dad's reputation when he could've been on the lookout for a new church to lead or to make Mama the laughingstock of her extended family.

I feared word of my worldly sexuality spreading would draw judgment and criticism to my family, and then I feared they'd cut me off over it. I'd only just started feeling like I had them back, and to lose them again would've taken a greater toll on me than I cared to deal with.

We have more fun than could be accurately portrayed on social media, anyway, I thought, scrolling past pictures of my friends with their partners.

Our dates started taking the form of that night under the dam but with a much more positive beginning. I'd pick him up, charging him one adorable lopsided smile to unlock the car doors, and we might stop in somewhere for a couple burgers or some quick tacos, but we'd usually end up adventuring out to watch the sunset from cold Cooper's Rock or exploring the snow-dusted grounds at Friendship Hill, whatever the coin toss decided. Those were my favorite dates, the ones where we ended up walking around some random place and talking about anything that crossed our minds, totally oblivious to the harshness of winter around us.

One Sunday in January, we were walking down a tree-lined street leading to the manor at Friendship Hill sharing stories about past lovers and past haters, about who we were and who we aspired to be, about everything. Snow fell lightly in the fields around us the way it did in my favorite Christmas movies, and his biggest curls waved at me from under the edges of his beanie every time the wind hit him in the face.

Amias's life spilled out before me like pour art in stories layering and swirling together to paint a meaningfully complicated and beautiful history. He spoke relatively openly about most aspects of his life—including a more descriptive version of how he met Matt, which I hated hearing but listened to because it led him to me —but I noticed a lack of any stories about his family.

It seemed more serious than him not wanting to talk about them, too. It felt more like he couldn't talk about them, like talking about them might've hurt him in some way, which I understood, so I didn't push it.

I perfectly enjoyed seeing the bits of him he wanted me to see. It was more than enough for my tiny little brain and overgrown heart to fully process at the time anyway. The other stuff could wait until he felt ready.

He also got a crash course in Monte 101, though I did tell him about my family and friends. I filled him in on their dogmatic religiosity and my previous commitment to that same lifestyle. I told him about my old friend Merida, the same one who preached down to him at the only rally he ever attended, and how she explained to me why he left his old school for Richwood.

He told me he remembered her clearly and that she was right about why he left his old school, but he didn't want to go into it, which, again, I didn't mind.

I filled him on the friends I'd made in college and their push on me to explore the world. I also told him about the douchey guys I'd found myself with over the last few months, the ones who had me in the pits before he came back into my life and saved me.

I did keep some secrets, though. I didn't want to scare him off or traumatize him more than he already had been, so I kept that terrible night in June that I couldn't forget about in a box where he couldn't find it. That night was the biggest reason I wanted to avoid sharing my truth with folks back home for as long as possible— because I knew it was coming at some point.

That day clung in the back of my mind like peanut butter to the roof of a dog's mouth, the day everyone would eventually find out about us, but it was my baggage and my problem to deal with. I just felt lucky to finally have someone to lean on and share the burden with, someone who was there for me even when he didn't know why he needed to be with open arms or a shoulder to cry on.

Things were great for us most of the time, but there came two major challenges. The first was something I chose not to share with Amias. It was at the end of Valentine's Day, and I had just gotten back to my room after an evening walk around the arboretum with Amias when I received a most unexpected text.

It was from Braxton.

"Hey, Monte. Been thinking about you lately. Hate the way things ended between us. Maybe we could get together soon and rehash things or see where we might go? Please text back. Miss you. xoxo."

Something along the lines of *How fucking dare you?* found its way into the reply box initially, but as I slept on it, his out-of-the-blue message began to weigh differently on my heart. I hated myself for that. He was my first shot at anything with a guy, and he knew how to have an awfully good time in the bedroom when he wasn't punishing me. But he punished me, and that was something I knew I never had to fear with Amias.

Amias never ignored me or made me feel guilty. He never beat me or manipulated me. He never reminded me of the past and gave me hope for the future. Braxton had nothing on him. So, I deleted his number and never heard from him again.

Then, there was another hurdle, perhaps a larger one, but one I knew would be likely to come. It came while we were snuggled up on Amias's couch watching Brother Bear: something on his phone. At first, I couldn't figure out what pulled his attention away from the movie and what eventually pulled him away from me. He spent the rest of the night against the arm on the opposite end of the couch glaring at his phone, casually keeping the screen directed away from me, and went to sleep facing the wall that night.

I wished I could've gone to sleep. My guts twisted and my head throbbed as my mind repeatedly ran over scenarios in which I awoke to an empty townhouse. It had been pretty obvious who texted him, but I didn't want to ask questions. If the end was near, I didn't want to know it, so I kept my mouth shut and tried to move on.

I came to learn days later Matt had texted Amias some pages-long disgustingly heartfelt apology followed by several other texts and drunken voicemails virtually begging Amias to let him move back into the townhouse and to sign a lease on it again for the next year. He repeated over and over how much he "loved" Amias and promised to be a new man with a new outlook, burping and slurring words together as he screamed into the phone or typed in all caps, misspelling every other word.

Amias didn't even dignify his pleas with a response.

Instead, he chose me—again.

* * *

In the weeks where spring was starting to feel like a cool summer in the sun and a warm winter in the shade, Imani and Avery invited me to a "Patty's Day party" in Fairmont, a thirty-minute drive south from Morgantown, and since Imani knew the host somehow, she worked it out so we could stay overnight.

And being the angel she was, she managed to get me a plus-one for Amias.

I hadn't been to a party since before classes started back for spring semester months ago, so I accepted eagerly with my eyes on the opportunity to cut loose with Amias in a place where we could shake our inhibitions. We'd been together for nearly three months and walls were coming down as far as getting to know one another went, but I still noticed a vague discomfort about us as new lovers struggling to find the way forward in a world seemingly rigged against us.

We hadn't talked about what we were. We hadn't talked about what we expected to happen between us in the future. A good swift kick in the ass from a bottle of liquor sounded like just the thing we needed.

After my morning shift on the Saturday of the party, I got dressed and grabbed some grenadine and orange juice at Kroger, and Amias and I decided to throw in on a bottle of tequila for the celebration.

I'd picked him up so many times by then he figured out how long it took me to get from Honors to his townhouse, seemingly to the second. Out the door he marched as I turned up onto his driveway, looking like the tastiest stalk of celery I'd ever seen. He strode across the lawn in his signature *not from 'round these parts* attire for the holiday: a lime green romphim and gold accessories.

"Howdy-doody," he joked, sliding into the passenger seat. "Boy, I've got this timing down pat."

"Seems like it. You're ready for the party, huh?"

"You bet your ass. This is my first party in ages, and I'm not holding back." He fastened his seatbelt. "This'll be my first time seeing you tequila-drunk, and I gotta admit, I'm pretty excited about it."

An involuntary hoot burst through my lips. "Oh yeah? Let's be drinking buddies. Anytime you drink, I drink and vice versa. No skipping. No quitting."

He agreed enthusiastically, and we started down the highway toward Fairmont.

"So, uh, Monte… Can we talk about something?" Amias shifted in his seat and began tapping his thumbs together in his lap.

Oh, fuck, I thought. Google Maps said we still had about fifteen minutes left in the car, but I gripped the steering wheel, ready to turn around in the median if the words he was about to say wrecked me.

I all but knew where he was headed. Something had come up: either Matt was back again or Amias needed space or the world was ending. It didn't matter. I could feel the roadblock coming, and I preferred the world ending to the other two options.

"Sure."

It took him a good ten or so seconds to ask his question, but he finally did.

"What are we? This thing happening between us, I mean. What would you call it?"

"Well, uh…" I always knew one of us, most likely Amias, would ask this question sometime soon, but I didn't expect it on the way to a party we both planned on getting shwasted at. I skated safely through Valentine's Day without having to answer it, so I didn't imagine I'd have to on St. Patrick's Day.

He grabbed my hand. "I mean, I know what we're doing. We've been having some of the best months of my life, but what should I call you?"

"I know what I wish we were calling each other." My

weak heart nearly stopped.

"I do, too."

"Well then, let's make it official."

"Monte, will you be my boyfriend?"

If I could've bottled the feeling that overtook me when I heard that question slipping through his devilishly sexy lips and taken a drop of it every day for the rest of my life, I would've in a heartbeat.

"I'd love nothing more."

Amias's eyes, as round and bright as two full moons in the black night sky, shined on me from the passenger seat, and if the road hadn't demanded so much of my attention, I surely would've leapt across the center console and ravaged him with kisses and strokes.

Our hands often clasped together when we rode around in the car, but after we became boyfriends, they locked so tightly I hoped they may never come apart. He was mine. I was his. It was official, for the first time. I had everything I wanted and nothing I didn't, and I felt like nothing could've ruined it for me.

It was around seven in the evening when we finally cruised through the giant metal gates guarding the grounds at Riverview Estates, the subdivision where Imani and Avery's friend lived. We rolled over hill after hill of similarly styled homes with perfectly manicured yards and expensive cars in driveways until coming up to the one with numbers matching the address Imani gave me.

416 Corinthians Lane. The driveway and parking area on the street overflowed with cars and trucks, and a man seemingly in his forties guided me across the narrow ditch and into the front yard.

Amias and I peeled our hands apart and stepped out

into the unusually warm air, which felt more like early May than late March.

"Hey man! Glad you made it!" Imani waved to us from the crowded wraparound porch with a blunt in her hand. "Follow me, I wanna smoke!"

She carved a path wide enough for us to travel single file behind her, and massive speakers blared someone's country-pop playlist from every direction while people from eighteen to upwards of fifty bounced recklessly to the beat with cups full of alcohol. Imani led us off the back of the wood and stone porch and along a path of concrete pads inlaid in a bed of black and white gravel to a gazebo.

The gazebo, which was covered in vines and blue flowers blooming far too soon, sat quietly at the edge of the backyard. A hill fell steeply twenty yards to the neighbor's privacy fence on the other side of it, and white flecks of paint littered the grass around it. We slipped through the curtain of vines and dangling blue flowers and took a seat on the aged white benches lining the railing.

"So, y'all have been pretty close lately, huh?" Imani asked after everyone got to take a hit.

Amias and I looked at each other with big, toothy grins.

"What was that?"

"Amias asked me to be his boyfriend." Those words came out of me with more pride than I'd ever felt, and my cheeks turned as red as the brilliant sunset trickling through the dangling vines behind him.

"Aw, I'm so happy for you guys!" Imani's face straightened up sarcastically, and she looked at me. "I guess this explains why I haven't heard much from you this semester."

"Oh, shit." She called me out, and to be honest, I did feel bad about how I practically abandoned my friends when Amias came into my life. The way things had been with him kept me from feeling too guilty, though. It was hard to feel guilty for living my dreams. "I'm sorry, dude. We've just been spending so much ti—"

"It's cool, bro. I'm just picking. I'm really, *really* happy this is who's been distracting you." She looked to Amias and puffed her chest out so far I thought it might explode. "You should've seen this fucker when I met him. He was a total mess until I showed him the art of being independent."

I raspberried in denial, but the more I thought about it, the more I realized she wasn't wrong. I had no idea how to do anything unrelated to worship when I got to college. I didn't know what I wanted to do or who I wanted to be, and Imani had given me every opportunity to consider the world from perspectives I may have overlooked without her like a worldly Sunday school teacher. And Amias... well, Amias felt like the one person on Earth I needed to be around. Things could only go up with him by my side, and even if they didn't, I had his smile and care to get me through.

We finished off the blunt and made our way inside the grand suburban home, pushing down the hallway and past rooms full of drunk people to a stainless-steel-loaded kitchen and open living room.

Imani handed each of us a Jägerbomb from the tray on the bar and told us to down them on three. "Three!"

The drink splashed across my tongue, and I instantly decided I would not be having another. The pungent flavor stuck in my mouth long after I swallowed it, turning my tongue into a waterslide. I looked over and saw Amias with an equally strong but adorable reaction, twisting the muscles across his face with his eyes closed. Imani grabbed another Jägerbomb and wandered off, letting us know she was going upstairs if we needed her.

Amias and I mixed ourselves a couple tequila sunrises with the tequila, orange juice, and grenadine we brought and finished them off, and I made sure we stuck to the drinking buddy rule we agreed to on the way over. Then we poured another round. And then another.

Fiddles and guitars blared from speakers embedded far too high in the wall to be turned down without a remote, but the noise still somehow faded behind Amias with every reckless stranger and something heavy falling over down the hall. I looked into his eyes and matched his smile with mine, and I swore I heard our heartbeats sync up. I felt the looseness of the alcohol and the power of his presence and closed my eyes, leaning in.

A warm face.

Two warm faces.

Two warm faces, pressed against each other.

Two soft hands.

Four soft hands.

Four soft hands, tangled around each other.

I stopped thinking I never wanted to leave those moments because I knew the future held more, but I did think about how nice it would've been for those moments to become more than moments and to bleed into every second of every day.

"You guys should come upstairs!" Imani shouted from the staircase. "It's a lot better up here!"

I reluctantly pulled my head away from Amias's but kept my eyes on his, and his eyebrows arched abruptly over those velvety brown eyes I saw whole beaches in, a bit redder where they were once white. "I'm down. If you are, I mean."

"We'll follow you!" I grabbed what was left of our mixers and tequila from the wet counter.

The stairs felt like they might go all the way to the moon, but when we finally reached the top, we were met with a long corridor lined with family pictures and framed art like a family-only Hall of Fame. The raucous party melted away with the lights behind us. Imani walked us around one corner and then around another and through a large door into what appeared to have been somebody's mancave.

A large pinball machine sang wacky tunes and flashed colorful lights from the back wall, and a bright neon sign reading "CHEERS, BEERS, AND MOUNTAINEERS" glowed proudly over it. A humongous T.V. played an old university football game on mute while Imani's group huddled around a record player and display of vinyl in the corner, using whatever was available as a seat, drinking and smoking to The 1975.

I recognized a few people Imani had run into at parties back in Morgantown and a few people from Chapmanville, and I noticed Avery sitting closest to the record player. The rest were folks I'd never seen before and would probably never see again, like most house parties I ever went to.

That was what I liked about parties, though: the anonymity of it all. Nobody was sober enough to recognize you and those who probably would've been able to couldn't because of the shitty lighting.

I don't know how much time passed before Amias and I realized we were out of orange juice and were running low on grenadine and tequila, but we decided to stop drinking. Or maybe we had to. We were in the middle of a game of drinkless beer pong on a table by the room's only two windows when someone walked up behind me and covered my eyes. I turned quickly to see who.

Fucking Shech.

"Hey, you beautiful thing, you. Your ass looks as good as it did in December."

I wanted to throw up, but it had nothing to do with the alcohol. His voice grated at my eardrums, and his fingers, orange with Cheetos dust, left greasy smudges across the lenses of my glasses. I hated him more than words could describe.

He noticed Amias. "Oh my. How'd I get so lucky? To be surrounded by you two beautiful specimens."

"That's pretty clinical-sounding, don't ya think?" Amias looked at him with a straight face and chuckled sarcastically. "I think I'd use something less creepy next time."

Shech, for the first time since I'd met him, seemed to be out of words to say. I wanted to laugh or maybe say something to back Amias up, but I couldn't.

"Monte, are you okay? You're looking a little rough." The worrisome tone Amias used was new to me, and it was not my favorite thing to hear from him.

"Looks rough, but ten out of ten—would bang," said Shech with the kind of wink old men gave young girls at church.

I jumped up and darted out the door, down the stairs, and out into the dark backyard by myself, fighting my tightening lungs and rubbery legs every step of the way. With the heat provided by the sun long gone, I found myself running for shelter in the dimly lit gazebo, guarded against the mountain wind behind thick, flowery ropes.

Within minutes, feet clomping down the stone pathway made me regret coming out by myself. Somebody was approaching the gazebo—a shadowy silhouette marching toward me with nothing but a few leafy vines hanging between us. I tensed up for a moment, worried an axe murderer trying to make their mark by terrorizing the local party-goers might burst into the gazebo and make me their first victim or, even worse, Shech might've followed me, but Amias's fuzzy hand pulled back the green veil. His smile outshined the speck of yellow light wavering in the old bulb overhead when our eyes met.

"Everything okay, boyfriend o' mine?" Amias asked, drunkenly using our new label and my new favorite word. He'd been joking when he used it then, but that made it no less true. It was a word I'd never used and one which had never been used on me. I pinched myself to make sure I wasn't just dreaming of him again.

"I'm fi—" I hiccupped. "—ne. I've got you, and that's all I need."

He plopped down on the bench next to me, and I scooted closer to take some of his warmth and maybe provide him with some of mine in return.

"Well, I've got you, and that's all I need. So we've got all we need then. I guess that makes us a couple of happy fuckers." Amias wrapped his arm around my neck and pulled me in even closer.

"I guess it does."

CHAPTER 20: BLUE BIRD

Amias and I were too drunk to make the drive back to Morgantown from Fairmont but too sober to be in the same room as Shech, so we opted to spend the rest of the night drinking in the gazebo. It also helped that I couldn't find my car keys anywhere, but I wouldn't have driven even if I did.

Amias and I sat on benches in the gazebo pressed together, and then I lay flat on my bench and he on his, pressing his head to mine. My mind kept obsessively running over everything about him even with him sitting right next to me, which I didn't expect. I always thought my addiction to thinking about him would dissolve once we had one another, that my mind would go back to normal, but it didn't. If anything, thoughts of him grew stronger the more I got to know him, and they became much more powerful once I was able to touch him every day.

I looked at my phone to check the time, maybe to see if I was even capable of thinking about anything else anymore.

It's 3 a.m., and I'm wondering if you might be thinking of me, too.

Just then, Amias reached around and tapped me on the forehead. He pointed to a crack in the ceiling. "There's Ursa Minor, also known as the Little Dipper. And, and over there is Ursa Major, whose ass is so nice we call it the Big Dipper. Or, sort of." He pointed to a patch of water damage and hiccupped, chuckling at himself.

I snickered. "Oh, hush. You're just drunk."

"No, I'm not. Well, I am, but I'm right about this. I don't know where they are right now, but Ursa Major is the Big Dipper and Ursa Minor is the Little Dipper."

"Okay, okay. I believe you. But what do you mean you don't know where they are? They're right there." I pointed to the crack and water damage.

He laughed and inched closer, sliding his head between mine and the corner where our benches came together. "I think we're like that."

"Like what?"

"Different, but the same. The Big Dipper and Little Dipper in a world of Ursa Majors and Ursa Minors."

"What do you mean?" I started feeling like Imani's spirit of digging had possessed me.

"We're different from the people we grew up around in some ways, but we're essentially the same when you look at us."

I thought he had a bad case of drunk guy word vomit, but he sounded like he had a point in there somewhere. I remained quiet to see if he would go on.

"I mean, we're human. That's what I'm trying to say. We love in the same way as other people, only we felt like we had to wait so much longer to be out, and we're still not out all the way. Why do we have to be 'out' in the first place? I hate that."

He looked at me, blushing. "Oh shit, I don't mean to say I hate it, but I *hate* it. If you wanted to bring a girl home, there would be no second thoughts. You'd just do it. Not you specifically, Monte, but I mean *you*. There'd be no painful explanation. There'd be nothing but happiness, assuming they liked the person you brought home, or actually the woman. But why can't it be that simple? Why can't it just be the person you brought home? Who decided it absolutely has to be a woman you take home?

"I don't expect you to answer me or anything. I know it's something to do with tradition and history and some other bullshit people can't seem to let go of, but I think on these things all the time. It hurts me to know how much time we wasted not being together, and all because we had to look like other people."

I knew exactly what he meant. I understood his pain. I wanted to say something, but for some reason, I couldn't.

"I'm sorry. I'm rambling, and I'm drunk as fuck. You probably think I sound crazy, but I can't even blame this on the alcohol. These are sober thoughts leaking out because of the alcohol."

"You don't sound crazy."

We turned our heads simultaneously, and his satin lips tasted so sweet on mine, overpowering the tequila taste in my mouth. The bench creaked under him as he turned his body and sat up, pulling away from me slowly. He slipped out of his green romphim and kicked it onto a bench on the other side of the gazebo.

I sat up and undressed, and Amias lay back down, too dizzy to pull his underwear any lower than his knees. His dick, long and stiff and beautiful, rose between the tops of his thighs like a lone skyscraper in a field. I struggled to climb over him without falling, but once I stabilized myself on all fours, my mouth gravitated toward his throbbing cock.

His hand scratched my back gently as I sucked, alternating between each of my shoulders when the arm he was using began to tremble. Chilly winds moaned around the gazebo, seeping through the vines with the ambrosial scent of their flowers, and Amias moaned back. His lungs began to pump rapidly. The muscles in his legs hardened, and then, he finished.

I stumbled back and wiped my face.

"Your turn," he said, unable to roll up into a sitting position.

"Can we just lie together?"

He tapped the spot above his head where I had been earlier. I pulled my clothes back on and covered him up with his on my way over. The music from the house had gone off and many of the lights, too, and the only way a passerby would've known anybody was home was by the echoes of laughter from the porch and an upstairs room illuminated by the unsteady blaze of a television.

My head lay so close to his I could know his desires without hearing his voice—*Closer,* he thought, or maybe I thought, but it didn't matter because he and I were one and the same now. My eyes fell shut when I slid impossibly closer.

The sun woke us up earlier than anybody else, peering through the green vines as soon as it rose. I sat up, hair stiff and sticking straight up, and peeled back the leafy curtain to get a glimpse at the citrusy orb rising behind the wispy clouds over the mountains. A blanket of fog covered the river as it ran through downtown Fairmont in the distance, blowing down the valley like smoke beneath a fiery sky.

Amias sat up and looked out with me.

"It's beautiful, isn't it?" I asked.

"I could look at it with you all day."

Absolute perfection.

I gave him a *Good morning* smooch and poked fun at his messy hair, and he poked back at mine. We stepped out of the gazebo, backs sore, and walked across the obstacle course the backyard had become. Destroyed lawn furniture and crushed red cups were strewn about as if a tornado swept through overnight, and the mulch from the flowerbeds was scattered everywhere. Some people had fallen asleep on the porch furniture, some on the cold concrete floor in the garage, and the rest had presumably fallen asleep inside or taken an Uber home.

"Jesus Christ. Who in the world would ever want to host a house party?"

"Beats me. Let's dart." Amias pulled my keys out of his pocket and threw them to me.

The drive back to Morgantown seemed more hellish than beautiful. The sun became less awe-inspiring as its brightness grew in intensity, triggering pins and needles to scrape around inside the most delicate parts of my skull. The majestic mountains rose rather inconveniently, and the road maneuvered over and between them like a roller coaster. My stomach flipped and flopped emptily, growling a little, and I began to salivate.

Choke it down, I thought, swallowing gallons in an effort to contain what I knew was coming.

It worked, and we eventually made it back to Morgantown. That same afternoon, after I dropped Amias off and had time to nap off a gnarly hangover in my room, Imani hit me with an invitation to join her for a blunt. I never turned down an offer to smoke, so I met her on the rail trail at the bottom of Third Street as soon as I could. She was leaning against the fence on the other side of the path looking at her phone when I hopped over the four-foot wall instead of walking around and taking the ramp.

"Yo, thanks for the invite."

"No prob Bob." She shoved her phone into her pocket and slapped me on the ass like a coach.

We didn't say much else on the quarter-mile walk from there to the tunnel. We mostly spent the trip leisurely soaking in the colorful, newly bloomed tulips and greening hillsides the warmer weather was bringing to Morgantown. The occasional cyclist or runner yelled, "On your left!" and whizzed past us noisily, and the river splashed as small waves created by a boat speeding by crashed onto the riverbank.

We hobbled down the hill and over to our space on the wall by the tunnel. The creek ran out of the tunnel's rusted grates at full force, muddied and foamy from the waves of rain that seemed to endlessly soak West Virginia in the spring. The sun was shining now, though.

Imani reached down to her boot and pulled out the blunt, sparking it as soon as she could. "So," she started. "...how did the night go with Amias? Or sorry, your boyfriend."

"He's amazing, isn't he? We sat in the gazebo and talked until we fell asleep."

"Yeah, I'm sure you did a lot of talking. At least he seems to make you happy. You deserve that."

"Thank you, Imani. Like really—thank you. You are the

one who pushed me out of my comfort zone, and it led me to the most perfect thing."

"Nah, don't thank me. I was just joking around last night. All that shit was in you, bro. You just needed to be around people who cared enough to bring it out. This perfect thing you've found—yeah, that was all you."

"Well, I know." But I wasn't sure if I did. "I just had a lot of help from you."

"That's what friends do. Especially best friends. You were bound to venture out of your comfort zone because we all have to at some point. I was just here for it, and I'm happy I was. Now let's get back to you and Amias. How's that going, honestly?"

Her humility was nauseating—or maybe it was the hangover—but I smiled at her anyway. "Honestly, it's going well. Actually, it's going great. Better than anything I've ever had or seen. He makes me so incredibly happy."

"I can tell. Any plans for the future?"

"For now, we haven't talked about it. I'm just happy we're finally together, but I'm hoping he's in it for the long haul."

"He seems like he is. He was so worried about you last night when you needed to step outside. I'd have thought you'd been together for years if I didn't know you."

And once again, Imani hit the nail on the head. Amias felt like someone I'd been with for years or even lifetimes, like we'd known each other when we hadn't. He was, singlehandedly, every dream, urge, and hope I grew up clinging to. I just didn't know it at the time because I didn't want to.

So many years of my life had been wasted trying to be normal—what music, television, peers, and the church told me to happily accept as normal. What I wished they'd told me was "Find what makes you happy and chase it." I wished they'd asked about what gave me peace and not forced me into what kept the peace. It wasn't worth obsessing over, though, because I had people who said and asked those things now.

Imani tapped the roach out on the side of the wall when we'd smoked it so low it burnt our fingers, and we headed back to campus.

Over the next couple weeks, Amias and I spent even more time together. I almost dreaded going to parties where people were certain to be too loud and to do things I wasn't interested in anymore. I preferred getting wine drunk with Amias and binging The Office or Over the Garden Wall.

One evening the week before spring break, we were supposed to be watching Call Me by Your Name, but Amias kept glancing over at me from his spot on the couch. Out of the corner of my eye, I noticed and returned one of his glances.

"Can I help you, fool?"

He pondered for a moment. "I've just been thinking about something."

"Thinking about what?"

"Nevermind. It's probably nothing." He looked back at the television, so I did, too. It was only for a moment, though.

"Can I ask you a question?" He spun around to face me with a tear glimmering in his eye, throwing his legs across mine.

"Sure?"

"What happened the night we met up in City Park? You were crying and left a mess, and I was so worried about you. I spent months worrying about you, actually, wondering if you ever made it out of that situation."

I gulped down a half-gallon of saliva. "I think I told you that night. Don't you remember?"

"No. Can you refresh my memory?"

I sat my wine glass down. That night was the absolute last thing I wanted to be thinking about and the last thing I wanted to share with someone so perfect.

My family apologized and made nice with me, sure, but they didn't know I was still possessed by the demon they tried to pray away when they did. Deeper I sank into the pits of my mind, terrifying myself with thoughts of everyone finding out my dirty secrets and cutting me off forever. I feared Amias might hear the story and assume I believed like them or that I could believe like them again someday and run the other way. I feared having nowhere to run for shelter. I feared everything about telling him the truth.

He'd know how impossible it was for me to come out to my parents. He'd know there was no chance of ever meeting my family or posting pictures together or tagging each other in flirty statuses—never ever.

"It was just a family issue, a little bit of nothing."

"I don't think it was nothing, Monte. You were so shaken up. It broke my heart to see you that way, and it still does when I think back to it." The tear in the corner of his eye rolled down his nose and disappeared around his lips.

I gazed past him, out his living room window, and into the backyard. A blue bird sat, perhaps the same one as before, chirping loudly on the windowsill. Oh, how I wanted to be that beautiful blue bird, free to sing my song from every branch I landed on, able to drop what-

ever weighed me down and fly away from the past forever.

"Monte..." Amias pulled me out of my trance. "I won't
make you share anything with me if you don't want to.
I just want you to know I care about you and don't want
you to think you can't share things with me. I won't
promise to be able to remove the pain, but you don't
have to hurt alone anymore." He reached his palm over
and rested it on my thigh before placing a tender kiss on
my cheek. "I'm not going anywhere."

My eyes closed when the familiar but unwelcome sting
of saltwater grew unbearably intense. I couldn't begin
to fathom how someone I hadn't known for a full year
could care so genuinely about me, but then I remembered the way I felt about him, and it made perfect
sense.

Be the blue bird.

I shared with him everything that led us together that
night—from telling Delilah about my feelings for this
new guy at school to secretly meeting up with him after
she told everybody. I told him about the things Dad
found on my computer and the way they pleaded with
the man upstairs to have the gay demon removed from
within me. I told him everything.

I couldn't help but feel concerned for our future as I
spoke. I felt terrible because I didn't know if I'd have had
the strength to be with someone whose parents wished
I didn't exist and constantly prayed for our relationship
to fail.

But he was better than me—better than anyone. His
face didn't ooze with pity or judgment, and his eyes
didn't drift toward the stairs like he was waiting for the
moment I stopped talking to split. He just listened. He

shook his head when I quoted the things they said and raised his eyebrows in the center when I told him how they made me feel, but he didn't say anything or try to tell me how to deal with it.

"Montgomery, I had no idea... I'm sorry about all of it but especially the shit you had to stand there and hear them say. I hope you don't believe any of those things. I hope you know how wonderful you are." He kept most of his tears confined to the rims of his eyes and forced a sympathetic smile.

I wiped a tear from my cheek, and a new, magnificently hot sensation expanded in my chest like a bomb had gone off. I suddenly felt like I couldn't breathe, like I was drowning, and then I opened my mouth.

"I love you, Amias."

His smile grew so wide it nearly touched his earlobes, and the outer corners of his eyes wrinkled. "I love you, too."

I shouldn't have doubted him. He was such a special person—one who genuinely cared and would've gone to any length to show someone how much they meant to him. I felt like the luckiest man alive—as I was starting to always feel—when he wrapped his arm around me and pulled me closer, nearly sucking my lips off until we fell asleep tangled around one another.

* * *

I got myself into the terrible habit of staying at his place until way too late only to drive back downtown exhausted and missing him. I thought about asking if we could stay together more often—hopefully in the townhouse—but I never wanted to come off as clingy or overstep some sort of boundary. When I stayed there, I ate his groceries and used his utilities, and I never gave him a dime for any of it. But the day before I had to move out of Honors for Spring Break, he put all those worries to rest by asking me to stay with him.

I told my parents I was staying with my aunt and uncle, and I told my aunt and uncle I went home. What I actually did was spend the week with Amias in his townhouse. We had to work all week, but Meghan gave us the last weekend off. So we decided to spend Sunday afternoon at Dorsey's Knob where I could study, he could relax, and we could enjoy a picnic together.

The hilltop park, loaded with students looking for ways to pass time besides drinking and smoking, had few places left where we could enjoy a little privacy, but we searched high and low until happening upon a small clearing between a few trees and a pond. Cattails lined the pond and lily pads covered it, and on the other side, a disc golf course stretched out in several fields behind the tree line. We set up our picnic blanket for later and our hammocks for now, climbing into them for an afternoon study session.

After an hour or so, we both started dropping hints that it was time for a break, so I wriggled out of my hammock and plopped down on Amias's Ron Jon blanket. I'd just begun rummaging through the ice-filled cooler for our meal and Gatorades when something caught my attention.

Amias had not yet gotten out of his hammock. He hadn't even stopped lounging in the white rays like a sunbathing cat. He looked at me with eyes squinting in a sliver of sunlight and hair like golden waves. His pearly white half-grin, better for my soul than the fresh mountain air, curled into a full smile when I grinned back.

"Why don't you come over here?"

I shot up off the blanket and skipped toward him. He grabbed me by my waist as soon as he could and pulled me against the hammock.

"I can't get in. We'll be on the ground in a split second," I said half-jokingly, pulling away.

"No, we won't Monte. I bought a two-person hammock, and I did it for a reason." He winked at me.

I looked over each of my shoulders to make sure nobody could see and joined Amias in his oversized hammock. I slid in next to him, showering his body with kisses and rubbing my hands messily through his thick hair.

Amias brought his lips to mine, and boom: fire like the very first time we kissed, like every time we kissed. He stumbled up onto his knees and towered over my body. Each of his fuzzy, toned legs flexed under his weight along my sides, squeezing between my torso and hips and the hammock tightly. I was just starting to turn over on all fours when he stopped me.

"No, no, no. I want to see your face. Please?"

I wasn't sure how that would ever be comfortable given the tightness of the hammock, but I did it anyway —not that I took much convincing.

One by one, our clothes came off and scattered in the grass around us. He grabbed the small bottle of lube hidden in the zipper pouch behind him and used his hand to slather it on himself generously.

He raised my legs above my head and pressed his dick into me over and over again. I let out a hushed moan with each thrust, trying desperately to keep the sound muffled. Framed between my thighs, Amias halfway smiling from the pleasure and halfway straining from the effort threw my heart into overdrive. I grabbed the lube and quickly rubbed some on my right hand. Then, with him in focus, I grabbed my dick and started stroking.

The hammock swayed slightly, and the sun shined through the trees in small lines and half-circles of light. Amias let out one final breathy exhale and a moan, both erotic and risky, and finished. His beauty, his action, his sounds—everything about that moment and every moment with him was perfect to me. As soon as he could control his arms again, he started on my dick with his sticky hand. I finished fast and hard with another dangerously loud moan.

"Monte!" Amias fell back into the hammock. "Someone's gonna hear us!"

It was a moment before I could respond being that I was out of breath and still couldn't see straight, but the world eventually came back to me. "Fuck off," I said with a laugh. "I can't control myself around you."

He looked up at me with a smile that read something sarcastic like *No, you fuck off,* but I meant what I said. Sex with Amias felt otherworldly. His skin on my skin, his breath on my neck, his flesh in my flesh—it sounds vulgar and shallow, but it wasn't with him. It was a connection of our emotions, our minds, and our bodies and a moment of togetherness so intense and raw we couldn't contain the sensations.

Life with Amias felt like so much more than life.

CHAPTER 21: BRIGHT THINGS

The week of final exams arrived and brought with it a thorny silence as students across campus prepared for the make-or-break grades of the school year. Summer break sat just on the other side of a week in hell, so teasingly close with its barbecues and pool parties I could practically smell the charcoal and sunscreen. Houses and clubs that had been crammed with drunk people all year sat empty now, and every table at the library was a jumbled mess of computer screens, notebooks, and students with unkempt hair and headphones of all sizes. I thought myself lucky to have avoided dependence on caffeine, too, because the lines at every café in walking distance stretched out the door from daylight till dark. With each passing day, though, more people finished their exams and turned in their final papers, and Morgantown shrank back into the small West Virginia town it looked like.

Imani and Avery left on a Greyhound bus on Friday, each happy with the way their first year at college turned out. I felt alright about my year as far as school went. First semester kicked my ass, but second semester was better.

Amias was happy for me, of course, but it was his encouragement to look to the future that taught me to live outside the past, freeing me up to focus more of my attention on what mattered. He was the sole reason an otherwise average or even terrible year turned out to be the best one of my life.

On the last day campus was open, Amias and I spent the afternoon moving my things out of Honors. Boxes rose from floor to ceiling like a mini-metropolis, and the only thing left to do, aside from lugging it all downstairs, was clear the walls. I removed my clock and calendar, my family pictures and Polaroids from parties and dates over the year, and lastly, the painting Mama gave me the day I moved to Morgantown.

Everything that had happened since she gave it to me, everything I had been through, it all came to mind. I didn't feel like the son she'd known when she bought it, but it still felt weirdly personal as if she bought it for the *now* me and not the *then* me. The menacing clouds and stormy seas, the vibrant tornado of colors brightening the dark, and the man taking shelter on his small stone island—it felt like she'd known what the future held for me before I did. I packed it gently away with my other valuables and wall art and marked the box "Fragile."

Some boxes went in his car and some in mine for the move to what had become my break-time bedroom in my aunt and uncle's home in Westover, but I rarely slept there anymore. I told them I was crashing at a friend's place or working a double at the hotel and stayed with Amias. The fact that he was a boy worked in my favor in this instance because nobody questioned our friend-ship. It was easy to make everyone believe we were just friends, and I began to see that maybe we could spend time in public and around family as long as I fought the urge to constantly touch him or suck on him, which was easier said than done.

His lease on the townhouse was set to end in July, and since Matt's nursing income left when he did, Amias was doomed to be in a regular apartment by August. He still had it for a couple more months, though, and we liked to pretend the whole place was one giant bedroom.

He had me on the kitchen counter, out on the upstairs balcony, in the garage, in the shower, over the banister at the top of the stairs—anywhere he could fuck me, he did.

But we also did other things. One of my favorite things we did on our days off was take spontaneous all-day road trips to places we'd never been together. The southern end of the Monongahela National Forest took a Saturday to explore, from the Falls of Hills Creek to Cranberry Glades to the Highland Scenic Highway. One weekend, we found ourselves paddle boating at Babcock State Park, and the next, we watched peacocks at the Palace of Gold.

Some evenings, we chose to wander out to Pittsburgh or Charleston to picnic in a random park and explore museums, and I'd get lost watching him look around at the high-rises, fascinating exhibits, and people in every direction. Our trips never demanded much money and if we stayed overnight, we slept in the car or at a cheap motel, but they were the best trips of my life.

I felt as though my life had become a movie about someone I wanted to be, someone with courage, an authentic smile, and a massive heart with someone in it. With Amias, I forgot I wasn't normal and that out there, lots of folks were praying people like me would stop existing. His goodness and unhindered focus on finding his happiness—and now mine, too—kept every bit of negativity the world may have been waiting to shoot at us away.

Like me, he wasn't perfect. Spending so much time together meant his quirks had time to make themselves known, and they sometimes aggravated me. He would do lazy little things like leave his dishes next to the sink or leave the shower curtain open, but we always seemed to work it out. The good in him far outweighed any minuscule bumps in the road.

University orientations picked up in the middle of May, and thanks to never-ending lines, clogged streets, and an atmosphere so thick with moisture you could've swum in it, every person who entered the hotel was already at or quickly approaching their boiling points.

But even when the line of furious, exhausted guests extended out the front door and down the sidewalk, I had him on the computer next to me, and I had the night in his townhouse to look forward to.

I've found my treasure, I thought when I caught him smiling at me for no good reason. He could've just been cussed out by a guest who thought they booked a suite but actually booked a standard room, but it didn't affect the way he looked at me.

Weeks of insanity-inducing days went by before Meghan or corporate took notice of how well we handled orientation rushes, but her pats on the back and empty cards from corporate declaring us a "family" offered limited motivation. The people who chose to stay and work in Morgantown through the summer talked to us at the front desk about how tired they'd grown, and like Meghan said happened every summer, nearly every maintenance and housekeeping worker had quit and been replaced.

Amias and I came dangerously close to following in their footsteps and finding work somewhere with less intense rushes when Meghan received an exciting notification from corporate: the remaining members of the original staff, of which there were few, would each receive a bonus on our next paychecks. On their own, the bonuses weren't really enough to do much, but pooled together, Amias and I figured we could put them toward something fun.

One Monday evening in late May, while perusing travel blogs and articles for someplace to relax, we stumbled upon a cabin on the rim of the New River Gorge and booked it for the weekend almost instantly, sold by the quaint, cottagey vibe of the cabin and, more importantly, the hot tub overlooking the gorge. The weekend-long reservation cost almost the full amount of our bonuses, but I didn't give it a second thought and it seemed that neither did he.

I longed to be with him someplace where the memories we created would be the only memories we had of that place—as if it were *our* room even if only for the weekend. I would never know what it would feel like to sleep in *our* bed alone or to wake up in it without the love of my life next to me.

We spent Friday evening loading my car with overnight bags and a cooler chock-full of sandwich ingredients, soda, water, and beer, and we put a few of my boxes from Honors in the trunk. I'd called Mama earlier in the week to see if we could drop some of my things off at home on our way to the cabin, which I told her I rented with a friend.

My insides prickled with anxiety when I told her that lie—but not just because it was a lie. To refer to Amias as my friend when he was undeniably so much more felt wrong, or blasphemous maybe, like I was pretending the only person in the entire universe who had ever been genuinely good for me was just the same as everybody else. He deserved so much better than that.

Every terrible memory from the way I had to survive before him resurfaced: of having to cover what gave me happiness in layers of lies and excuses to preserve everyone else's, of being so insecure I forced my voice an octave or two lower when speaking in public, and of blaming myself for the misery and anxiety I felt around the people who were supposed to help me find something meaningful to follow in this life. I dreaded going back there, but I couldn't keep my aunt and uncle's home cluttered with my things any longer.

With clear skies above us and the open road ahead of us, we took off. It was a long trip, but I didn't mind being locked in a hotboxed car with Amias. He held up a carefully crafted blunt once we got out of Morgantown and shuffled his "Best Hits of All Time" playlist, which was almost exclusively Fleetwood Mac and Sylvan Esso.

"Ya know, my dad took it the hardest, my coming out," he said randomly, looking at the green sign signaling we'd crossed the border into Nicholas County.

"I'm sorry to hear that," I replied, lost in thought over how my father would take the news if he ever found out. "What happened?"

"He pretty much told me to 'stay straight' or 'leave *his*

home.'" He paused, fighting off a tremble in his voice, and looked out the passenger window. As if on purpose, his playlist ended and left a silence only disturbed by the roar of the car down the road and our conversation. "So, I left *his* home."

"I'm so sorry Amias." Those wounds had gone untouched for years, and I knew there was nothing I could've done to fix them right there. I just had to be better for him. No matter what.

"It's okay," he said, recomposing himself. "I'm happy now."

He grabbed my hand as tightly as he could on the center console and I his, but he kept his gaze directed out the window.

"I was fifteen, so of course I couldn't stay anywhere long. I spent a few nights on one friend's couch and then a few nights on another friend's couch before I realized... before I realized they weren't coming for me. Nobody was. I was completely alone with no money, no bed, and no car. Those were some of the worst nights of my life..." He trailed off like he wasn't able to say another word, but he did.

"I eventually had to put any amount of pride I had left aside so I could go back home where I had access to basic necessities. Dad couldn't leave me be when I got back, though. It was just like him to be that way. He couldn't act happy to have me back or relieved to know where I was. No, he had to let me know he won and tried to embarrass me for being a kid who needed things. He busted through my door the night I came home to tell me he was taking my bedroom door away and to remind me that if I was going to be back under his roof, I needed to agree to his terms. So, I did."

A long, heavy silence flooded the car, seemingly muting the thunder of the road, and increasingly steeper mounds of earth and stone rose higher and higher on either side of us. The sun shined through the clear blue sky so glaringly I got sunspots from the reflections on cars around us, and the air conditioner fought with all its might to dry the sweat forming on my skin.

Amias gripped my hand, somehow even more tightly this time. "Ya know, Monte, I'm really glad I met you."

"Ya know, Amias, I'm really glad I met you, too." I returned his affectionate grip, again.

His smile shined in the corner of my eye, and the warmth I only ever felt around him overwhelmed me. I forgot for a moment we were headed to a place where we wouldn't be able to keep holding hands, so I gripped his hand for as long as I could.

The red reflectors at the bottom of my childhood driveway turned my blood ice cold, and my hand pulled hesitantly from Amias's as I began to imagine him as someone he could never be. He became a close friend, perhaps closer than Imani or Merida, but no closer than that. We could no longer kiss or hold hands. No more playful glances or cute smiles. Those things were inappropriate for friends to do. Friends could only high-five one another and had to sit in ways that guaranteed no thigh-touching.

God, it fucked me up having to think of him that way. I had half a mind to speed up and drive past the driveway.

I can come up with an excuse later, I thought, dreading going back to my old life even for twenty more minutes.

Amias told me repeatedly he had no issue keeping things hidden until I was ready to show my family the truth, but he hadn't said it with a smile. His words came out slowly as if trying desperately not to crawl off his tongue and into existence. It hurt me to force him into living my lie and to make him call me his friend, but it was easier than starting the best weekend of our relationship by having to defend it.

Mama came around the corner of the beige double-wide I hadn't seen in months with her arms open wide when she heard my car revving up the driveway. She enveloped me in a hug as quickly as I could get the door open.

"Oh, Monte, it's so good to see you! I was thrilled when you called me." She looked at Amias stretching his legs on the other side of the car.

"This is Amias, my friend from school." My hands collapsed into tight, numb fists, and my throat felt like a tiny straw.

"I remember him." Her smile grew wide, and he offered a faint smile in return. "It's good to see you, too, Amias. I hope you're doing well."

"It's lovely to see you again, Mrs. Lee, and it's always nice being back down this way. I'm just excited to see our cabin." I felt panicky, afraid the words "our cabin" might've been too specific.

"Oh, always so polite with you. Relax a bit and call me Cathy. I bet you're both ready for a little time away. Let's get those boxes inside, and you guys can hit the road again."

We loaded our arms with boxes from the trunk and carried them in. Juliet and Remi shouted "Hey," from the pool as we marched across the back porch, and Dad kept his attention on the smoky kabobs and steamy onions sizzling on the grill. I hoped we'd make it inside before he noticed us, but the sound of his metal tongs clanking against the table told me we didn't. He jogged across the deck to get the back door for us.

"Hey, guys! I'm glad you could drop by." Dad motioned us inside.

"I'm glad we were able to stop in and see everybody," Amias said, stepping past.

I realized I'd been so distracted the last time I came home I forgot to look around. The place felt quieter and colder than I remembered, like a home I'd never lived in. Hatchets were supposed to have been buried, but the house seemed to hold onto the negativity of the past with a firm grip, a firmer one than I cared to hold onto it with myself.

Mama stacked her boxes on the empty, dust-covered dresser in the corner of my bedroom, and Amias put his boxes next to hers.

Almost time to go, I thought, walking toward the dresser. The cross hanging on the wall caught my attention as I placed my boxes on theirs, filling me with a familiar sense of anxiety. I remembered putting it there. I remembered the person I was when I put it there and the life I led before I met Amias, before I questioned what I was told and discovered I could make my life one worth living.

Bleak and frigid and lonely before, but Amias's voice reminded me I meant something to someone.

He'd been chatting with Mama until my arm bumped the stack of boxes we just made, and the one I placed on top fell to the floor. My heart raced faster than it had in a long time as I considered what terribly revealing things might tumble out before us: my bong, my condoms, my dildo, or worst of all—my Polaroids with Amias.

The cardboard flaps covering the end of the box flung

open, and the word "Fragile" flashed by in my handwriting. Frames and books I remembered packing away fanned out in all directions on the floor. I bent over to start picking things up, hopefully before Mama could start helping me, and slid all the books and frames together. That's when I saw my sandwich bag of Polaroids had landed face-up on the back of a canvas at Mama's feet. They weren't necessarily romantic or sexy pictures, but I smiled with Amias more than I'd ever smiled before.

I stopped and watched as Mama bent over slowly, reaching her arm out for the bag. She grabbed it and looked at its contents for a few seconds before grabbing the canvas. She read the inscription she left on the back, and then she flipped it over, giving the painting a long look. I wanted her to look up so I could tell what she was thinking, but that was also the exact thing I hoped I wouldn't see for a long time.

The rapid thumping of my heart against my ribs rattled every bone in my body as Mama slowly raised her eyes, as shiny as a moonlit lake. She pointed a smile at Amias and then a bigger one at me, and she reached the canvas and bag to me. "You're perfect, Monte. I loved you then, I love you still, and I'll love you always— exactly the way you are and exactly the way you were born."

I grabbed my things from her, legs wobbling, jaw trembling. I might've believed her, but it didn't matter. I wanted the moment to be over. *I'll tell this truth later,* I thought, putting everything back in the box and shoving it up on the dresser.

A few teary goodbyes later, Amias and I were back in the car, but my mind was stuck in my old bedroom.

I found myself replaying Mama's words over and over, worried she might share what she'd seen with Dad or stage another prayer. And this time it was more than conceptual bullshit. Dad would've probably had a conniption if she told him I brought my boyfriend into his house. My shoulders felt lighter the further we got from the house, and once it was out of sight, Amias's soft hand caressing mine made me forget it all.

We crossed the New River Gorge Bridge on the way into Fayetteville a little while later, and within twenty minutes, the car was rumbling down the long driveway to our cabin. The building itself sat high up off the ground, starkly contrasting the cold cobblestone carport. It was a two-story log cabin overlooking the New River Gorge on one side and surrounded by forest on all others. The owner, a friendly man from Fayetteville, greeted us on the front porch with a set of keys and a smile before leaving us alone for the weekend.

The humble kitchen into which the front door entered greeted us first with a wave of crisp air conditioning, the kind I loved hotel rooms for. It was a small kitchen for such a large house, although it had been nicely appointed with a wet bar on the far side and a pot rack over the tiny island. Glass bottles hung from the ceiling, each one holding a bright, vintage bulb—the Thomas Edison kind—and the gold they radiated bounced from wooden surfaces in every direction.

Beyond the kitchen sprawled a giant, two-story living room with a giant window taking up the entire far wall, flooding the room with natural light. A flat-screen T.V. mounted over a brick fireplace flashed pictures of mountains on the right, and on the left, a set of leather furniture sat at the base of a wooden staircase.

We dropped our bags on the couch and stepped out onto the balcony. A crystal-clear hot tub sparkled in the center of the balcony as a small waterfall poured into it, spraying chlorine fumes all around us. The view beyond the railing made me feel like an ant on the rim of the New River Gorge. The densely forested valley dropped eighty stories or more beneath us, spotted with jagged rock cliffs and divided by zigzagging country roads, and the rusty New River Gorge Bridge, bustling with weekend traffic, rose prominently over the chasm further downriver. My heart nearly exploded when I looked over at Amias and considered how fortunate I was to have ended up with the perfect man in the perfect place.

Amias and I spent the first evening like we had any other. We connected my laptop to the T.V. and watched Fried Green Tomatoes, cracked open a bottle of wine, and kicked our feet up.

"Am I allowed to post the pictures we take this weekend?" Amias asked out of the blue, pointing to a selfie we'd taken earlier on the porch.

"Sure, you can take all the pictures you want this week."

"That's not what I asked, Monte."

I knew what he was asking. I just didn't want to answer, or I couldn't. It didn't matter to me.

"I just wanted to see if you wanted to talk about it. You haven't said much about your plans for coming out or if you even have any."

"I know... I just—" I choked on my saliva.

Amias pulled back. "Ya know, this is super, *super* personal. I just wanted to see if it was something you needed to talk about."

I had picked up this habit of looking at Amias any time

I felt low; something about his beauty or his energy or *something* always seemed to pick me up.

"I love you, Amias." God, it felt just as good as the first time.

He stopped and raised his eyes to mine. "I love you, too, Monte."

I threw the wad of blankets into the floor and moved closer to him, peering into his beautiful brown eyes. And for a divine second, that was all I did. I removed the obstacles so I could look into him, and he could see into me.

Like a shooting star plummeting to the earth in fiery delight, I fell to him and planted my lips on his. He gripped the back of my head with a firm grasp, massaging his fingers around my scalp, and pressed his chest and stomach into mine as our lips twisted into a sloppy pink mess, and his warmth absorbed me.

Harder than ever, my throbbing dick gained the attention of both Amias and me. He paused his vicious lip-sucking, pulled down my pants, and began sucking my cock. With each graceful dip and triumphant rise, it throbbed harder and larger, and before I knew it, I hungered for something I'd never had before.

I rose quickly to my knees over Amias and turned him onto his stomach. With the side of his face pressed to a throw pillow, I leaned down over him, closed in on his one exposed ear, and whispered, "I want to fuck you so badly right now."

Slightly out of breath and with a hint of excitement, he responded, "Please."

I thrust into him, and the lambent, yellow light from the antique table lamp shined across him, illuminating every sexy bony rivet and flexing muscle as it did. There came a time when I could no longer feel my body. The stinging of my overworked thighs, the debilitating huffing caused by my lungs' desperate fight for air, my heartbeat rippling across my body as my blood vessels struggled to supply my muscles with enough fuel to keep going—it all disappeared and gave way to more meaningful and more powerful feelings.

I felt me.

I felt him.

I felt us.

Nothing else mattered.

Like a million times before but with an intensity unparalleled in my universe, the burning of an orgasm started deep within me, curling my toes. My body and mind tingled with a numbing exhilaration, and visions of him before, him now, and him in the future flashed through my mind. The giant living room faded to blackness with everything else in the world.

My breathing halted, and for a moment I must've died. I pulled my dick out and erupted all over Amias's back, losing control of my legs and falling onto the couch next to him.

There we lay for a while, me on my back looking at Amias and him on his stomach looking at me.

"I love you," he said.

"I love you, too."

I felt invincible with him, safe from whatever wanted to bring suffering, safe from worry and strife. It didn't matter who did or didn't support me because he did, and because he did, I did. He taught me what it meant to love somebody, to wake up every day thinking of them and to go to sleep every night dreaming of them. In my life, I'd never felt something so destructively powerful or mind-clearingly beautiful. I didn't want to, and probably couldn't, live without it ever again.

Using my reflection on a mirror on the china cabinet across the room, I fixed my bedhead and straightened out the ruffled hairs in my beard. Then, after leaning against Amias and holding my phone out in front of us, I snapped the world's most lovely selfie. Straight away, I tapped the share button, selected Facebook, and wrote out the following caption:

I am so lucky to have met and fallen in love with the man of my dreams. I love you, Amias Parker.

I looked at him and pressed post.

There was no anxiety.

There was no judgment.

There was no worry about being alone.

I was mine and he was his and we were ours, and as long as that was the case, the future held bright things.

MONTE'S PAINTING

Digital art created by Kirstin Burwell

ABOUT THE AUTHOR

Trey Burwell

Trey Burwell was born and raised outside the old lumber town of Richwood, West Virginia and graduated from West Virginia University in 2019. Trey currently resides just a couple hours west of his hometown in the city of Charleston, and his life is made whole by his small family consisting of his husband Anthony, his dog Kenai, and his cat Archie. He enjoys spending weekends with his husband at the countless parks and forests within a short drive of Charleston and traveling home to Richwood to visit his extended family. Because I Remember You is Trey's first book.

Find Trey on Facebook or email him at bytreyburwell@gmail.com.

Made in the USA
Middletown, DE
14 March 2022